Praise for *The Sweet Life*

"Suzanne Woods Fisher has written another winner! Filled with her signature heart, *The Sweet Life* is an uplifting reminder of the joy of restored relationships, the importance of bravery, and the hope of second chances."

Liz Johnson, bestselling author of *The Red Door Inn*
and *Beyond the Tides*

"Suzanne Woods Fisher has gifted us with an inspiring, irresistible story in which following the ice cream leads to a whole bunch of heart. Fisher is a winsome storyteller who never disappoints, and that's certainly true here as she celebrates variety as the spice of life, love, and ice cream flavors. *The Sweet Life* is an effortless charmer!"

Bethany Turner, award-winning author of *The Do-Over*

"Restoration and reawakened dreams gather in Suzanne Woods Fisher's Christian romance novel *The Sweet Life*. . . . In it, a painful separation leads to a spiritual revival that's fed by the flavors of a small-town ice cream parlor."

Foreword Reviews

"This story is uplifting and inspirational, emphasizing what is important in life. The small-town setting, humorous banter, colorful characters, and healing make for a wonderful story."

No Apology Book Review

"*The Sweet Life* is a wonderful beach read, set at the Cape, with lots of ice cream sprinkled throughout. Nothing could be better on a hot summer day!"

Romance Junkies

Praise for *At Lighthouse Point*

"*At Lighthouse Point* rounds out Fisher's charming modern-day Three Sisters Island trilogy. . . . Christian faith and prayer are central to the book's message, and themes of trusting God's steadfast plan and empathy toward others are grounding beacons amidst the tumult of the unexpected."

Booklist

"*At Lighthouse Point* is a charming read, with gentle truths and great characters. I'm glad I got to revisit their little island."

Interviews and Reviews

"All three books of this series were fun reads where each sister learns something about themselves."

Write-Read-Life

the
SECRET to
HAPPINESS

Novels by Suzanne Woods Fisher

the SECRET *to* HAPPINESS

SUZANNE WOODS FISHER

Revell

a division of Baker Publishing Group
Grand Rapids, Michigan

Published by Revell
a division of Baker Publishing Group
Grand Rapids, Michigan
www.revellbooks.com

Printed in the United States of America

Library of Congress Cataloging-in-Publication Data
Names: Fisher, Suzanne Woods, author.
Title: The secret to happiness / Suzanne Woods Fisher.
Description: Grand Rapids, MI : Revell, a division of Baker Publishing Group, [2023] | Series: Cape Cod creamery ; 2
Identifiers: LCCN 2022029170 | ISBN 9780800739485 (paperback) | ISBN 9780800743154 (casebound) | ISBN 9781493441310 (ebook)
Subjects: LCGFT: Domestic fiction. | Novels.
Classification: LCC PS3606.I78 S453 2023 | DDC 813/.6—dc23/eng/20220623
LC record available at https://lccn.loc.gov/2022029170

Published in association with Joyce Hart of the Hartline Literary Agency, LLC.

23   24   25   26   27   28   29   7   6   5   4   3   2   1

Cast of Characters

Callie Dixon (age 28), recently fired executive chef, cousin to Dawn, niece to Marnie.

Dawn Dixon (age 28), half owner of the Main Street Creamery, ice cream maker extraordinaire.

Marnie Dixon (a woman of a certain age), mother of Dawn, half owner of the Main Street Creamery.

Kevin Collins (age 28), fiancé to Dawn. Studying for his master's degree in preservation architecture.

Lincoln Hayes (a man of a certain age), Chatham resident, full-time volunteer to charitable causes, lover of ice cream, friend to all.

Leo the Cowboy (age 6), lover of any and all ice cream.

Bruno Bianco (age thirtysomething), professor at 4Cs (Cape Cod Community College), author of *The Secret to Happiness*.

Jesse (age 23), friend and colleague of Callie, works at Penn State's Creamery.

Brynn (age 28), former roommate of Dawn's.

Nanette (age seventysomething), Chatham resident, runs a T-shirt shop, known for being on the nosy side of nosy.

Mrs. Nickerson-Eldredge (age seventysomething), Chatham resident born and bred, chair of the Historical Commission. Considers herself to be the guardian of Chatham.

Richard Dixon (age 61), father to Callie, brother-in-law to Marnie.

Glossary
of Popsicle Making

base—the egg-dairy-sugar (cream) mixture or juice-water (fruit) mixture that is the main ingredient in all popsicles

blender or food processor—to mix or purée the base

cornstarch—add a tablespoon of cornstarch to cream-based popsicles to make them creamy. Acts as a stabilizer to keep popsicles from getting icy

cream base—whole milk plain Greek yogurt (lower water content than usual yogurt = less water crystals to make popsicle icy). Other options for a cream base: full fat coconut milk, heavy cream, almond milk

dips—milk/dark chocolate or white chocolate, melted, to coat frozen popsicle (all or part). Allow to harden before returning to freezer

freezing—popsicles require 4–8 hours to freeze solidly

fruit base—ripe or slightly overripe fruit. (Most fruits work well.) Juice or water works well as liquid for fruit-based popsicles

herbs—bring extra flavor to popsicles (organic herbs such as mint, cilantro, basil, rosemary, lavender)

molds—silicone molds (easy to clean and unmold)

sprinkles—add preferred toppings (chopped nuts, sprinkles, raspberry dust) after dipping in chocolate or white chocolate

sticks—food-safe and environmentally friendly wooden sticks to hold popsicle

sweetener—honey, agave, maple syrup, sugar (ingredients lose flavor when they freeze, so it's best for purée to have a strong flavor and be heavily sweetened before freezing)

zest—adding citrus zest (lime, lemon, orange, grapefruit) enhances flavor and adds texture

I doubt whether the world holds for anyone a more soul-stirring surprise than the first adventure with ice cream.

—Heywood Broun, sportswriter

Chapter
ONE

The cold never bothered me anyway.
—Elsa, "Let it Go," *Frozen*

Penn State Ice Cream School
State College, Pennsylvania
Friday, January 21

Two months ago, Callie Dixon had been the executive chef at one of the largest convention hotels in Boston, a hotel so highly esteemed that the Food Safety Conference chose to hold their annual meeting there. Today, she was serving up bowls of ice cream to amateurs who had hopes to become the next Ben & Jerry. She wore a shapeless smock and a hair net that made her look like a cafeteria lady, and her salary had dropped from six figures to minimum wage.

Even worse, she was lucky to have the job. A temporary job that would be over after Penn State's Ice Cream School ended. From that point on, she had no idea what she would do. Her sterling reputation in the culinary world was ruined.

And it wasn't her fault! Well, mostly it was. But not entirely.

During the conference, the hotel's event planner had kept circling through the kitchen, clapping her hands, telling the staff to step it up because attendees complained of waiting too long for their meals. Flustered, Callie had neglected to put a sauce for tomorrow's chicken entrée in the refrigerator. It stayed on the counter overnight, warming to room temperature, bacteria dividing and multiplying. Sauces could be tricky like that.

The next day, her sous-chef assumed it had been put on the counter, ready for him to use, and a meal contaminated with C. perfringens had been served . . . resulting in food poisoning. And the rest of the conference was ruined for over two hundred attendees.

While her boss informed her that he was sorry to have to let her go (oh, just say it. *Fired!*), he was sure she realized someone had to take responsibility for this. It was no small mistake. It was catastrophic. Then he added, "Callie, you do seem extremely distracted lately."

No, she wasn't extremely distracted lately. But yes, she did understand that someone's head had to roll. What irked her was how pleased the event planner looked as Callie bid her goodbyes to the staff. This woman—who'd been at the hotel for ages and ages—had never been a fan of Callie's. They'd had numerous run-ins, holding vastly different opinions about menu options. Quite simply, she did not like Callie. (That in itself was absurd! Who didn't like Callie?! During high school, she was president of the student body, homecoming queen, and—her favorite—voted most likely to become a benevolent dictator. Once a month, she went down to the shelter and fed the homeless. Everyone liked Callie! Except for the event planner.) The unfortunate sauce incident became the golden opportunity to have her fired.

And just like that, Callie's meteoric rise in the culinary world . . . was DOA. Who would ever hire a chef responsible for poisoning the entire Food Safety Conference?

But that was how she ended up at Penn State's Ice Cream School. When Jesse, her friend who helped run the school, heard what had happened at the conference, he insisted she come to Penn State during January. "No one's hiring in the winter months, anyway," Jesse had said.

True, but timing wasn't going to be the problem in finding a new job. It was her name. It was mud. She was no better than the dirt beneath people's feet.

So she packed up her bags and she drove to State College. Penn State's Ice Cream Short Course had been held every January since 1892. Past participants read like a Who's Who in the world of ice cream: Baskin-Robbins, Ben & Jerry's, Dreyer's, Dairy Queen, on and on. There was also a three-day Ice Cream 101 workshop held later in the month for serious ice cream lovers and small business owners.

Today was day one for that workshop. The class had been listening to the principal instructor give an overview of ice cream making and were about to taste samples made with different grades of milk.

Callie carried a tray full of ice cream cups to the table in the back and set a cup in front of a woman.

"Callie? Is that you?"

Callie stopped to see who had recognized her. A woman, middle-aged-ish, pretty features, blue eyes, her strawberry blond hair held back in a ponytail.

"Aunt Marnie?" Marnie Dixon had been married to her dad's eldest brother, Philip, and Callie hadn't seen her in years. She'd been unable to attend Uncle Philip's memorial service. There simply wasn't time. No, that wasn't true. She'd been so absorbed in her work that she didn't *make* time for it.

Marnie was peering up with a puzzled look on her face. "Are you okay?"

"I'm fine!" But Callie was hardly anything close to being fine. *Change the subject*, she thought. *Quick.* "What in the world are you doing here?"

Marnie lifted the ice cream cup. "I came for this."

The man sitting next to Marnie cleared his throat to remind Callie of people waiting for ice cream. She handed a cup to the man and kept working her way down the line, but her attention stayed on her aunt. "But . . . why?"

"Didn't you hear our news? No? Dawn and I moved to Cape Cod and bought an ice cream shop."

"GET OUT!"

Chairs clattered as everyone spun to look at Callie. She looked around the room at the confused group. "I didn't mean get out, like 'go,'" she said to everyone. "I meant, like 'you've *got* to be kidding me!'"

"Perhaps," the instructor said, "you could save this conversation for after class."

"Right," Callie said. She emptied her tray of ice cream cups and bent low as she swept past her aunt. "You and me. During the break. I want to hear all about this." Marnie grinned and gave her a thumbs-up.

Wow . . . Aunt Marnie had left Needham and bought an ice cream shop on the Cape. Gutsy! Bold! Brave! She tried to remember the last updates she'd heard about her cousin Dawn. She was rocking it as a CPA and engaged to her high school sweetheart, and . . . hmm . . . whatever happened to that wedding, anyway?

Callie went back to the kitchen to get more cups of ice cream from Jesse. He looked up from scooping when he realized she was standing right in front of him. "What's that big smile for?"

"Because I just saw someone special!"

He grinned. "Ah, shucks. Thanks."

"Funny." She rolled her eyes. "My aunt is attending the workshop. My favorite aunt of all. The world's best aunt."

"Yeah? What makes her the world's best?"

"Aunt Marnie's the type who always remembered to send cards. Cards for birthdays, cards for graduations, cards for Valentine's Day, for Easter. Sometimes cards to just say she was thinking of me. She's just . . . wonderful."

"What's she doing here?"

"She and her daughter are running an ice cream shop on Cape

Cod." She turned the tray around so he could add more cups on the other side.

"I didn't know you had a cousin."

"Lots of them. But Dawn and I are closest in age. Close in everything. More like sisters than cousins. We adore each other."

"Yeah? I've never even heard you talk about her."

"You know, life gets"—she shrugged—"busy."

He put the last cup on the tray. "Well, you've got some spare time now."

She snorted. True. In fact, she had a surfeit of spare time. A frightening abundance of it. Callie had never done well with downtime. She avoided it.

"Maybe it's no accident that you're here now, and your aunt is here now."

"What do you mean?"

"Why don't you go visit your best-aunt and sister-cousin on Cape Cod?"

"Not happening." She shook her head. "I've got my next best job to find."

He paused. "Callie, have you ever thought that there's a reason you got fired?"

She froze. "Uh, because the sauce that smothered the chicken should've spent the night in the refrigerator instead of on the counter."

He rubbed his chin. "Well, that's one way of looking at it. Maybe this . . . pause . . . could give you a little time for personal reflection."

"Personal *what*?" Her eyebrows shot up.

"Never mind. All I'm saying is that a little breather right now could do you some good."

She took all that in. Then she let out a long sigh.

He added the last few cups on her tray. "Everybody needs a little help sometimes."

"Tell me about it." Callie nodded, as if she knew exactly what Jesse meant. She certainly knew what it was like when someone needed help. She just wasn't clear on how to ask for it.

* * *

Marnie
Dawn! Guess who's at Penn State's Ice Cream School?

          Dawn
          Who?

Your cousin Callie! She says she's in between jobs.

          Mom—do NOT invite Callie to Cape Cod.

I didn't invite her.

          Good.

She invited herself.

Chapter
TWO

An ice cream a day keeps the tension away.

—Marnie Dixon

Penn State Ice Cream School
Friday, January 21

Marnie was shocked. She barely recognized her niece Callie, not until she heard her unmistakable sandpapery voice. She hadn't seen her in years, but the girl she remembered had *presence*. Callie would burst into a room and spray exuberance over everyone like a can of whipped cream. A tad overwhelming, even Marnie had to admit, but she was happy, upbeat, confident. Over-the-top positive.

It was only in that one split second, when Callie yelled "Get out!" that Marnie saw the old Callie. This young woman in a hair net and a big floppy smock and a defeated countenance was a stranger.

No, not entirely a stranger. Marnie had seen this side of Callie once before.

It was the summer Richard, Callie's dad, had remarried. Marnie'd had a hunch that her brother-in-law might've been ready to move on sooner than his daughter was ready for such a change, so she invited Callie to come stay with them in Needham. Callie and Dawn were about the same age, each was an only child. Marnie thought it would be an ideal opportunity for the two cousins to get to know each other.

Big mistake.

Callie made a contest over everything, and Dawn, daughter of Philip Dixon, couldn't resist competition. The two girls competed over the most ridiculous things: how quickly they brushed their teeth, to playing the piano, to side-by-side lemonade stands—and Callie always won. Always.

The summer ended with Dawn discouraged and frustrated. Callie left their home transformed into a happy little girl again. The best summer of her life, she had said. A magical summer. She asked to come back the next summer, but Dawn threw a fit and Philip, of course, supported her. He didn't like seeing his daughter come in second, even to his own niece. Summers after that were planned by Philip. Dawn attended every camp for gifted children that Philip could find. When Richard heard about those camps, he signed Callie up for the very same ones. The relentless competition between brother and brother, cousin and cousin, continued.

Marnie had wondered if part of Philip's obsession for Dawn to be successful had a lot to do with how he felt about his brother, Callie's dad, who was always on his heels of achievement. Just like Callie and Dawn, the two brothers had competed over everything. And Philip had always come in second, just like Dawn. And just like Callie, Richard had seemed oblivious to how others felt when they constantly came out as the loser.

What Philip and Dawn could never see was that Richard and Callie made them better, pushed them further than they might have pushed themselves, inspired them to stretch and reach and grasp. Because of Callie's and Richard's can-do attitude, Dawn and Philip were influenced to try things they might never have tried. Learning how to play musical instruments, running for class offices at school, trying out for sports teams.

And then there was ice cream.

As a teenager, Callie had made pints of homemade ice cream to sell to neighbors and friends. She'd made quite a name for herself—the local paper had sent a reporter and photographer to do a piece on her. She'd become a bit of a phenomenon, and boy o' boy, did Richard make sure Philip knew about that! Philip and Dawn's interest in ice cream making skyrocketed after that news, so much so that they attended Penn State's Ice Cream School. Look where that hobby had taken Dawn—she was making ice cream in her own shop on Cape Cod! And loving it.

The last few years had been so tumultuous that Marnie hadn't kept up with extended family like she usually had. She wasn't exactly sure what had been happening in Callie's life, but something was clearly wrong. She had a bone-deep feeling that Callie needed them, much the way she had during that summer when she was ten years old. In a strange way, she could see past the young woman standing in front of her to the hurting little girl inside.

What if this had been Dawn? What if Marnie had ended up like Callie's mom?

But the clincher came with Callie's last remark. "Aunt Marnie?"

She looked up. "Yes?"

"All those cards. Thank you for sending them."

So! So they had made a difference, after all. Marnie had never been sure if it was worth the effort. She'd sent cards off to Callie with regularity—birthdays, graduations, holidays—but she'd never heard anything back. Philip had said she was wasting her time, that it was like mailing something into a galactic black hole. But Marnie hadn't stopped other than the last few years, after Philip died, and life had turned upside down. She supposed she'd sent those cards because she felt some kind of responsibility to her sister-in-law, to try and provide some kind of "mothering" to Callie the way her mom would've, had things been different.

So when Callie asked if she could come visit them in Cape Cod, Marnie said yes, knowing Dawn would object. How could she not? Still, she was glad she was here and Dawn was there.

She felt her phone vibrate in her pocket and was relieved she remembered to leave it on silent. Not thirty seconds later, it vibrated again and she pulled it out to see a text come in.

Dawn
Mom, pick up! We need to talk about Callie's visit.

> **Marnie**
> Can't talk. In class. Instructor discussing prepackaged bases.

Avoidance strategy! Not fair.

No kidding. Marnie smiled and tucked her phone back in her pocket.

● ● ●

Main Street Creamery
Chatham, MA

Dawn had been in the middle of experimenting with a new ice cream flavor this afternoon when her mom texted her about the coming of Callie. Since then, she'd been marinating in resentment.

What was Mom thinking? A visit without an end date! In *this* tiny house.

Callie's personality would fill up the house like a balloon. All personal space would be gone, pushed to the edges. The girl never stopped talking. She even sang in the shower!

And the *kitchen*. She shuddered. *Don't even get me started on that.* The kitchen belonged to Dawn. It was her personal terrain. Mom knew that, Kevin knew that, Mom's very good friend Lincoln knew that. Leo the Cowboy knew that. Even Nanette, the nosy T-shirt retailer across the street who respected no boundaries whatsoever—even she knew that.

But Callie, being Callie, would be blind to that reality. Dawn had it all pictured in her mind just like a movie: she'd done it at Dawn's first apartment in Boston. Who could forget that exasperating event?

Mom had been gently nagging Dawn to invite Callie for dinner sometime, so she finally did. Callie had sat on the kitchen stool and watched Dawn as she cut an onion. It wasn't a minute before she hopped off the stool and took the knife out of Dawn's hand. "I just want to show you a better way," she said. She started chopping the onion with her fancy chef-y techniques, then picked up the green pepper and sliced it expertly, then diced the tomatoes. Dawn ended up on the stool, watching Callie finish the entire meal. Most irritating was that the meal ended up tasting far, far better than Dawn's version.

As Kevin later said, you can't ask a chef to dinner. It just doesn't work.

After that, Dawn sort of ignored Callie. She wasn't rude about it, she just didn't engage much. Callie would text her and she would respond with a thumbs-up or thumbs-down or "Ha! Ha!"—the cyber way of saying "I read your message but I'm too busy to text back." Once a year or so, Callie would invite her to come have dinner at the restaurant, but she would decline, using tax season as her excuse, which wasn't entirely an empty lie. Tax season loomed large for a CPA.

Her thoughts slid toward Kevin. He had proposed to Dawn just a few weeks ago on New Year's Day—symbolic, he had said, of their new beginning together. They hadn't made many wedding plans, not even setting a firm date, but they had sent Mom off to Ice Cream School so she could get up to speed to make ice cream properly while they were away on a long honeymoon. That was the only decision that was firmly in place—the "take-two" honeymoon. This time, Kevin and Dawn were going on an African safari. Dawn wasn't going to shortchange Kevin from the kind of honeymoon he really wanted. Not this time. But once Callie got wind of a wedding in need of plans, she'd take it over just like she took over everything.

The steady hum of the ice cream machine reminded Dawn of the task at hand. She grabbed a container to check the results of this Kevin-inspired flavor. He was studying for his master's degree in preservation architecture and had been working on some renovation projects in nearby towns. Last summer, when the Main Street Creamery opened, they'd made quite a splash with locally inspired ice cream flavors. Since then, Kevin kept encouraging Dawn to branch out to other towns. "I challenge you to come up with something delicious for Mashpee," he said just last evening. Mashpee was a small town on Upper Cape, a place where the original Cape Codders—the Wampanoags—had a reserve.

Dawn could never resist a challenge.

This afternoon, she set to work on a flavor that celebrated the town of Mashpee. To the base that she had made earlier and refrigerated to cool and cure, she had stirred in mashed green peas, green matcha powder, curry powder, and fresh mint leaves, poured the mixture into the machine, closed the gate, turned the switch on, turned the refrigeration button on . . . and waited. She listened to the sloshing sound as the dasher started to whirl, and set the timer for seven minutes. When it was done, she opened the gate and let a small amount ooze out to sample flavor and consistency. Sweet. Creamy. Cold on the tongue. A curiously savory taste. But way too soft. She set the timer for another minute, placed a bowl beneath the barrel, and opened the gate, allowing a small amount to slide out. She heard the front door open, and a rush of cold air swept into the shop. She closed the gate and popped her head around the corner to see Kevin. "Hi! You look cold."

He smiled when he saw her. "I look cold because I am cold. The wind cuts right through my clothes." He unzipped his coat and hung it over a chair, then his scarf. He looked around the shop. "No customers?"

"Not many this afternoon. Hold on, I have something for you." She grabbed two spoons and went to meet him with the bowl. "Are you too cold to try a new flavor of ice cream?"

"It's never too cold for ice cream."

She held out a spoonful for him to taste. "It's still a little soft."

"Great flavor." Kevin swallowed the scoop. "But an odd color."

Dawn looked into the container. "I was mixing in curry to the base when Mom texted with bad news. I think I got distracted when

I added the curry. Too much. The turmeric in the curry turns everything bright yellow. I thought the green peas and matcha might tone it down, but it turned everything kind of . . . brown." And not a luscious chocolatey brown . . . a disgusting shade of brown. But the taste—that was surprisingly good. She'd have to keep fiddling with it.

"What bad news could your mom possibly have from Ice Cream School?"

She dropped her shoulders with an exaggerated sigh. "My cousin Callie is coming for an open-ended visit."

"Callie, as in, the cousin who outdid you in everything?"

Dawn frowned. "She didn't always outdo me." She sighed again. "Well, yes. She did."

Kevin took another spoonful of ice cream and swallowed it whole. "This flavor is strangely addictive."

"I know, right?" Dawn dug in her spoon to try another taste. Creamy, sweet, yet slightly savory.

"Is Callie still working as a chef at that fancy downtown hotel?"

"Not just any old chef. *The* chef." She frowned. "She was only twenty-five years old when she was promoted to the head chef position. Uncle Richard made sure everyone knew what a big deal that was." And it *was* a big deal. Dawn had to give her that.

"Callie's always been a real slacker." He grinned at her.

Kevin wasn't taking this seriously. "It's just that . . ."

"You're jealous of her."

"Insanely jealous."

He grinned and tugged at her hand to pull her close to him. "You know, don't you, that you have no reason to be jealous of Callie."

She resisted his tug. "You think I don't remember how you and your goofy friends used to drool around Callie."

"That was back when we were idiots. We've matured since then. Me, especially."

"Yeah? Let's wait 'til you see Callie."

"I don't have to." He leaned forward to kiss her on the tip of her nose. "You're the only one I'm looking at."

She smiled. "Good answer," she said, and kissed him again. The bowl nearly slipped from her hand, and she remembered there was ice cream waiting to be scooped out and popped into the freezer.

With her hand on the gate, she froze. *This machine!* Her gleaming 6-quart Emery Thompson ice cream maker! If Callie dared to try out Dawn's precious ice cream maker, her beloved baby, she would send her packing . . . no matter what guilt trip Mom laid on her.

She heard a text come in on her phone and glanced over at the counter, cringing when she saw the text came from Callie.

Hello to my favorite cousin! Did your mom tell you that we bumped into each other? Did she tell you I'm coming for a visit? It'll be just like old times!

That. That's exactly what worried Dawn.

Chapter
THREE

There's nothing better than a friend, unless it's a friend with ice cream.

—Unknown

Penn State Ice Cream School
Sunday, January 23

Callie knew she must've seemed pathetic to Aunt Marnie, asking if she could come stay with her for a while. She could visibly see her aunt's reluctance, hesitation written all over her face. If Callie were in a better place, she would've backed down, would've avoided humiliating herself to her aunt and, eventually, to her cousin Dawn. She dreaded the pity on their faces and the assumptions they'd make. She dreaded how sorry they'd feel for her.

But she was desperate, lonely, and scared.

"The thing is," Marnie said, "the ice cream shop is not really a home. More like a place of business."

"But then . . . where do you live?"

"Well, upstairs. The living quarters are just two small bedrooms and a bathroom. The ice cream shop is downstairs."

A fog of panic rose up through Callie's middle. If Aunt Marnie said no, where would she go? What would she do? She knew she wasn't coping well. "I won't take up much room. Just a corner."

"Another thing . . . Dawn and Kevin just got engaged. They'll be getting married soon."

Callie scrunched up her face. "I thought Dawn *was* engaged to Kevin."

"She was. But then the wedding was called off. And now it's on." Marnie hastened to add, "And it's a definite *on* this time."

"Well, that's great! Maybe I can help."

"Help?" Marnie swallowed. "How, exactly?"

"I can . . . work in the ice cream shop so that Dawn has time to plan her wedding." When her aunt continued to hesitate, Callie ordered herself to be tough. If Aunt Marnie said no, she might completely lose it. She might cry! And she never cried. Never ever.

Then came a moment when her aunt's face shifted. She seemed to get it. "You're really sure coming to Cape Cod is what you want to do?"

Callie nodded. It wasn't a want. It was a *need*.

Somehow her aunt then said exactly what Callie had hoped she'd say all along. "Of course you're welcome, Callie. You're family. Come to Chatham. Stay as long as you need to."

The first thought that ran through Callie's mind was, *That might take a tiny bit longer than anyone might imagine.* Happily, she didn't say it out loud.

When she told Jesse her plans, he was pleased. "Go!" he said. "The change will do you good. Besides, you have nothing to lose."

Oh, but Callie did. She had everything to lose.

Jesse didn't understand. No one did. No one could. Losing her dream job was terrible, mortifying, but the *reason* why she had made such a rookie mistake . . . that was impossible to forget.

• • •

Main Street Creamery, Chatham, MA
Sunday, January 30

Upstairs at the Creamery, Dawn was reconfiguring her small bedroom to fit both a twin bed and an air mattress. Leaning against the doorjamb, Mom watched her struggle. "Maybe there'd be a little more room if your bed could be up against that wall."

Hands on her hips, Dawn squinted, trying to visualize it. Mom was probably right. She had a better spatial sense than Dawn did. Together, they pushed the twin bed into the corner, then stood back to assess the room, satisfied. "Better," Dawn said. She twisted her hair into a knot at the back of her neck. "How long do you think Callie plans to stay?"

"Honestly, I don't know if she knows. She just seemed to want to be with us."

"Couldn't you have put a limit on it?"

Mom sighed. "Let's give her a little time. She seemed very appreciative, Dawn. She's looking forward to seeing you."

Dawn dropped to her knees to pull the air mattress, borrowed from Mom's very good friend Lincoln Hayes, out of its box. "Well, we'll soon be seeing quite a lot of each other." Too much. She could take Callie only in small doses. She was the single most talkative person she'd ever met.

"You haven't seen Callie in a couple of years, have you?"

"Nope." Dawn hooked the pump up to the air mattress and turned it on. As air filled up the mattress, Mom brought sheets, blankets, and a pillow from the hall closet. Spreading a sheet over the mattress, Dawn said, "Don't you think it's odd that Callie has never been in love?"

Mom arched an eyebrow. "How do you know she hasn't?"

"I asked her once and she said she hadn't."

"Maybe she just hasn't met the right person yet."

"I know for a fact that plenty of guys would've liked to be the right person."

Mom lifted a shoulder in a shrug. "Seems like your generation is waiting longer for love than mine did."

"But most everyone wants to find love." Dawn stood up and stretched while Mom spread a blanket on top of the mattress. "What about the guy at the Ice Cream School? Think there was something between them?"

"Jesse? He's quite a bit younger than Callie. He was right out of high school when he came to work at the hotel. Callie trained him in her kitchen. No, there's nothing between them other than friendship. More like the brother she'd never had."

"Well, I think it's strange that we've never heard mention of anyone special in her life. I mean, Uncle Richard would've trumpeted it, like he did everything else Callie accomplished."

"Love is not an accomplishment. It's just a . . . gift. And when the time is right, like it's been for you and Kevin, it'll happen for Callie." She frowned. "Dawn, your cousin is coming here because she needs a little breather between jobs. She doesn't need us overanalyzing her. I hope you're going to give Callie the breathing space she needs."

Dawn plumped the pillow and set it on the makeshift bed. "There is no breathing space in this bedroom for a long-term houseguest."

"I offered to have her stay in my room."

"No, that's too weird."

"How is it weird?"

"No one wants to sleep in the same room as an—"

"As an old lady?" Mom scowled.

Dawn grinned. "You said it, not me." Her grin faded. "Tell me again . . . why is she coming here?"

"I told you. She's out of work."

"So why isn't she looking for a job?"

"I don't know the circumstances. But I do know Callie's always put a lot of importance on her career plans. Maybe she's having a hard time bouncing back."

Dawn zeroed in on her mom. "So you think that's why she's coming here to stay for an indefinite period? Her plans have fallen through?" Plans were always falling through! Look at Dawn's wedding to Kevin last year. That was a colossal fall-through. What about Mom's breast cancer? That changed everything. Sure, losing a job was a big deal, but Callie was resilient. She was the epitome of toughness. She was happy. Always. Annoyingly so.

Downstairs, the door opened and a voice called out, "Aunt Marnie? Dawn? Hello? Is anybody here?"

Dawn exchanged a look with her mom. "She's here."

She followed her mom downstairs to greet Callie. The very second she set eyes on her cousin, all of her outrage melted away. She hadn't seen Callie in years—she'd done her best to avoid her—but the cousin she remembered had been effervescent. She glowed. Light came off her and illuminated everything and everyone around her. And personality plus! She had this bottomless-energy thing about her, like those TV weather people. Happy all the time. Her happy didn't have a dimmer switch.

But *this* Callie? She walked into the Main Street Creamery like a shell of her former self. She was pale, eyes bloodshot, her tangled blond hair was pulled back in a sloppy braid that ran down her back, strands escaped that loosely hung on her shoulders. Her clothes were mismatched and her shoes weren't shoes at all, but pink fuzzy slippers. Dawn couldn't help but notice how thin Callie had gotten—tall and thin as a willow. She hardly even looked around the room before she just sank into a wooden chair like she was utterly exhausted.

"Callie, can I fix you something to eat?" Mom asked, her voice soft and tender, like she was talking to a sick kid sent home from school.

"Thanks, no. I'll just sit for a moment, then take my stuff to my room." Callie's impossibly big dark brown eyes—such beautiful eyes—blinked in confusion as she gazed around the ice cream shop. It seemed to just occur to her that this wasn't an actual home, but a place of business. Hadn't Mom described the shop to her? "Do I . . . have a room?"

"Sort of. You're staying with me in my room. Upstairs." Dawn forced a smile. "Just like old times." She swept her arm in a half circle. "Different surroundings."

"I've never been to Cape Cod before," Callie said.

"Really? Even though you lived in Boston most of your life?"

"Living someplace," Callie said, ". . . you end up missing the touristy stuff."

Dawn couldn't argue that. She'd only been to Cape Cod a few times as a child. "Actually, coming to the Cape in winter might be a better introduction to it. It gets pretty crazy in the summer." She didn't add, *You're not planning to stay until summer, are you?*

Callie gazed out the window. "Is it always this foggy here?"

"Pretty much." Mom sounded like she'd been given a compliment. "Locals call it sea fog. They're very proud of it."

Callie looked around, her eyes sweeping the ceiling, the floors, the fireplace. "This building must be really, really old."

Mom's smile bloomed. "Over two hundred and sixty years old."

Dawn pointed to a horseshoe over the fireplace. "It was built by a blacksmith named Daniel Baker. We found some of his old nails and horseshoes when we were doing some work on the foundation." *Some* work . . . ha! They did a massive amount of work. This building should have been condemned. Kevin would be horrified by that thought, but it was true.

"Daniel Baker and his wife, Prudence," Mom said, "raised ten children here."

Callie's eyes went wide. "Ten children? Here?" She swept the room with a puzzled gaze. "If it were any smaller, it would be a doll house."

"Somehow, they managed," Mom said. "It's in an ideal location. Right in the heart of the town. A blacksmith was one of the most valued individuals in the colonies."

"I suppose there'd be lots of horses needing new shoes."

"Well, sure, horses needed shodding," Dawn said, a little pleased to know something Callie didn't seem to know. "And then farm tools were essential. Door hinges, door handles. Guns needed repair. If a community didn't have a smithy, they would poach one from another town by offering a choice piece of land."

Mom grinned. "We figure if the place could handle Daniel and Prudence Baker and those ten children, and all the horses that were shod, and all the tools that were hammered into existence . . . then it can put up with the two of us trying to run an ice cream shop."

Callie listened to Mom as if she had trouble imagining the scenario. "Ten children?" she repeated. "Raised here?"

Dawn leaned across the table. "Callie, are you feeling okay?"

Callie seemed surprised by the question. "I'm great!"

Right. She was three blocks short of great.

The door opened and in walked Leo the Cowboy. He looked at Callie, then at Dawn. "Just checking to make sure the lost lady found you."

"Leo, you have to remember to close the door behind you." Dawn jumped up to shut the door. "This is Leo, our resident cowboy."

"We've met," Callie said. "While I was driving along Main Street."

"She didn't know where she was going," Leo said. "She kept driving up and down the street, slower than Mrs. Nickerson-Eldredge."

Dawn had to bite back a smile. "Don't tell me you asked a six-year-old for directions?"

"Six and a quarter." Leo's small chest puffed with pride.

"He was tossing a rope to lasso a park bench," Callie said. "I figured a daring cowboy like him might know where the nearest ice cream shop would be."

Leo looked up at Callie. "Are you married?"

Callie looked startled. "No."

"Do you have a boyfriend?"

"Nope."

He looked pleased, and then a big grin spread over his little round face. It figured. Callie had been here ten minutes and she'd coaxed a smile out of serious Leo. So whatever *was* wrong with her cousin, it hadn't stolen her magic touch.

Dawn took Leo's hand and squeezed. "Seems like a cowboy should get a reward for helping a damsel in distress. Let's go see if we can rustle up some ice cream." They went into the kitchen as Mom took Callie upstairs to show her around. As Dawn scooped a bowlful of Leo's favorite flavor—chocolate—and sprinkled it with mini-marshmallows, she wondered what Callie would think when she saw the tiny living quarters. She would've loved to see the expression on her face when she stood at the open door of the barely-enough-room-to-walk-in bedroom and realized she'd be sleeping on a cold air mattress.

• • •

Callie never should have come. She'd only driven to Cape Cod because she felt desperate, although she couldn't articulate exactly what she was desperate for. She thought she'd been doing a pretty good job of mimicking a normal conversation with Marnie and Dawn until she realized she was shaking. Not trembling, not the way you do when you're cold and your chin shivers, making it hard to talk. Instead, it felt like a shudder that was traveling from toe to head, the way her mom's seizures used to start. That now familiar tightness, concrete evidence of all that was going wrong with her life . . . it began to squeeze her chest.

Could Marnie and Dawn tell? Had they noticed?

She told them she needed to use the bathroom and hurried to close the door behind her. She heard Dawn lug her suitcase up the stairs, but she stayed in the bathroom. She wasn't up for another attempt at conversation.

After a while, Dawn knocked on the door and said, "Callie, I need to get going. Your suitcase is in the bedroom and Mom is downstairs, if you need anything."

"Thanks," Callie said.

"You sure you're okay?"

"I'm fine!" Callie said through the door. "Couldn't be better!" She felt a funny little pressure in her throat, like she might cry. But she didn't cry! Callie. Did. Not. Cry.

She washed her face and then went to Dawn's bedroom. The room was even smaller than she'd expected. Dawn had pushed her twin bed against the wall to make room for the air mattress. In between was a narrow path that led to a night table with a goose-necked lamp. She forced herself to unpack, although the only thing she wanted to do was flop down on the air mattress and sleep. But then, as soon as she did, she couldn't sleep.

Too much to process, she guessed. Her mind was spinning. She kneaded her calves, tight from the drive. How could life change so quickly? Then again, maybe she'd always known this grim fate was going to be her future. Maybe this was why she was always in such a hurry to reach milestones.

She lay on the air mattress and tried not to think about her future, how gray and dismal and bleak it seemed, but it was a strategy that never really worked. Just the opposite. The more she tried not to think about it, the more she thought about it. It was like being told not to think about a circus clown, and suddenly all that filled your mind was a large man in a polka-dot outfit with a bright red, round nose.

Callie'd had a lot of time to think lately. One thing she had firmly decided: She would never, ever cook for anyone again. She would never return to the kitchen. Too much responsibility to bear.

Giving up felt good. Maybe *good* was too strong a word, but it certainly took the pressure off. And that might be the best she could hope for. With that in mind, she felt herself unspooling like the string of a kite caught up in the wind.

● ● ●

Monday, January 31

Early the next morning, the winter sun shone brightly as Marnie bundled up to head out for a walk. As she was zipping her coat, Dawn came downstairs to stop her.

"Mom, you can't leave."

"I'm just going to the beach. I'm meeting Lincoln."

"We planned to make ice cream this morning. I thought that was the reason you went to Ice Cream School, so you'd be up to speed to take my place after the wedding."

"Yes. That is the plan. But it's not even seven o'clock in the morning. I'll be back in an hour or so and we can get started." She glanced at the stairs. "Unless Callie is still asleep. Maybe we should wait to use the machine until she wakes up."

Dawn scoffed. "Nothing can wake that girl up. She's always been a champion sleeper." She took a step closer. "How could you have extended an invitation to come here when she's in that kind of condition? What were you thinking?"

Marnie slipped one foot into a boot, then another. "Well, she did

35

seem stronger at Ice Cream School. More like herself." But she knew what Dawn meant. Callie's condition was alarming. She looked fragile, weary, and beyond weary, defeated. "Just give her a little time."

"Oh no. Stop pretending she's okay. She's not!" Her brow furrowed. "Do you think she's on drugs?"

"No drugs."

"Head injury?"

"None that I know of."

"Then what? Because something is"—she waved her arms in the air—"way off."

Marnie wrapped a scarf around her neck. "Dawn, you're overreacting." Normally, that would be true. Dawn had always overreacted when it came to Callie. But probably not this time. "Callie's just in a little funk. I'm sure she'll snap out of it soon." She hoped so. "Have a little empathy. Callie's been working hard these last few years. Really hard. Maybe she just needs a little time off."

"Do you have any idea how long she'll be here?"

Marnie rolled her eyes. "She hasn't even been here twenty-four hours."

Dawn clapped a palm against her chest. "Mom, I have to share a bedroom with her."

"Don't forget that I offered to share my room. So if you're going to be hospitable, then be truly hospitable."

"Has it ever occurred to you," Dawn said in a smug tone, "that the root word of *hospitable* is hospital?"

Stuffing one hand in a mitten, Marnie paused. "Meaning . . . ?"

"Callie should be with professionals. We can't be responsible for her."

"She's not asking us to be responsible for her. She just needs a little time with family. She's where she needs to be."

"You know that feeling you get about people sometimes when it's like they're on the edge of a cliff—and even the tiniest breeze could tip them over?"

Marnie sighed. "Overreacting again."

"Mom, do you think she can be fixed?"

"I think she can be helped."

"She's been sleeping since she arrived. She's nearly comatose!"

"And you were worried she would push you out of your kitchen. She hasn't even been near it!" With that, she slipped out the door and headed due east to meet Lincoln and his dog Mayor.

Twenty minutes later, Marnie reached the sand and went straight down to the water's edge. The air was cold, but it was low tide, the surf was gentle, and the sun had just barely lifted above the horizon to shed light on the water. She drew in a deep breath of salty air. She loved it here, absolutely loved it. In April, it would be a full year since she'd moved from Needham, where she'd lived for most of her life, yet it felt like she'd always been here. Or maybe, she felt as if she'd always belonged here.

Marnie heard a bark and turned to see Mayor bolting toward her, kicking up sand as he ran. She braced herself. The big golden retriever was known for misjudging the sand, resulting in body slams on innocent victims. This morning, he veered off at the last second to chase a seagull.

Lincoln jogged up to join her. "Morning!"

She involuntarily held her breath at the sight of Lincoln Hayes. At sixty-two, he still looked like a young man with an athletic build—broad shoulders, narrow hips. The only giveaway to his age was his salt-and-pepper hair, cropped close. When she first met Linc, her impression was an older Clark Kent. She still saw him that way. Like Superman, he had swooped in many times to rescue the Main Street Creamery.

"Sorry to be late," he said.

He smiled and she couldn't help but smile in return. "No problem."

Mayor ran up to them and shook, spraying water all over them. Then he bounded off into the waves again.

"And now another sorry is in order." Linc cleaned off his glasses with the corner of his shirttail.

They started walking up the beach, their usual route. She couldn't help but notice how their hands kept brushing against each other as they walked. Each time it happened she felt a little jolt, even through the thick mitten.

"Did your niece arrive?"

"She did. In a manner of speaking."

"What do you mean?"

Marnie stopped. "When I saw Callie at Ice Cream School, it was clear that something seemed off, but we didn't have much time to talk. I was kept busy by the workshop and she was working. That was over a week ago, and she seems far worse now."

"Worse . . . how so?"

"She seems like a ghost of the girl she was. She's been sleeping practically nonstop since she arrived."

"What do you think has happened?"

"I don't really know any details." She gave her shoulders a shrug. "But it's a pretty good bet that Dawn won't rest until she figures it out."

● ● ●

Dawn
You won't believe what I found out!

Kevin
What?

Callie's all tangled up in a lawsuit.

Uh, seems like that shouldn't be something to celebrate.

Of course not! It's terrible.

But a little corner of her heart—a shameful, ugly part of her—just couldn't help but gloat.

Chapter
FOUR

Life is like an ice cream cone. Enjoy it before it melts.

—Unknown

Tuesday, February 1

Sometime after midnight, Callie tiptoed out of the bedroom to go downstairs to get a glass of water. A step squeaked about midway down the stairs and she froze, hoping the sound didn't wake up Dawn or Aunt Marnie, then hurriedly tiptoed down the rest of the stairs. Someone had left on the light above the stove, giving the kitchen a soft illumination. It was a nice little galley kitchen, tidy and clean. She looked in the cupboard and found a glass, filled it with water, and took a few sips. On the counter was a rack with muffins that were cooling. Callie leaned over to examine them. They looked odd for muffins. Their texture too tight. Over-mixed. Rubbery.

"Callie, are you hungry?"

She spun around to see her aunt at the end of the kitchen. "Did I wake you?" That squeaky stairstep!

"No. I was still reading."

She was just being kind. Callie knew her aunt's bedroom light was out. Marnie took a few steps toward the refrigerator and Callie moved back so she could open the door. This was a one-cook kitchen. That wasn't necessarily a bad thing. Small kitchens could be incredibly efficient. But she did wonder how Marnie and Dawn managed working together for the ice cream shop in this narrow space. It would have to be highly organized for two people not to bump into each other all the time.

"During the winter months, we've been trying to keep the Creamery open with coffee and baked goods. We had been buying goods from a bakery, but the baker left for Florida, so Dawn's been making muffins in the evening to sell each day. You're welcome to have one."

Callie cast a glance at the rubber muffins. "Not right now."

Marnie held up a white box. "Kevin brought some Chinese takeout for supper. I can warm it up. Does that sound appealing?"

It sounded awful. But Callie didn't want to be rude. She saw a bunch of bananas on the counter and grabbed one. "This hits the spot. Thanks for the offer, though." She started toward the stairs, but Marnie called her name. She turned.

"I'm always available," Marnie said, "if you'd like to talk."

There was such compassion in her aunt's voice, such kindness in her face, that Callie nearly inhaled a deep breath and exhaled the whole story. Almost. But she caught herself. How could she even talk about this without seeming like a wounded animal? No one needed to hear such a depressing story at this late hour. At any hour.

Instead, she lifted the banana and gave her aunt what she hoped was a bright smile. "I'm pretty bushed. I'll see you in the morning." She hurried up the stairs, skipping over what she now knew was the giveaway squeaky step. She tiptoed back to bed and lay down, staring at the ceiling.

She must have fallen asleep, because the next time she opened her eyes, light was outlining the edges of the window curtains. She made herself get up, grab a robe, and go downstairs. She found Dawn at a small wooden table in the front room, staring at her computer. "Morning."

Dawn looked up, first with a smile, but it quickly faded. "That's my robe."

Callie looked down at the blue chenille robe she had on. "Is it?"

"Yes," Dawn said, frowning. "You slept so long that I wondered if you'd passed away."

"Not dead."

"I even checked on you. Just to make sure."

"Still here."

Dawn rose, passed around Callie to head into the kitchen, and returned with a cup of coffee, then handed it to her.

"Thanks." The warm ceramic mug felt wonderful in her hands. It might be sunny today, but it was cold. Really cold. "Does it get warmer as the day goes on?"

"Nope. The ocean air keeps everything dank and cold."

"Sea fog, your mom called it." It was a nice term for something that seemed like a quivering, smothering blanket of cold.

"She's out in it now with her very good friend Lincoln."

"A very good friend?" Callie asked. How long ago had Uncle Philip died? Going on two years, she realized. It would be nice if Aunt Marnie had someone special in her life.

"Yep. Lincoln Hayes. I'm sure you'll meet him. He's been wonderful to us." Dawn disappeared back into the kitchen.

Callie walked around the front room, admiring the touches. The first thing she noticed was the amount of light pouring in from those long, narrow double-hung windows. She put a hand against one window, feeling the cold seep through. Original, no doubt. No wonder this place was so cold. The wood floors were rough-hewn, nicely weathered. An old brick fireplace anchored the room, though it didn't look like it was used. The antique tables and chairs were perfectly mismatched. Aunt Marnie's doing. She'd always had flair. Uncle Philip used to say that Aunt Marnie had fantastic taste in junk. She would head out to a tag sale and come home with a box full of odd castoffs: roof snowbirds she turned into bookends, a wooden coffee grinder she transformed into a lamp, a weathered lobster trap she fashioned into a coffee table. Trash became treasure. It was one of the reasons Callie had always loved Marnie. How could she not? Marnie could find beauty in anything. She was a caretaker. She liked to help things flourish.

The only two modern pieces in the room were an upright freezer by the door and, closer to the kitchen, an ice cream display counter. Behind the glass, Callie counted twelve containers, though only six were filled with ice cream. The entire room was well designed, Callie thought, turning in a circle. Appealing but functional.

She sat down at a small table near a window to sip her coffee. Outside, she saw a middle-aged couple walking a dog. She wondered if they had any realization of how precious that ordinary moment was, such a sweet and simple part of the day, or if they were too caught up racing through their to-do lists. Like she'd always been.

Dawn slipped into a chair across the table and set a scone on a plate in front of Callie. "I can make you some eggs."

"This will be fine." She had no appetite, but to be polite, she tore off a corner of the scone and tasted it. She started to chew, then stopped, and couldn't help herself—she made a face.

Dawn saw. "What's wrong with it?"

Callie swallowed. "Just a little dry." Truthfully, it was appalling. Shocking ratios. Too much baking soda, not enough salt. Terrible, terrible, terrible.

Dawn frowned. "For the last few months, we've been getting baked goods from a local bakery. Then right after Christmas, the baker fled town for Florida sunshine, so I've been filling in."

"Maybe you should offer customers a little soft butter to go with the scone. A little jam, perhaps?"

"Baking uses different, um, skills than ice cream making."

"Well, yes and no. They both require acute attention to detail."

Slightly frowning, Dawn picked up the scone plate from Callie. "Can I get you something else to eat?"

"Maybe later. Coffee's fine for now." Had she said something wrong? Dawn whisked the plate back into the kitchen. When she returned, she sat across from Callie, her face compressed into a sympathetic frown.

"So," Dawn said, hands around her own mug of coffee. "So, you got fired for poisoning the entire Food Safety Conference."

Surprised by her bluntness, Callie choked so violently on the coffee she'd been sipping on that Dawn had to grab the mug from her.

"Sorry! It's all over the news."

Callie felt a sting of alarm. "All over the news, as in . . . your local newspaper? Here?" In a tiny town that was practically slipping away into the Atlantic Ocean?

Dawn tipped her head toward the table where her computer sat. "On the internet."

Even worse! Her thoughts zigged and zagged like a balloon losing air.

Dawn handed back her mug. "Guess it's still a tender subject."

"No," Callie said. "It's not a tender subject."

Dawn wrinkled her nose. "So it wasn't your fault?"

"Well," she hesitated, unable to meet her cousin's eyes. How to explain something she still hadn't fully come to grips with? She wasn't ready to talk about it, especially with Dawn. She sat up straight and adjusted her voice to sound noble. "Let's just say, as the executive chef, I took full responsibility for the mishap."

"And you got fired."

"It was a mutual decision," Callie said.

"In December," Dawn added, as if to say she was already up on all the details.

"In December," Callie said, sitting up even straighter. "In a way, it was all for the best. Time for a change."

"Did someone really die?"

"No!" Though one person was hospitalized for dehydration after throwing up all night. "No. No one died."

"Well, that's good to hear. I mean, when I read about the lawsuit . . ."

Callie glanced away. So. She blew out a puff of air. So that had made it into the news too. She'd only learned about the lawsuit last week while working at Ice Cream School. It was the tipping point that made her want to run away to her aunt's home. To hide. She cringed, thinking of how her dad would react to news of a pending lawsuit.

"So you're really okay with . . . everything that's happened?"

"Of course!" Dodging the heart of the question, Callie added, "I'm always okay."

"Nobody's always okay."

"I am!" Callie declared, her voice falsely bright. Of course she wasn't okay. But even if she had wanted to discuss how troubled she'd felt these last few months, which she did not, her cousin would not be the one she'd turn to. She wasn't sure who she should turn to, but it definitely wouldn't be Dawn, who'd had a nearly picture-perfect life. She could never understand.

"Okay," Dawn said at last, in that unconvincing way, but at least she was finally dropping it. "So what's next?"

"Working on that now." Callie lifted the mug and tried to keep her voice un-irritated. "In fact, I have emails I need to respond to. Lots of opportunities to consider."

"Really? I mean, that's great." Dawn's expression screamed epic fail. "Uh, well, with your skills and experience, I'm sure you won't have any trouble getting a job."

Sure, because "poisoning the entire Food Safety Conference" looks great on my résumé.

Way too much conversation. Callie rose. She needed to be alone. Pronto. "Thanks for the coffee." With that, she went back upstairs, set the coffee mug on the floor, and flopped facedown on the air mattress.

* * *

Marnie arrived home later than expected. She and Lincoln stopped for a coffee and bagel at a shop and time got away from them. When she returned to the Creamery, she found Dawn going over bills at a table she'd pushed against the window to maximize the winter sunlight. Unbuttoning her coat, she braced herself. "Bad news?"

"Not bad," Dawn said. "But not good. I had thought we'd break even by selling coffee and baked goods through the winter months.

But there's just not much foot traffic. We're squeaking by but just barely."

Marnie shared her concern. It was their first winter, and they'd had a lot to learn about the rhythms of the Cape. The autumn months had seen a dwindling of customers, but she'd expected that. The shock came after Christmas. In the quiet, cold, gray mornings of January, she and Linc would walk through town, past dark houses that had been closed up for the rest of the winter. She had never imagined so many locals would have fled for warmer climates. She'd never thought the Creamery would be this empty of customers.

The door opened and Kevin walked in. He dropped his messenger bag on the floor and hung his coat up on the rack. He often stopped in for a quick bite at the Creamery after work and before class.

Marnie grabbed a muffin from under the glass cloche for Kevin. "Any sign of Callie?" She set the muffin on a plate and handed it to Kevin.

"Briefly," Dawn said. "She came down, had coffee, and went back upstairs."

Kevin pulled out a chair next to Dawn and sat down. "She sounds," he said, in between muffin bites, "depressed to me."

"Callie? Not a chance. Callie Dixon thinks depression is a word confined to economics."

Marnie poured two mugs of coffee and brought them to the table, handing one to Kevin. "Did she tell you anything more today?"

"Not really." Dawn seesawed her hand in the air. "But she did confirm what I had dug up on the internet."

Marnie gave her a puzzled look. "Such as . . ."

"Food poisoning at the Food Safety Conference," Dawn said. "Callie got axed." She drew an imaginary line across her neck. "There's a lawsuit pending. My guess is she'll have trouble getting hired. Anywhere."

Kevin blew out a whistle. "That's a hard thing."

"Very hard," Marnie echoed.

"I suppose," Dawn said, sounding unconvinced.

Marnie threw her daughter an exasperated look. She was a little disappointed in Dawn's lack of empathy for Callie. "Everyone hits a brick wall sooner or later."

"It's just that this is . . . Callie. There isn't a mountain she can't scale." Dawn pointed a thumb toward the stairs. "Just watch. Somehow, she will land on her feet. Somehow, the worst thing will end up being the best thing." She folded her arms against her chest. "It's the Callie Magic."

Marnie hoped Dawn might be right. Callie had always seemed unstoppable. While it was Dawn who'd been given the nickname Teflon Dawn, it was really Callie who was Teflon-ish. Nothing seemed to faze her. If she got knocked down (and Marnie doubted she'd ever been knocked down), she was the type to get right back up.

Until now.

A small but niggling voice kept nagging Marnie that maybe there was something else going on with her.

● ● ●

Callie didn't mean to eavesdrop, but the Creamery was a small, compact structure. No insulation between the downstairs and the upstairs. Quite possibly, judging by how chilly the house was, there was no insulation in the walls either. Marnie's voice was soft and low, hard to hear clearly, but Callie could definitely make out a man's deep voice. Kevin's, maybe? And she could hear Dawn's voice quite clearly. She found Dawn's confidence that she would land on her feet to be touching. Imagine that. Callie Magic. Her cousin wasn't terribly demonstrative or expressive, but Callie knew they held a special bond.

She'd always treasured Dawn. They used to be close, spending every summer together at various camps. When they were young adults, she would've liked to spend more time with her, but their schedules didn't easily align. Dawn, even more than Callie, was always too busy to get together.

But the time they'd spent together in summer camps became the highlight of Callie's childhood and teen years. It was too bad their lives took such radically different turns after high school. She still had trouble getting her head around the fact that her cousin now ran an ice cream shop on Cape Cod. That news had gobsmacked Callie. It wasn't the ice cream part that was hard to understand, it was Dawn leaving her hotshot CPA career behind. But the love of making ice cream, that she understood. In fact, Dawn was the reason Callie had first ventured into the kitchen. Aunt Marnie had sent a birthday card and mentioned that Dawn had been making ice cream with her dad, so she decided to give it a try. Instantly, she fell in love with the process of it. Even better, she quickly discovered that everyone loved ice cream. She became the most popular girl in high school.

And culinary school wasn't even on Callie's radar until she'd heard Dawn bring it up to another camper during the summer after their junior year in high school. Callie had planned to apply to a number of colleges in the Northeast—all the ones Dawn had talked about for the last three summers. But culinary school? Where had *that* come from? Intriguing.

So when Callie returned home after camp, she researched culinary schools, applied to the very one Dawn had mentioned to the camper, and ended up—to her dad's delight—receiving a full scholarship. She'd expected to hear similar news from Dawn, couldn't wait to compare notes and make plans (maybe become roommates!), but then she learned that her cousin was heading to college to study accounting. *That* came out of the blue.

She heard Dawn say something downstairs that jolted her out of her memory sifting. "Sure, getting fired is no fun, and a lawsuit sounds terrifying, but this is bounce-back-Callie we're talking about. There's got to be something else going on. I think that maybe it's a secret she's keeping. Maybe that's what's got her in such a mood."

Callie put her earbuds in and turned on her Calm app, squeezing her eyes shut. Dawn was right. She was keeping a secret. Something big. The lawsuit *was* terrifying, but it was the least of her troubles. Here's where her favorite cousin had it wrong: Her life couldn't be reduced to a mountain that needed scaling. More like a star that was just about to implode.

FIVE

Someone should open an ice cream shop with flavors like *Don't Be Sad!* and *You Deserve Better!*

—Callie Dixon

Wednesday, February 2

Callie had spent the last twenty-four hours studiously avoiding Dawn and Marnie, which was no easy feat in a house the size of a shoebox. She needed quiet, restorative time alone, though it didn't feel particularly restorative. Just being near the buzz of activity of Marnie and Dawn's life, their excitement about the coming season, the discussion of Dawn and Kevin's still-to-be-organized wedding . . . it made Callie feel worse. Was that possible? The world was spinning on its axis without her, and it didn't even seem to take notice of her absence.

It also felt odd that she had learned so much about this little town by the sea simply by listening and watching.

She knew that light ebbed around four thirty in the afternoon, and the sun set by five o'clock. Garbage truck pickup started early Wednesday morning. Mail arrived in the middle of the day.

Customers for ice cream or coffee or rubber muffins popped in mostly during the afternoon hours, though they were few and far between. Shockingly so.

And then there were the people of Chatham, whom she had started to recognize by their voices. Kevin and Lincoln, who spent long evening hours at the Creamery. Nanette, from across the street, had an extremely recognizable voice. Tinny and loud. She popped in and out of the Creamery frequently, talking nonstop in a stream of consciousness.

Nanette and Michael hadn't remembered to put out their garbage cans last night, so early this morning they scrambled outside, shouting at each other, at the first sound of the rumbling garbage truck. Callie had a hunch it was a weekly occurrence.

Another memorable voice: Mrs. Nickerson-Eldredge, who stopped by twice to have tea with Marnie. Callie imagined her as the prim librarian type, gray hair pulled tightly into a bun on the top of her head, doughnut-like. A permanent frown of disapproval etched on her face.

And then there were the sounds of the larger world that pulled at Callie's attention. Birds, all kinds, that could tolerate the cold winter. Seagulls, waterfowl, and the haunting sounds of the loons. She heard the loons mostly at sunset, when the town was quieting down for the night.

This was the village of Chatham she had come to know, without leaving Dawn's tiny bedroom. It was a wonder to her that Boston was only eighty-seven miles away, yet it might as well have been across an ocean. This place was a different life entirely from the hustling, bustling city.

She had discovered one benefit of the Creamery's paper-thin walls. Callie could tell when the house had emptied out. This morning, she heard Dawn greet Kevin and head out for a run. And then she heard Marnie leave, most likely to meet her very good friend Lincoln. The coast was clear. Callie threw off the covers, grabbed Dawn's robe, and went downstairs. She just couldn't handle talking to anyone, but she knew she needed to eat something.

She looked around the small galley kitchen, opening cupboards and drawers, trying to find utensils and dishes. The kitchen, clearly, was Dawn's domain. Things were organized in a system logical to her cousin but to no one else, just like the kitchen had been in Dawn's Boston apartment. A cardinal sin in restaurant work—kitchens should make sense to everyone. Callie shook her head, disappointed. If the Creamery hired more employees for the summer season, this kitchen would need a complete overhaul.

She opened the least-likely-cupboard-to-find-mugs-in and voilà! She found them. She grabbed an empty mug, filled it with leftover coffee. While waiting for the lukewarm coffee to heat up in the microwave, she noticed two large mixing bowls on the counter. One was full of flour, the other with sugar and spices. It looked like Dawn had just started to make something, then got interrupted and left the house. A recipe card was on the counter next to the bowls. The microwave beeped so she took out her mug. Sipping her coffee, Callie picked up the recipe card to skim. Chai muffins. She smiled. Nice twist.

Then her eyebrows furrowed when she read through the ingredients for spices. She found a spoon and dipped it into the spices in the mixing bowl. Just as she thought. The recipe was all wrong. All wrong.

She set down her coffee and adjusted the spices in the dry mixture, adding in ground cardamom and ground cloves, increasing the cinnamon and nutmeg. People didn't realize how spices interacted with each other, stimulating different parts of the tongue. She mixed the sugar and spices with a spatula. There, she thought, rinsing the spatula and putting it back in the drawer. Everything looked the way it had when she came downstairs.

That small spurt of creative action had sapped what little energy she had, so she found a small yogurt container in the fridge, grabbed a spoon, and went back upstairs.

A few minutes later, she heard Dawn return home from her run. Spooning the yogurt from the cup, she listened to the comforting sounds of clatter in the kitchen. It reminded her, just a little, of her restaurant work, and the thought filled her with nostalgia. And sadness. Those days were behind her. At the grand old age of twenty-eight! She tossed the empty yogurt container in the wastebasket, turned over, and punched her pillow.

Not much later, the most delicious cinnamon-nutmeg scent floated up the stairs, filling the bedroom. Callie's tummy rumbled. She hoped Dawn hadn't overmixed the muffins this time.

She heard the front door open and close, and Aunt Marnie's voice call out. "Dawn! What are you making? I could smell it all the way to the street."

"Mom, you've got to try one of my muffins. They're incredible! Just amazing. I've made this recipe before, but they've never turned out like this."

Callie smiled, pleased. It was the least she could do for Marnie and Dawn. Then her smile faded.

So pathetic. The highlight of her day was adding spices to a muffin mixture.

●　●　●

During the winter months, a couple of times a week, Marnie had been tagging along with Lincoln to help with his volunteer work. It was something he did, Monday through Saturday mornings, to redeem what he felt had been a life of acute self-centeredness. Marnie thought he was a little hard on himself, but it did sound as if he had been a champion workaholic. He'd been extremely successful in his career doing some kind of technology work, but success had taken a toll. His wife had divorced him and his two children were distant. His son, especially.

The former Lincoln Hayes was not the man Marnie had come to know this last year. Lincoln was one of the kindest, most thoughtful persons she'd had the pleasure of meeting. Generous to a fault. Almost embarrassed by his wealth. He couldn't do enough for others. Philanthropy was his full-time work.

Marnie and Dawn had known Lincoln for six months before he invited them to what he called his "cottage." To quote Dawn, "*That* was the understatement of the year." Lincoln's cottage was a magnificent seven-bedroom estate with a pool and pool house, a full wrap-around deck, panoramic views, floor-to-ceiling windows, gorgeous hardwoods, a state-of-the-art kitchen. It had a wonderful fusion of indoor-outdoor living, designed for entertaining. It was a house, but it wasn't a home.

Nothing about that estate matched up with the Linc she had gotten to know. He seemed more at home in the Creamery, wearing jeans and a flannel shirt with a hammer in his hand, than he did in his hotel-like house. He told Marnie that he liked the chaos at the Creamery. He liked the confusion. Which was good, because they had plenty of chaos and confusion to spare.

And Marnie felt the same way. She had always lived modestly, with a bent toward making old things new, to give them life. She had an almost insatiable need to make things lovely again. Her favorite way to spend a day was to roam through tag sales and look for cast-off treasures to restore or repurpose. It was her *thing*, the way philanthropy was Linc's thing.

Linc had been kind enough to offer free room and board to Kevin while he was working on his master's degree, but he declined. Kevin felt he needed to support himself during this career shift from a commercial architect to a specialty of preservation architect, and he also wanted to be closer to Dawn at the Creamery. Dawn confided to Marnie that Kevin felt uncomfortable in Linc's enormous house, like he might get lost in it and never be found. Marnie had been a little sorry to hear Kevin turned down Linc's generous offer. It would've helped him save money while he was in graduate school, and she knew that he and Dawn had talked about buying a home after they married. Chatham was not inexpensive.

But Marnie was also disappointed Kevin had turned the offer down because she worried Linc was lonely. Frankly, she hadn't been worried about him until she saw the size of that house. It was just ridiculous.

But she didn't say as much to Kevin or Dawn. Marnie had learned, through much trial and error, to *try* and stay out of the decisions made by young people even if she thought they were making mistakes. Maybe . . . especially then. They needed the experience. Somebody famous once said, "Good judgment comes from experience. Experience comes from bad judgment." Marnie knew there was truth in that saying, but it was hard to hold her tongue. She liked imparting her hard-earned wisdom. She had lived nearly sixty years on this earth. Sixty years of experience stored inside her like a library full of books. What good was knowledge if she couldn't share what she had learned? But then she remembered what her wise and wonderful friend Maeve often said: "If they aren't asking for help, they aren't listening."

The bottom line was that Kevin and Dawn hadn't asked for her advice. Nor had Callie.

And that was why she hadn't put any pressure on her niece to reveal what had brought her to Cape Cod, what had sent her to bed, and what had kept her there. If or when Callie wanted to reveal more, it was up to her to start the conversation. At least, that's what Marnie planned to do. To wait. There was plenty of time, she had decided. But now, she wasn't quite sure that was the best plan.

"Ready to go?"

Marnie startled. "Linc! Oh yes, almost done." They had spent the morning at the Family Pantry in Harwich where she'd been filling boxes of donated food. She must have slowed to a stop while her mind was pondering those nagging family issues. She quickly added the last few cans and closed the lids on the box. "Ready."

"You looked like you were a million miles away."

"Just thinking about Callie."

"Let's stop for a sandwich at the bakery down the street. You can tell me more over lunch." He waited until she zipped her coat and put on her gloves, then held the door open for her. He was thoughtful like that, always treating her like she was something special.

Over a bowl of lentil curry soup, she told him how Callie hardly interacted with them.

Linc had ordered a grilled cheese sandwich and a cup of tomato soup. He took a spoonful of soup, then reached for the saltshaker. "She's still staying in her room?"

"Yes. She rarely comes downstairs. It's so unlike her. She's always been such a flaming extrovert. She's driven Dawn crazy with her enthusiasm. Over everything." She told him about Dawn and Callie growing up together, about the girls' relentless rivalry, egged on by their fathers' relentless rivalry. "It's like Callie's a different person. She arrived at the Creamery and just shut down."

"I wonder," Linc said, dipping the corner of his grilled cheese sandwich into his soup, "if your niece might be depressed. I knew of a man who kept going and going, like the Energizer Bunny, and when he was forced to stop—for different reasons—he sank into a deep depression." He spread out his hand in a line. "Flat on his bed. Grounded."

"Kind of like Callie." Marnie took a spoonful of soup, thinking about Linc's energetic friend. "Maybe you're right. Maybe she is depressed." She asked how he'd coped.

Linc chewed, then swallowed. "Who?"

"Your friend."

"Oh. He, well, he had to do a lot of soul searching. He went back to church. He tried to make amends for some of the mistakes he'd made."

She pondered that, thinking that while it would be good for Callie to go to church, she wasn't sure she'd be interested. The church Marnie attended was on the formal side of formal. Dawn and Kevin complained often about it—the music, mostly—but not enough to find another church that suited them.

Linc polished off the last bite of his sandwich. "How about you? What about after your husband died? Were you depressed then?"

"Very. But not flat on my back, not like Callie. My friend Maeve helped me through that period."

"How did she help?"

"She knew me well enough to know the things that made me feel better—and then we did more of those."

"Like what kinds of things?"

"Matinee movies. Tag sales. Bike rides. She even got us some black spandex outfits so we would look the part on those bikes." She smiled. "Dawn said we looked ridiculous, but we thought we looked pretty hip for two ladies on the generous side of middle age." She took her last spoonful of soup and swallowed, wiping her face with her napkin. "It helped, all those things. They added up, reminding me of what it felt like to be happy again. And then, Dawn got engaged and there was her wedding to plan—her first one—and out of the blue came my breast cancer diagnosis. And then Dawn's broken engagement. Suddenly, here we were, in Chatham, and I was buying the Main Street Creamery. I think the reason I bought it had something to do with Maeve's help to seek out those things that made me feel happy again."

"And then you met me."

She smiled. "And I met you."

"Maeve sounds like a very good friend."

"The best."

"Well, being here in Chatham, walking along the beach and soaking up the oxygen-rich air, it has a way of curing what ails a person."

"I hope you're right," she said. It was so un-Callie-like to be depressed. There must be a reason for it, something bigger than getting fired. Even bigger than getting sued. Maybe Dawn was right. Maybe Callie had a secret.

"Have you thought of just . . . asking her?"

"Dawn has asked. She got nowhere. Callie's good at deflecting questions. I've been waiting to see if she might volunteer information, but lately I've been thinking I should be more forthright." She scrunched up her napkin into a ball. "How's your friend doing?"

"My friend?"

"The one who was down-and-out."

"Oh. That guy. He's good! Better than good. In fact, you could even say that his life has never been better."

It wasn't until later in the day that it dawned on Marnie that Linc had been talking about himself.

• • •

Dawn and Kevin had met for a late lunch at their favorite Indian restaurant, sharing tandoori chicken over basmati rice. She'd been telling him that she felt she needed to do something drastic to help Callie get back on her feet, and he didn't seem convinced.

"Why can't you just let her be?" Kevin reached out to tear a corner of naan bread, then mopped up his sauce. "She's only been here a couple of days. Maybe she just needs time to work out whatever is bothering her."

"I know Callie. She's always been highly structured. Full of plans. This just isn't like her."

"Maybe you don't know her as well as you thought you did."

"Kevin, I grew up in her shadow. She soared at everything she ever tried. She soared while I plummeted."

"You didn't plummet."

Not plummeted, exactly, but Dawn had felt that way around her cousin.

"Dawn, don't you think it's time to stop feeling like you're in a race with Callie?"

"A race? I guess it's a race I didn't sign up for." But she did try to run in it. She did try her very best to beat Callie. She just never could. So finally she stopped trying. She vividly remembered that moment. She was eighteen years old.

It was spring of Dawn and Callie's senior year in high school. Callie had been accepted to every single college she had applied to. Dawn had choices, good ones, but not the one she'd hoped for. What she *really* wanted to do was to go to culinary school, but her dad was against it. He was pushing hard for her to go to college. There was a lot riding on that—she'd be the first in her family to go. There'd been many arguments between Dawn and her dad that year. Then, out of the blue, Uncle Richard called to brag that Callie'd been given a full ride to a culinary school—the very one Dawn had hoped to go to—and with that, Dawn made an abrupt turn. She chose the college path. In fact, she chose a major of accounting and finance, as far away from Callie's direction as she could get. Her dad was thrilled. Over the moon.

"All I'm saying," Kevin said, "is that maybe you should consider that Callie's come to Chatham for a reason. Maybe she just needs a place to be. Maybe she needs to be left alone."

Dawn shook her head. "She's been here four days and hasn't even gone to the beach yet."

"It is winter. It's cold and bleak and foggy."

She ignored his objections. "I can't believe I'm saying this, but I miss the old Callie. The happy Callie. The talkative Callie."

He lifted his hands in a helpless gesture. "Then give her time. Dawn, sometimes you miss what's most important."

"Like what?"

"Well, like . . . with us. Like with our first wedding that took on a life of its own."

Oh. That. She picked up her fork and pushed some rice into the tandoori sauce. Then she set it down again with a sigh. "You're probably right." Frankly, Kevin's logic let Dawn off the hook. She couldn't be responsible for Callie. She just couldn't.

But at that moment something rose up in her, and she had to try.

Who was Dawn to try and bring life back into this cousin? Just about a year ago, she had been nearly as down-and-out as Callie was now. What made the difference?

A lot of things, she realized now. Being here, in Chatham, mostly. Being in this little town by the sea changed her life.

● ● ●

Dad

Callie, I've been trying to call you. Your phone goes straight to voice mail. Pick up!

Callie cringed. Then she turned off her phone.

Chapter
SIX

When I was a kid, I used to think, "Man, if I could ever afford all the ice cream I want to eat, that's as rich as I ever want to be."

—Jimmy Dean, American singer

Thursday, February 3

Callie was sitting up in bed, researching information on her computer, when the bedroom door blew open. Startled, she practically tumbled off the bed because she'd been sure the house was empty and had even been contemplating a trip downstairs for an apple or orange or banana. There stood Leo the Cowboy.

"Leo! Don't you know you need to knock before you open a door?"

"Cowboys don't knock."

"What happened to your guns?" Did he have toy guns in that gun belt? She couldn't remember.

He frowned, patting his empty holsters. "My dad won't let me have guns. Sometimes, I use sticks."

He walked in and sat on her air mattress, bouncing up and down a few times, then looked around the room, blinking. "Why is it so dark in here?"

"Easier on the eyes." She closed her computer. "What brings you to my office?"

"Office?" Leo's face scrunched up. "I thought it was Dawn's bedroom."

"Well, it's both." She smoothed out the blanket. "Are you looking for Dawn and Marnie?"

"No one's downstairs."

"I figured as much. I can tell when they leave because the door bangs shut and the windows rattle. How'd you get in? Didn't they lock the door?"

"I always come in the back door."

"Oh." Good to know that door stayed unlocked. "So, what exactly do you need?"

"I came for ice cream."

"Ice cream? Really? On a cold day like today?"

"I eat it every day."

Callie knew that, actually. Leo was a daily visitor to the Creamery. "You love it that much?"

"It's the way I get my calcium because I don't like milk."

"Oh. Well, that makes sense."

He shot a glance at her. "What's calcium?"

A grin slipped over Callie. "It's what makes your bones strong."

Leo nodded. "Maybe I should have two helpings."

It occurred to her that he was expecting her to serve him up. "Can you get it yourself?"

He shook his head. "I can't reach."

She swung her legs over the side of the air mattress to stick her feet in her slippers. "Okay, buddy, let's go get you some ice cream." She grabbed Dawn's blue robe out of the closet and put it on. "Then you can get home before your parents start worrying about where you are."

"My dad says that worry is a waste of time."

Callie stopped short at that. It sounded so simple, like turning off a faucet. Managing worry wasn't that easy!

Down in the kitchen, Leo showed her where bowls and spoons were kept. He stood next to the freezer. This boy knew the drill. "You know, you could probably work here."

"I do. I'm the taster."

Searching through a drawer for an ice cream scooper, Callie paused to look at him. "Wait. You're serious, aren't you?"

"When Dawn was making vanilla ice cream, she needed my help to choose the best one."

"Vanilla can be tricky. So pure. Lots of integrity." Callie closed one drawer and tried another. No scooper. Then she scanned the room and saw the scoopers in a special glass container on the counter. Of course! After all, this was an ice cream shop. She grabbed one and went to the freezer. "Okay. What flavor do you want?" She opened the freezer and stopped short. Rummaging the shelves, scanning the containers, she was alarmed by the chaotic organization. "Where is all the labeling?"

Leo came up underneath her arms to peer up at the shelves. "I don't read."

She looked down at the top of his cowboy hat. "Even if you could, you probably wouldn't be able to find what you're looking for."

"I like chocolate best."

"I'm sure there's some in here." She finally found what she thought was chocolate on the bottom shelf. Dawn had scribbled dates on each container for when the ice cream had been made, but there was nothing to indicate which flavor it was. The containers weren't sorted by flavors or by dates. Callie shuddered. This freezer was a hodge podge. It might make sense to Dawn, but anyone else would have to spend precious time hunting for what they were looking for. And some of Marnie's and Dawn's own personal frozen food was interspersed with the ice cream containers. Imagine what the Health & Safety Department would have to say about that! Callie was very familiar with vigilant inspectors from the state of Massachusetts. They struck fear in the heart of the kitchen staff.

She scooped out a bowlful for Leo and handed it to him. He looked at it suspiciously. "It's weird looking."

So it was. Kind of a tired, drab, mud color.

Leo took a tentative bite and spit it out. "It's not chocolate."

Callie grabbed a spoon and took a bite, paused to let the ice cream melt in her mouth, filling her palate, before she swallowed. "Definitely not chocolate." She took another bite, then another. It had a disgusting appearance, but the taste held an oddly pleasing combination of flavors. She tasted another spoonful. Was that a note of curry? Interesting. Bold, daring, innovative. Good for Dawn.

But Leo was waiting for chocolate. She looked through the freezer until she found what was definitely chocolate—packed with chocolate chips—and gave him a new bowlful. Big scoops, so that he would hit his calcium requirements for the day.

As Leo ate, Callie started moving containers around in the freezer. She decided to work shelf by shelf, rather than the preferred style of removing everything. She had to work fast because the temperature rose the longer the freezer door stayed open. The worst thing in the world was for ice cream to melt and refreeze. Ice crystals formed on the top and, well, if that happened, it had become worthless. Toss it out.

Leo slipped in under her arms again to peer up at her. "Whatcha doing?"

Man. He was a cute little guy. Were all kids this cute? He was a towhead, a beautiful child with round, chubby cheeks and big blue eyes. Were they blue? Or green? "I'm organizing the containers of ice cream so Dawn and Marnie can find what they're looking for much more quickly."

"Can I help?"

She stopped. Her experience with children his age was nonexistent. She didn't really know what to expect. Could kids really help?

"I help Dawn and Miss Marnie a lot."

She closed the freezer for a moment and leaned against it. "When you said you don't read, did you mean you can't read or you won't read?"

"Cowboys don't need to read."

"No?" She folded her arms against her chest. "What about brand-ing cattle? Seems like a cowboy would need to be able to read brand-ing irons. Otherwise, they might get swindled."

"Swindled?"

"Other cowboys might steal their cattle."

As Leo considered that troubling thought, Callie went back to reorganizing the freezer. "This is an impossible task. I really need coolers to do this right. Everything should be taken out. But that creates a new problem. We don't want the ice cream to melt."

"Melted ice cream is the worst thing that can happen to ice cream."

Callie spun to look at him. "I'm very impressed that you would know that. Actually, the very worst thing that can happen to ice cream is for it to get melted, then refrozen."

He looked pleased with himself. "Nanette has coolers. She loaned them to Dawn when the old freezer died."

"Nanette's the one who lives across the street, right?"

Leo pointed to the door. "Nanette has the world's best T-shirt shop."

"What makes it the world's best?"

An earnest expression covered his little round face. "Nanette says so."

Callie couldn't not smile. Leo was good company. It was refresh-ing to be around someone who accepted her just as she was, didn't seem to mind that she lived in a borrowed blue bathrobe, and didn't ask about her future plans . . . of which she had none.

"Want me to go ask Nanette if we can borrow her coolers?"

"Thanks, but I don't think there's enough time today." Marnie and Dawn would probably be back soon. "I'll work on this a little at a time." She finished organizing the top shelf by creating zones—the key to organization. All vanilla-based ice cream containers went on the top shelf, in lines according to their made-on dates.

When she had finished, she turned to show Leo her top shelf re-org, but he wasn't in the kitchen. The front door was left wide open, filling the front room with freezing cold air. Good grief, she thought, as she shut the door and turned the lock. That little cowboy burst right into a room without a proper hello and left without saying goodbye. Where was that boy's mother?

Without him, the ice cream shop seemed strangely empty. Lonely. A wave of exhaustion rolled over Callie. In the kitchen, she cleaned Leo's cup and spoon and put them back where she found them. She looked around the kitchen to make sure nothing seemed disturbed. Then she went back upstairs, flopped on the air mattress, grabbed her laptop, and opened it.

● ● ●

Dawn had been prepared for a quiet and cold winter on the Cape, and for ice cream sales to go down. Way, way down, unless it was a super sunny day that broke into the fifties. No surprise there. She had to give props to her mom for planning ahead and insisting on adding a coffee bar plus baked goods. So far, the Main Street Creamery had been bringing in just enough revenue from coffee, scones, and muffins to squeak through the winter months. Actually, coffee sales had been steadily solid, but baked good sales had flattened out after the baker had left for Florida. For some reason, her muffins weren't selling. The Main Street Creamery still had a few months to get through before the tourists started to return, and the lack of revenue was starting to concern Dawn.

That was one worry on Dawn's mind. The other was her cousin Callie.

Dawn had spent some time today doing her favorite thing: making a list. She wrote down everything she could think of to help boost Callie's spirits. She had Kevin play lively tunes on his violin last evening. She invited her to get a manicure and pedicure—something Callie loved to do. After all, she was a girly girl!—but she flatly declined the invitation. Nothing worked. Everything on the list was crossed out.

Frankly, Dawn didn't have any idea what she was doing. She'd experienced some low points in the last few years, but she was never so low that she couldn't get out of bed.

She finally made herself do something she'd loathed to do: she asked Callie for advice in the kitchen. Long ago, Dawn had learned to never, ever ask Callie a question about cooking. It was like asking someone where the light switch was and getting a lecture on the intricacies of electricity.

It happened like this: In the late afternoon, Dawn had opened up the freezer to see how the second try at Mashpee ice cream tasted after time in the freezer. Making ice cream was one thing—most ice cream tasted great right out of the machine. But freezing ice cream, keeping it cold, that was the tricky part. A lot of problems could occur. She had to hunt for the container and finally found it on the second shelf, which seemed strange because she thought, for sure, she had put it on the bottom shelf with the family food. Someone had gotten into it too, and she knew just who the culprits were. Mom and Lincoln. They must've tried it after she told them about it. Tried it, didn't like it, and were too nice to tell her so. This had been a common scenario. She wished they would just give her direct feedback if they didn't like something. Instead, they danced around it.

She opened the container and sniffed. No smell, which was a good thing. Ice cream shouldn't have a smell. She took a taste. Delicious! But the color was definitely off-putting. She knew Callie might have a solution.

She went upstairs to find Callie facedown on her air mattress. She sat cross-legged next to the air mattress and watched Callie for a moment, just to make sure she was still alive. Should she poke her? "Hey," Dawn whispered. "I'm here."

Callie rolled over. "Hey."

Phew! Still alive. "I have a question. I'm working on an ice cream that has mashed peas in it."

Silence.

"I know that might sound disgusting, but it's not. Other than the color."

"Did you blanch the peas?"

Dawn hit her forehead with the palm of her hand. "Of course! No wonder the ice cream turned gray." She waited a while to see if Callie

65

might open up, might want to start talking. After all, she'd lobbed her a softball. The old Callie would've hit that ball right out of the park.

But that was the old Callie. The new Callie didn't say another word. Dawn sat there for a long time, a weird heaviness between them. When Dawn's bottom went numb, she gave up and went downstairs.

She tossed out the Mashpee ice cream and started again. This time, she blanched the peas first. And this time, the color of the ice cream came out perfectly. Almost like green grass.

Later, over supper with Mom and Linc because Kevin had a class, Dawn lamented. "There's got to be something else to do for Callie."

"Linc wondered if she might be clinically depressed."

With a sigh, Dawn turned to her mom. "So what should we do to help get her un-depressed?"

"Nothing," Mom said. "It just takes time."

Oh no. There was no way they were going to let the Main Street Creamery become a lengthy rehab ward. Dawn shook her head. "I think we need to take action." Immediately. Swift, decisive action.

"I agree," Linc said.

"Right?" Dawn said, glad to have a bit of support.

"There's a class at the community center," Linc said, "that meets on Saturday morning right after the cancer support group. It's called 'The Secret to Happiness.'"

"Interesting," Mom said. "Who leads it?"

"Bruno Bianco."

Mom's eyebrows lifted. "The author?"

Linc nodded.

"Think Callie would be a fit in the group?" Mom looked unconvinced. "I wouldn't want her to think that we're trying to find a way to get her into therapy."

Dawn gave a sly grin. "Even though we are."

"*You* are," Mom said.

"That class," Linc said, "seems to have a good turnout. I have yet to meet Callie, but judging by the size of the class, I think the topic must've hit a chord with all kinds of people."

Dawn clapped her hands on her thighs. "Excellent. Then it's official. The campaign to reclaim Callie's happiness is now underway. Somehow, I'm going to get her there this very Saturday morning." She brushed her hands back and forth, like, *I've got it covered.*

And then she tried not to notice the look on her mother's face. A look that said, "Dawn, leave that poor girl alone."

She grinned. *Not a chance.*

● ● ●

Dawn
I've discovered an ace in the hole for Callie. This will rouse her out of bed!

Kevin
???

There's a class at the community center on Saturday morning. It's all about finding happiness.

Oh yeah? How are you going to get her there?

TBD

Chapter
SEVEN

An ice cream a day keeps the tension away.

—Unknown

Friday, February 4

Around two o'clock in the morning, Callie was still wide awake, restless. Antsy legs. Another sleepless night. She lay in bed, adjusting and readjusting her pillow, unable to stop obsessing about the phone call she'd had with her dad a few hours ago. Her mind kept replaying their conversation, like an elf in her brain kept pressing *repeat*.

"Any promising interviews?" Dad didn't bother with niceties, like *Hello*. Like, *How're you doing? Feeling okay? Need anything?*

"Some," Callie had said. "I'm still hoping for a few more." Only a half lie.

"Hoping for more? You lost your job in December!"

She could picture him throwing up his hands in despair.

"The point is," Dad said, "you can't just assume a job will come to you. You have to be proactive. Go after it." When she didn't respond, he said, "Look, I know you've had a disappointment, but there's no reason you can't pull yourself together, lickety-split, and get back in the saddle."

Lickety-split? For someone who had spent his career in sales, working with people, he could be remarkably obtuse with his own daughter. "Excellent point, Dad. I'll get right on it."

"I know the work world is changing, but people still love to eat. You don't want a big gap between jobs that you'll have to explain. You don't want to give up everything you've been working for."

Did he really think that's what she wanted? "Got it."

"Vacations on Cape Cod are nice, but it's time to update LinkedIn. Get on all those sites. Network. Make connections."

"Right." That's exactly what she was doing. Vacationing at the Cape. In February. In Dawn's teeny room.

"I'm not sure you see the time pressure here," her father said.

"I'm pretty sure I do."

"Your health insurance will run out soon."

"Yes. You've mentioned that before."

"And don't even get me started on that lawsuit."

"Pending," Callie said. "It's not definite yet if the Food Safety Conference will press charges."

"There you go! Think positive. Don't dwell on getting fired. Stop hiding from the world. Mind over matter."

"Yep. Absolutely. Mind over matter." She felt like her eyeballs were going to start spinning.

"Each day, set goals for yourself. Do the bare minimum."

Spoken like a person who had no idea how it felt when the bare minimum was having enough energy to take a shower.

"Work is an elixir. It'll make all the difference."

"You don't have to worry. I've got this."

Dad wasn't having it. "Callie, you're not a quitter."

Maybe not—but she wanted to be.

Still wide awake at three o'clock, she tiptoed around Dawn and went downstairs to make a cup of chamomile tea. In the kitchen, she turned on the stovetop light and noticed Dawn had left some muffins cooling on a rack. Her cousin's habit was to bake after dinner for the Creamery's next day's provisions. Fresh, but not restaurant fresh. Callie's baker used to arrive in the early morning hours so that pastries were astonishingly fresh.

She picked up a muffin and sniffed. Pumpkin. She squeezed it, took a bite, and spit it out, offended by its texture. Terrible. Over-mixed. Overspiced. And what was it with Dawn and spices? She either under- or overestimated the potency of spices. No wonder there weren't any customers coming in to buy baked goods. Such a missed opportunity for the Creamery to boost sales. To weather the long winter.

She opened the refrigerator to find a dash of cream to add to her tea and her eyes landed on a container of leftover pumpkin purée. She picked it up, guessing the amount by the weight in her hand. She sniffed it, to make sure it was fresh. A carton of eggs sat beside it. She picked up the egg carton and checked the expiration date.

A little stirring of excitement filled her. Her eyes darted around the small kitchen. Should she?

She shouldn't.

Do the bare minimum, Dad had said.

Should she?

No. She really shouldn't.

But she felt protective of Marnie and Dawn. They shouldn't be serving rubber muffins.

She picked up the rack of Dawn's muffins and dumped them in a plastic bag to take out to the garbage. It pained her. Waste in a kitchen was a terrible thing. It was something that was drilled into culinary school students: Pennies were in the waste. That was because food margins were so small. But she couldn't even think of how to reuse Dawn's muffins. They were that bad. She turned on the oven to preheat and took an apron off the wall hook, slipping it on and tying it around her middle.

Just this once, she would make an exception to her no-cook/no-bake rule.

● ● ●

Marnie shared Dawn's worries about Callie. Her niece hardly ever came downstairs, and when she did, dressed in Dawn's blue bathrobe, her hair hung in her face and she didn't say much. She would eat a bowl of cereal or a banana or a yogurt, and head back upstairs. She was lost and sinking. And no wonder.

Last evening, as Marnie brushed her teeth in the bathroom, she heard Callie on the phone with her dad. Her brother-in-law Richard had a booming voice, and even over the running water, Marnie could hear how he kept hounding Callie to find a new job. Overhearing the conversation—if you could call it that—made her throat sour. It made her furious with him.

She wanted to go in and say as much to Callie, to empathize with her, but as she left the bathroom, she saw the light flick off under the door. So instead, she went to bed, but that phone call still bothered her. She recognized so much of her husband Philip in the way Richard pressured Callie. The two brothers wanted their daughters to reach their full potential—but only in the ways that they had already chosen for them.

It gave Marnie pause. She'd always assumed that Philip would've been pleased about her purchase of the Main Street Creamery. He had always loved ice cream, had always talked about buying a shop in retirement. But she hadn't considered how he might have felt to know that Dawn had left her secure career to throw everything into this venture. Nearly a year into it, Marnie was discovering it was a far more risky venture than it had seemed last summer, when Chatham was bursting at the seams with tourists who loved good ice cream. Listening to Richard on the phone call to Callie, she thought that maybe Philip might not be quite so pleased about the purchase of the Main Street Creamery. He was not one for risk.

It took a long while for Marnie to fall asleep, and she slept fitfully, dreaming that she had baked a pumpkin pie—Philip's favorite.

The next morning, she woke early and went downstairs to get coffee started. She was going to meet Linc to take a walk on the beach. As she filled the coffeepot with water, she couldn't help but eye Dawn's pumpkin muffins on the rack on the kitchen counter.

They looked unusually tempting, or maybe she was just unusually hungry this morning. As the coffeepot filled, she picked one up, sniffed it, and had to try it. Amazing. Moist, cakey, sweet without being cloying, leaving a lingering taste of cinnamon.

She polished off the muffin in three bites. *Nice work, Dawn.* If her daughter's baking kept ratcheting up like this, maybe there was hope for the Creamery during these winter months when the town's baker deserted them for Florida sunshine.

• • •

Later that morning, after Dawn had left to go on errands, Marnie made a cup of tea to take up to Callie. While she liked the idea of the Secret to Happiness class, and even appreciated Dawn's efforts to help Callie, she worried about her daughter's bull-in-a-china-shop methods. She wanted to see if she could break through Callie's shell before Dawn smashed it.

Upstairs, she knocked gently on the bedroom door. No answer. She knocked again, then let herself in. She froze at the sight of Callie, lying on the air mattress, eyes wide open as she stared at the ceiling. No wonder Dawn worried she had died! She seemed lifeless.

Marnie went over to the mattress and crouched down. "I brought you tea."

Slowly, Callie roused, pulling herself up to a sitting position. She took the tea from Marnie's outstretched hands. "Thanks."

Marnie waited a while. "Callie, it's time we have a talk."

Callie kept her eyes fixed on the teacup. "You want me to leave."

"No! Goodness no. But I do want to know what's happened to put you in such a state."

Callie took a sip of her tea before she answered. "I was fired from my job."

"Yes. I heard something about it. Is that what's made you feel so sad?"

Callie didn't respond.

"Getting fired must have been terrible."

72

Slowly, she nodded. "And then there's a possible lawsuit about the whole mess."

"Your dad must have had something to say about it."

Callie took another sip of tea. "His advice is to 'Stay positive. And get back in that saddle.'"

That sounded just like something Philip would've said to Dawn. "Callie, I've always been a believer in trusting my instincts. I just have this bone-deep feeling that there's something more going on with you than losing your job."

Silence. It went on so long that Marnie regretted asking. She was pushing Callie—exactly what she hadn't wanted to do. She shifted on her knees, preparing to get up and leave the room, when Callie surprised her with a question.

"What do you remember about my mother?"

Marnie settled back against Dawn's twin bed. "She was beautiful, like you. Warm and caring. She would light up a room with her joyfulness."

"That was before. What about after?"

After her diagnosis of multiple sclerosis, she meant. Callie was just a baby when her mom started having symptoms. "Well, the disease progressed quickly. Your dad tried everything, I remember that. Clinical trials, alternative cures. But nothing seemed to make a difference."

"Do you remember how old she was when she was diagnosed?"

"Twenty-seven or twenty-eight, I think. Why?" When Callie didn't answer, something seemed to click into place for Marnie. She stared at Callie for a solid thirty seconds. "Same age as you are now."

Callie kept her eyes lowered, focused on the tea she set on the floor as if it was the most fascinating thing in the world.

So, Marnie realized. So her instincts were correct, but she felt no pleasure in that. Only a stab of pain. So . . . something other than the job loss had been weighing Callie down. Marnie reached across to squeeze her hand. It was ice cold. "Honey, do you think you have MS?"

She could see a war being waged behind her niece's big brown eyes. Then Callie's chin did the slightest quiver, and she slowly nodded.

A helplessness tore through Marnie, an instant impulse to fix whatever was wrong. "Just because you're the same age as your mom was when she was diagnosed?"

She shook her head. "I have symptoms. Extreme fatigue, dizziness, shakiness." She looked at her. "Ever heard of the MS hug?"

"What's that?"

"A tight squeeze in the chest. Like a boa constrictor wrapped around you. It's pretty profound. Hard to breathe. Pounding heart."

Marnie took that in for a moment. It sounded truly awful.

"It's the reason I got fired."

"I thought it was because of food poisoning."

She shook her head. "That was my error. The food poisoning occurred because I had left a container of sauce out on the counter overnight. I had just finished making the sauce for the next day's entrée, and I poured it into a container to go into the refrigerator. It was a full container, very heavy, and as I started to pick it up, an MS hug started up. I put it down, and then the event planner burst into the kitchen, full of complaints as usual, and . . . somehow, the sauce got completely forgotten." She pulled her hand out of Marnie's grasp and rubbed her forehead. "I still can't believe I forgot it."

"When did you first start getting those MS hugs?"

"They started last fall. But this was the first time I'd had one at work."

"And you're sure that tight-chest feeling is a symptom of MS?"

"I know it is. I've read all about it. Cognitive decline too. Forgetting that sauce." She rubbed her cheeks with both hands. "I've never made a mistake like that before. Not ever, ever, ever."

"Everyone makes mistakes now and then."

"Not me. Especially one like this. When I first started working there, the kitchen was an accident waiting to happen. The chef was old school. No organization, no systems. Actually, he was just old. Period. I reorganized, I implemented checks and balances to keep mistakes from happening. It was the reason I was given the executive chef position when the old chef left." She let out a sigh. "And then *this* happened."

"Still. One mistake."

"This wasn't like forgetting to pick up the mail or take out the garbage. Two hundred people spent the night throwing up because of me." She thumped her chest. "Because of a mistake I made. And don't forget this was the Food Safety Conference, of *all* conferences. It will go down in history." She plopped back on the bed and covered her face with her hands.

"Callie, have you seen a doctor for a diagnosis? Have you had any tests?"

"I did." She dropped her hands with a sigh. "But the thing is, there really aren't tests to determine if you have MS. They kind of rule out everything else and what's left is probably MS." She gave a shrug. "Modern medicine still has its limits."

"So what did the tests say?"

"Inconclusive results."

"You had every possible test?"

"I didn't have the spinal tap. If that test found lesions, then most likely MS would be the culprit."

"What if," Marnie started, in a run-with-me-on-this tone, "you had *that* test, and found out you didn't have MS."

"Because it might determine that I *do* have it. Because if I knew, for sure, then I would become clinically depressed. This way, I still have a glimmer of hope."

Did she? She couldn't even get out of bed. "Callie," she said softly, "that's no way to live."

"If I do have MS, then whatever I do, I'm still going to die."

"Don't say that! Don't even think it."

"Aunt Marnie, I saw what MS did to my mother. I remember it, vividly. The shakes, the seizures. Mom had no control over body functions, she couldn't even speak. I can't tell you how many times the paramedics had to be called, and she'd be taken away in an ambulance. I just can't face getting a diagnosis. Not yet."

"So what does the doctor say?"

"He wants to see me again in six months." She let out a sigh. "After my health insurance runs out."

"That's it?"

"That's it for now, until more symptoms present more definitively." She glanced at Marnie. "Would you mind not telling Dawn? I'd like things to stay the same between us."

Really? Because, Marnie thought, it wasn't like they were terribly close. It wasn't like they truly talked to each other. But she didn't say what she was thinking. "It's not my place to tell Dawn. But I hope you'll tell her at some point. We all live in this house together, and we're your family. She worries about you." Marnie shifted on the floor. "Callie, would you consider getting a second opinion? My very good friend Lincoln seems to have all kinds of connections. I'm sure he could help you get to a specialist."

Callie shook her head. "No. Thanks, but no. My own doctor is one of the best. I know. I did the research."

"What if there's a chance that you don't have MS? Wouldn't you want to know?"

She lifted sad eyes. "But what if I do?"

Oh honey, Marnie thought. *You're already living like you do.*

● ● ●

Jesse
How's it going? Still feeling a little low?

> **Callie**
> Lower than low. I shouldn't have come to Cape Cod. I'm a burden to my relatives.

Not possible.

Oh, but it was.

Chapter
EIGHT

I'm always wearing Spanx, eating ice cream and feeling
a bit lonely.

—Sheridan Smith, American actress

Friday, February 4

Marnie spent the rest of the morning looking through an old photograph album. There was a picture she remembered that she wanted to show Callie. It was a picture of her parents, Richard and Beth, on a vacation at the seashore with Marnie and Philip. Beth was wearing a bikini—something Marnie could never have gotten away with—and she looked like a model, even with wet hair and sandy feet. Richard's eyes were hidden behind dark sunglasses, but he was clearly happy, with one arm draped around his wife's shoulders. They both looked happy in that picture, Marnie thought. Beth had just found out she was pregnant with Callie. Like Marnie and Philip, they'd been trying for a while. Marnie was four months along with Dawn, and Philip liked to joke that was why Richard and Beth finally had success at conceiving. Marnie and Beth exchanged an eye roll over that. Those two! Beth had said. Everything was a race.

It wasn't long after Callie was born that Beth suffered from vertigo. Pretty severely, if Marnie remembered correctly. The doctors couldn't find any reason for it despite test after test. Then some weakness developed in her hands. A memory stood out for Marnie. The family had gathered for some holiday—Easter, maybe. Callie was only a few months old and cried the way babies did, but Beth wasn't able to lift her. Richard had to pick her up and put her in Beth's arms. Marnie remembered talking about it with Philip on the drive home. Beth hadn't been diagnosed with multiple sclerosis yet, but Marnie sensed something dreadful was on the horizon.

"You and your intuition," Philip had said dismissively. "You conjure up things to worry about."

To be fair, that was often true, but not this time.

Beth's symptoms started to cascade—overwhelming fatigue, slurred speech, lack of muscle coordination, tremors, numbness, loss of bladder and bowel control. By the time Callie was three, Beth was in a wheelchair. By Callie's fifth birthday, Richard couldn't manage Beth's needs at home any longer and moved her to a full-time nursing facility. Richard, it seemed to Marnie, gave up at that point. He'd done all he could for his wife and could do no more.

Callie had never known her mother as the healthy, vivacious woman she once was. That's why Marnie wanted to find this picture for her. Those symptoms that Callie described for herself, as well as seeing her so fatigued—they churned up memories of Beth. They brought it all back to Marnie. And they filled her with that same dread she'd felt for Beth on that Easter day.

•   •   •

It hadn't taken long for Callie to become familiar with the rhythm of Dawn and Marnie's entire life by just listening to the sounds that floated up the stairs—their coming and going, the pleasant hum of conversation, the whirl of the ice cream machine and the hurried footsteps to the kitchen to sample the latest batch. She could even tell who was coming up the stairs by the creaks of the floorboards. Marnie's slower pace, Dawn's quick one. They talked a lot together.

They seemed happy living and working together, Marnie and Dawn, in this little shoebox. The sound of their chatter wafted up the staircase like the scent of onions caramelizing over a low flame. It filled the house.

Those sounds surprised her, because when Callie used to spend time at their home, Marnie and Dawn hadn't seemed particularly chummy. Dawn and her dad—they were the team. Clearly, things had changed since Uncle Philip had passed away. Marnie and Dawn were happy here, working together. Now they were the team. Which made Callie resent them in a way, which wasn't fair at all, but she just couldn't help herself. It stirred up something deep and overwhelming inside her—some familiar longing for her mother that she had no idea how to handle. And she hated things she didn't know how to handle.

Callie felt weird knowing as much about her aunt and cousin as she did, considering that she'd hardly been interacting with them. It helped to have Aunt Marnie press her for information this morning. It was a relief to tell her, to have someone else know her secret. She should have told Marnie sooner, but it was hard to say it out loud. It made it real.

As she lay on her back in the dimly lit room, she thought about her mom, wondering what it might have been like if she'd never had multiple sclerosis, if her body hadn't failed her so quickly and completely.

MS was more than just a disease. It was a thief. It stole hope. Dignity. Dreams. MS had already taken so much from her. Her mom, and in an extended way, her dad. And now it would keep on stealing from her.

Around noon, Callie heard Lincoln's booming hello downstairs. A few minutes later, he and Marnie left to grab lunch. The coast was clear. Callie went downstairs to get something to eat. On the kitchen counter was an old photo album, opened to a page of pictures of people standing on the beach. She looked more closely. She covered her mouth with one hand.

Her mother.

Young and happy, before the disease had made its intention known. An icy trickle started down Callie's spine, her heart started racing. Her ribs felt as if they were getting squeezed in a vise, making it hard for her to breathe without gasping. The horrible MS hug. She leaned against the counter with both hands, waiting for the hug to pass, trying to breathe. Count to four as she inhaled, hold it seven seconds, exhale slowly through her teeth for eight seconds. 4-7-8. She'd watched Dr. Andrew Weil's surefire cure to settle oneself down on YouTube.

It wasn't working. Why wasn't it working?

She wondered if this was a sign that the disease was progressing. Maybe this was its way of making its announcement that her life, as she knew it, was officially over.

She leaned her forehead against the top cupboard. With her other hand, she googled WebMD on her phone. There was nothing she hadn't already learned: Three out of four people with MS are women. MS affects nerves in the brain and spinal cord. The nerves get inflamed, swollen, irritated. They lose their coating, called *myelin*, that surrounds and protects them. A plaque forms around them. The plaque in the brain or spinal cord changes the electrical signals that zip up and down nerves. They can get slower, distorted, or stop altogether. Those signal changes cause the symptoms of MS.

She knew all that. It had started last fall, when she first felt waves of fatigue. Then came episodes of tightness in her chest. Dizziness. She'd gone in for initial testing, but everything came back negative. The doctor wanted to send her to a specialist for more tests, but she'd refused. She knew the answer: Only time would tell. There was nothing to be done, anyway. If she had MS, like her mom did, it would most likely advance quickly, like her mom's had. More and more symptoms would develop, eroding her body's coordination and, ultimately, control—to walk, to talk, to eliminate, to care for herself. Her mother's decline had lasted for eight years, and that was with medications. Callie had already decided she wouldn't take them. Wouldn't prolong her incapacity.

She was only twenty-eight years old and she was just waiting to die.

• • •

Dawn couldn't understand why Mom had done a complete about-face on the Happiness Campaign, to the point that she now discouraged her from insisting Callie attend the Saturday class. "Mom,"

Dawn said, "I think it's worth a try. If nothing else, it'll get her out of the house for a few hours."

Mom sighed. "Then don't insist, Dawn. Just invite."

Dawn made a face. "Of course!" But she wasn't going to take no for an answer. The longer Callie remained in bed, the more Dawn wondered if what she really needed was a full-time psychiatrist. As annoying as the ever-chipper old Callie was, this woebegone new Callie was worse.

Saturday's class would be a start in the campaign. On Friday afternoon, Dawn steeled herself and went upstairs to tell Callie about it. She opened the door a few inches.

Callie's head lifted from the pillow and she blinked a few times. "Oh, it's you."

"Who else?"

"I thought you might be Leo."

"Leo?" Dawn walked in. "Has he been coming upstairs to bother you?"

"He's not a bother. He just doesn't knock."

Dawn sank down on the floor next to Callie's air mattress. She looked at her eyes, dark circles from sleep deprivation, and she felt a wave of tenderness for her. "I don't blame you for feeling so bummed out about your job. I know it was your dream job. You were living the life. I get it. I really do. But I feel concerned that you're not getting out of this room. This"—she made a large circle in the air—"can't be good for you."

Callie lifted herself on her elbows, listening to Dawn babble on with a look of quiet benevolence on her face.

"Tomorrow morning, there's a class at the community center called the Secret to Happiness. There's a professor at 4Cs—"

"At what?"

"4Cs. Cape Cod Community College. Anyway, there's a professor who's written a book and Mrs. Nickerson-Eldredge talked him into teaching the class. Lincoln—he's my mom's very good friend"— whom Callie would know if she ever bothered to come downstairs when Linc was over, which was quite often—"he says the class is outstanding and full of all kinds of people." She was talking so fast she wasn't making any sense. "I'd like you to go tomorrow, Callie. I can go with you, if that would help. I just don't think sitting in this dark room during a cold winter will do much for you." *Or for me and Mom and the Main Street Creamery.* "So, I'm asking you to go tomorrow. Ten o'clock." When Callie didn't respond, she pushed a little more. "Actually, I'm not asking. I'm telling you. As your cousin, I must insist that you go. I can't let you languish in this dinky, dark room."

Finally, Callie let out a long sigh, and as soon as her shoulders sank, Dawn knew she'd won.

"OK."

"We'll leave at nine thirty."

"Okay."

"One more thing."

Callie gave her the side-eye.

"Wash your hair. Take it from one who has had some experience with hard blows in life . . . when you can't do anything else in life, do that. Do the bare minimum. Take a shower. Wash your hair. It makes a difference. OK?"

"The bare minimum," Callie echoed, and she plopped her head back on the pillow.

"Good." Dawn clapped her hands on her knees. "I'm glad we had this little talk." She tiptoed out of the room and gently closed the door, pleased with herself. This motivational talk went much, much better than she had expected. She held up her arms in victory.

The Happiness Campaign was underway.

● ● ●

Dawn
Significant progress made with Callie today!

Kevin
Dawn, she's your cousin. Not your project.

She's both!

Chapter
NINE

Living life without a purpose is like having an ice cream cone in your hand [and] letting it melt and drip without eating it. It was yours to enjoy, but you lost it!

—RVM

Saturday, February 5

Callie had overheard the worried conversations between Dawn and Marnie, so she wasn't taken by surprise when Dawn came up and told her—no, ordered her—to attend that class on Saturday morning.

She had tried to be a nearly invisible houseguest. She skipped meals. She only came downstairs when she knew the Creamery was empty. She hadn't come here to worry them. She hadn't come here for pity. So when Dawn brought up the Secret to Happiness class, she protested, but only mildly, though she had no interest in leaving this room.

Last night, as she mulled over the class's topic, the more intrigued she became. What *was* the secret to happiness? She'd thought she was a happy person. Everyone said so. Everyone counted on Callie to be happy, especially her dad. How many times had he said to her, "Your

83

mom wanted you to be happy, Callie. Make her proud. Be happy for the both of you." She'd felt the weight of it like a baton had been passed on to her. Be happy! So she was. That was her persona, her mantra, her MO. And it had worked . . . until this last fall, when she couldn't muster a happy thought for the life of her.

In the morning, though, she regretted saying yes to Dawn. Big mistake.

Callie had been anxious about leaving the Creamery, a place she'd been for only a week. But it felt safe to her. Pressure-free. Unlike being a passenger in Dawn's car on the way to the community center. She couldn't relax. She was shaky. Nervous. Every turn, every red light, every touch of the brakes made her wince with anxiety.

Dawn looked a little offended. "Why are you so jumpy?"

"I guess . . . I never realized you were such a late braker."

"A what?"

"You wait until the last second to brake."

Dawn rolled her eyes. "You have got to chill."

She bobbed her head. "Yes. Good advice. Chill." But she had no idea how to do that. How do you make yourself chill? She knew Dawn wanted her to be excited about this outing, but it just seemed like such a terrible, awful, exhausting idea.

Ten minutes later, Callie peered through a crack in the door to discover the room for the Secret to Happiness class at the community center was packed full. She closed the door and turned to Dawn. "No chairs left. Oh well. Next week, we'll come earlier."

"Hold it. Let me see." Dawn peeked in. "You're right. I'll go find the janitor. We'll get more chairs."

Before Callie could stop her, Dawn jogged down the hall. Then the door opened and a woman held it for her. "Come on in! There's one empty seat left, just waiting for you."

Callie froze. "It's okay. I'm fine right here."

"Nonsense! Plenty of room." The woman walked toward the front of the class with purpose, expecting Callie to follow.

Oh no. Not the front row.

Callie had always been a front-row kind of person. The first-to-arrive-for-class type. But that was her old life. Now, with each step, her heart thundered in her ears. The woman stood in front of an upright metal folding chair and waved her hand, a big smile on her face. Callie slipped into the chair, next to a stern-looking older woman who frowned at her.

"Hello," Callie said in a low voice. "Am I late?"

"Shush." The woman put her fingers to her lips to hush Callie.

She glanced at the clock. Seven minutes after ten. Not *so* very late. A man with shoulder-length hair, tucked behind his ears, stood at a podium next to a large whiteboard. She leaned against her frowning neighbor to whisper, "Is that the leader? He looks kind of . . . serious. Not exactly cheerful. I'm not sure what I expected. Maybe a stand-up comedian?"

"Shush."

Good grief. If Callie were to cast this woman in a movie, she would be a librarian. She gasped. "You must be Mrs. Nickerson-Eldredge!"

The shusher looked at her with a mixture of annoyance and tartness. Finally, she gave her a jab with her elbow. "He's talking to you."

"Who?"

"Him."

She looked up and realized the leader of this class must've asked her a question. From the look on his face, he was waiting for a reply. "Hello! Sorry to be late."

The long-haired leader patiently waited.

"I'm sorry, what was the question?"

"I wanted to welcome you to our class. Would you like to take a moment and introduce yourself?"

"No!" She said it so forcefully it was loud even to her ears. The room quieted as she spoke. "I mean, no thank you. I just want to sit. And watch. Listen, I mean. Sit and listen and learn from everyone." She waved her hands in the air. "Not in a weird, voyeuristic way. Nothing like that. Just in an interested way." She was rambling, but she didn't know how to stop the flow. "My cousin made me come." She shifted in her chair to look back at the door. Where had Dawn gone, anyway?

"Your cousin made you come?"

Callie spun around to face the leader. "She did."

"Why?"

"She thinks I'm depressed."

"Are you?"

"Depressed? No! Never. I never get depressed." She looked around at the class, all eyes on her, blinking at her like a herd of cattle. The whole room could tell she was having a moment. "I'm fine! I'm great, in fact. Really, really doing great."

"You're doing great?" He sounded doubtful.

"I'm always doing great." She said it confidently, in her most carefree, singsong voice. "Always."

"Really? Because nobody does great all the time."

Callie turned to look at the class again. Yeah, from the looks on these people's faces, that was probably true. They had kind of that gray, northeastern paleness look.

"Well," the leader said, "we're glad you're here. And, hopefully, you'll get something out of being here today."

She shifted back in her chair and gave him a smile. She tried to remember what Dawn had said his name was . . . Bruce? Bryce? No . . . something more foreign sounding, something lyrical. Something like Brutas. Bruno! That was it. Bruno Bianco. Did he look Italian? Maybe a little. No, not really.

As he talked, she assessed him. Hard to tell exactly how old he was, but she would put him somewhere in his thirties. Average height, lean and lanky, five-o'clock-shadow-y chin whiskers, black-rimmed glasses. He wore an L.L.Bean navy blue sweater vest that zippered down the front, covering a striped button-down shirt. His outfit finished with faded brown corduroy trousers and scuffed leather shoes. His longish dark brown hair had a cool vibe—smooth at the top, curly at the bottom. Why did guys seem to get the best hair? She'd always wanted curly hair. Hers was stick straight. She wondered if there was a woman in Bruno Bianco's life, because he wasn't bad looking, just a bit rumpled. Thrown together. Like there'd been no female to edit him.

His voice cut into her musings. "Who did last week's homework assignment about finding positive moments?"

Red flag, red flag. Callie's hand shot up. "Hold it. Is this a positivity class?" She knew she had a look on her face like this whole class was a scam, but she couldn't help it. That's how she felt. She'd been raised with her dad's "buck up, soldier" attitude. She knew it all. There wasn't anything more she could learn from this class. She could *teach* this class about being positive.

The look on Bruno Bianco's face! All amused. "No, this isn't the glass-half-empty class. That class meets in the basement on early Monday mornings."

Ripples of laughter slowly trickled through the class. Oh, Callie realized. He was laughing at her. She was always a little slow on that uptake.

"This class is about the latest scientific data that proves the ability to rewire one's brain."

"Why does my brain need rewiring?"

Bruno paused. "Well, maybe it doesn't. But I'm guessing that your cousin, the one who thinks you're depressed, might think it does."

Oh. Right. Dawn.

He turned his attention back to the class. "Last week, your homework assignment was the key to help your brain register joy."

Callie sat up. So there really was a key? A secret? Suddenly, she really, really wanted to know what it was.

"Can anyone remind us what the key was?"

The woman who opened the door and pulled Callie in was the first to speak up. "Each day, write down a few things that made you feel good."

"Yes, exactly," Bruno said. "Thank you, Eleanor."

That's it? Too easy, Callie thought. Way too simplistic.

"Doing so," Bruno said, "strengthens those brain circuits of good feelings. Brains are remarkably plastic. Their ability to adjust is astounding." He stepped in front of the podium. "Does anyone want to share about a few things that made you feel good?"

A man with bushy eyebrows—shaped like arrows that pointed to the sky—waved his hand. "My wife went to visit her mother. It ain't quite as nippy out as it's been. And I found my car keys this morning. They went missing a few days back." He let out a long-suffering sigh. "But I still haven't found a job."

"Keep at it, Clint," Bruno said. "This exercise is not about changing your circumstances but about enjoying life more by focusing on positive things. Because there are good things going on in each of your lives, every day, but you have to look for them. Pay attention to them. Appreciate them." He lifted his arms wide. "For the next few minutes, I'd like you to share your good things with whomever is sitting next to you."

The shusher turned away from Callie, as did the person on her left. She was on her own, which she didn't mind, but Bruno Bianco noticed. He pulled up a chair and sat down. "I'm Bruno."

"Callie."

"So what's really brought you here?"

She felt an odd hitch of shyness. She had never been shy! "I haven't been to Cape Cod, which seems unfortunate because I've lived in Boston for my entire life."

"Actually, I meant what brought you to the class today?"

She'd already told him this. "My cousin. She made me come." But did that sound rude? Like she didn't want to be here? It was true, but she didn't mean to be so blunt.

"Yes. You mentioned your cousin thinks you're depressed. But you're not."

"I'm not."

"Well, I'm glad you're here today, Callie. This is a group to help people figure out what makes a fulfilling and satisfied life. Not sure if that's what you're looking for, but—"

"I am!" burst out of her.

Surprised, his eyes widened. "Then, you've come to the right place. So . . ." He glanced over her head, scanning the room, and seemed pleased by the hum of conversation. Then he swung back and locked eyes with hers and picked up the conversation. "Let's talk about things that make you feel good." When he saw her hesitation, he said, "Want me to start?"

Callie nodded, relieved.

He held three fingers in the air. "I woke extra early and went for a walk on the beach as the sun rose on the ocean. Absolutely breathtaking moment. Something about it always feels . . . holy. The way the light floods the sky." He closed his eyes and took in a deep breath, as if he was reliving the moment. Then he let out the breath and his eyes opened. "I see the sunrise almost every single day and yet, somehow, it feels new every morning." With his other hand, he tucked one finger down.

She tilted her head. She'd been here nearly a full week and hadn't gone to the ocean yet. She'd caught a glimpse of it on her drive into Chatham, glistening and beckoning to her, but she hadn't heeded its call.

"Two," Bruno said, tucking down another finger. "A pod of dolphins swam past me this morning."

"Dolphins?"

"Yes. Cape Cod is known as a place for dolphins to get stranded. One summer, forty-five beached in one day over in Wellfleet."

"Why? What happened?"

"Cape Cod is a hook, and Wellfleet is yet another hook. The dolphins come in for food, and as the tide recedes, it acts like a drain. The dolphins get trapped."

"Did they all die?"

"Actually, no. Volunteers were able to refloat most of them. I remember, because it was one of my good things on that particular summer day." He folded another finger down. "And three . . . I didn't burn the waffles this morning." He folded his arms against his chest. "So what about you?"

She cleared her throat. "Me?"

"Yes. You. What are a few things that made you feel good today?"

"Today?" It had been a rough morning. She'd changed her mind about attending the class and Dawn had turned into a crazy woman—pulling her out of bed, helping her get dressed, sticking her feet in boots. She drove her to the center and practically pushed her into the building. No. There was nothing good to sift out of this morning.

Bruno was waiting.

"Um . . ."

"Maybe if you can't think of something today, what about yesterday? Or the day before?"

Yesterday? It was pretty much like the day before.

"Try. It doesn't have to be something incredible."

"A pod of dolphins swimming by is pretty incredible."

"True. But the best thing of all was that I noticed the pod. I was paying attention to what was going on around me. The more you look for good things, the more you'll notice them. And remember them. The brain is a funny thing. The more you focus on something, the more likely your brain is to focus on it. So what we focus on, we find." He leaned forward. "Isn't there one thing that made you feel good in the last twenty-four hours? It can be something small, like a great cup of coffee."

The way he fixed his gaze on her made her feel nervous. And when she was nervous, she did one of two things: she talked incessantly or her mind went completely blank. Right now, it was the latter. She could not think of a single thing to say. The silence stretched out. Her palms started sweating and her cheeks grew warm.

In a gentle tone he said, "For someone who is doing great, it's a little worrisome that you can't think of even one thing that makes you feel good."

Her eyes darted around the room. The murmuring had stopped and people were looking at them. "I think everyone is finished with their sharing and waiting for you to take over."

He startled, as if it just occurred to him that he had a class to lead. "Oh, right!" He jumped from the seat and went back to the front to gather everyone's attention. He picked up a stack of papers from the lecture stand. "This is a quiz," he told the class as he handed out worksheets, "to help you get an idea of where you fit on the resistance-to-change scale."

Callie only pretended to be taking the quiz. Afterward, as people discussed their results, she hardly listened. She was still trying to think of a few good things that made her feel good.

Aunt Marnie and Dawn.

Not that they made her feel good, necessarily, not with the worried looks they exchanged whenever Callie ventured downstairs. But Dawn had shared her tiny room, and her blue chenille bathrobe. And Aunt Marnie did say Callie could stay as long as she needed them. So that was something.

What else?

Stumped, she couldn't think of anything else. Not a single thing.

Finally, the class wrapped up. Bruno made a few closing remarks. Then he turned and looked straight at Callie. "When something happens in your life that you didn't expect, and maybe you didn't want, it can be a call to change. And change can be a good thing."

As soon as the class was excused, Callie hurried outside, blinking against the bright sunlight. She walked to the parking lot and looked around. Dawn's car . . . it was gone! She'd left!

She scratched Dawn off her good-things list.

Callie walked from the parking lot to the street, trying to stop a rising wave of panic. She couldn't remember how to get back to the Creamery. She hadn't paid any attention as Dawn drove through the winding streets. A sweep of exhaustion hit her. She was suddenly so very tired. She could feel tears start to prick her eyes. She wouldn't cry. Callie. Dixon. Did. Not. Cry.

She felt a little tug on her coat sleeve. She turned, and there was Leo the Cowboy, peering up at her.

"Are you lost again?"

She let out a sigh. "I am." *I really, really am.*

"You'd better come with me." He took her hand and led Callie home.

On the way, like a switch flipped on, Callie thought of something else for her good-things list. Something that genuinely made her feel good. Someone, actually. A little someone who had a knack for showing up at the right time.

Leo the Cowboy.

• • •

Marnie
Dawn dragged Callie to the Secret to Happiness class.

Linc
Uh oh. Not the kind of class to go to against your will.

Yep. A recipe for disaster.

Chapter

TEN

I go running when I have to. When the ice cream truck
is doing sixty.

—Wendy Liebman, comedian

Dawn had waited to make sure Callie had been settled in the Secret
to Happiness class before she decided to zip home to get an ice cream
base mixed so it could chill, curing, for a few hours before it went
into the machine. She planned to pop back down to the community center to get Callie when it was over, but then Kevin arrived at
the Creamery, full of news about a seventeenth-century house he'd
toured with one of his graduate classes, and she lost track of time.

"Horsehair in the plaster," he said, looking like a kid on Christmas morning. "This house was so old that the walls actually had
horsehair mixed into the plaster!"

She poured two mugs of freshly brewed coffee and handed him
one. "But why?"

"The horsehair strengthened it, kind of like a modern-day mesh."
He shook his head with a smile. "Those early settlers were incredibly
resourceful. They didn't let anything go to waste." He took a sip of
coffee. "Where's your mom?"

"She and Lincoln went on a hike."

"Something smells good. What are you making?"

"Ice cream. Caramel Chocolate with Nuts." She spun around to shake the pan that the pecans were dry roasting in.

"Guess what else was in this house?"

"What?"

"We found pumpkin pine. Big wide planks. Eighteen inches wide." He reached out and snitched a few pecans from the pan. "They're in excellent condition."

"I've never heard of a pumpkin pine tree."

"That's because," he said, chewing the pecans, "there is no such thing. It comes from eastern white pine. Very common. Practically everything built in the colonial era was made from eastern white pine. It's the patina of the planks that makes them so distinctive. The sap comes to the surface and gives it a pumpkin-y color. Your mom would love it."

"I bet. She'll want to install it in the Creamery."

"Impossible."

"Not now. Down the road."

"Not down the road. Not ever. You must know what a house with eighteen-inch planks means."

Dawn slid the pecans from the frying pan into a bowl. "I have absolutely no idea."

"Today we'd call them old-growth trees. But back in colonial America, it meant that the original owner of the house had some special connection to the king. Because the largest, oldest trees were reserved for the king and his cronies." He hopped up to sit on the counter. "If I had any money to spare, this is the kind of house I'd like to buy for us. Barely escaping a teardown. Just waiting for someone to restore it to its former glory."

Dawn kept stirring the sliced pecans. "Sadly, you're broke." Kevin had sunk most of his savings into his master's program. She glanced at him. "But I'm not. There's still my savings account."

"And you need to keep that account intact for a sense of security." He took a sip of coffee. "But we do need to think about where we're going to live after we get married. No offense to your mother, but I'm not living here."

"No offense taken."

"And we can't live at Nanette's."

"Definitely not."

She put the pan into the sink and turned to him. "You're loving this history stuff, aren't you?"

"Passionately." He slid off the counter and wrapped his arms around her. "Second only to my passion for you, of course."

She smiled. "Of course." She reached up to kiss him, and as she did, she felt a blast of cold air sweep through the Creamery. Her eyes popped open to see Callie peer around the stairwell into the kitchen. "You're back!"

"My apologies for interrupting this intimate moment."

She sounded annoyed. Dawn wiggled out of Kevin's arms and took a few steps forward. "I was going to come get you when the class was over."

"It ended thirty minutes ago."

Really? Dawn felt her stomach clench. "I'm so sorry. I got involved with—"

Callie shot a glance at Kevin. "Kissing."

"—making ice cream." This should've been an opportunity for Dawn to feel sympathy for Callie, to offer some encouragement and comfort. An apology for forgetting her. But instead of sympathy, she just felt irritated. After all, it was just a few blocks away. She gave a little fist bump in the air. "Good for you for finding your way home. Well done."

Callie tipped her head, as if studying Dawn.

Kevin looked back and forth between the two of them. "I feel like I walked into a movie halfway through."

Callie lifted her chin and gave Kevin a bright smile. "Sorry. Hi. It's nice to see you again, Kevin. It's been years. In fact, I didn't even recognize you at first."

"Have I changed so much?"

"Something's different." Callie squinted. "Oh! No beard." She gave him an approving smile. "It makes you look older. In a good way. Hipper. Less geeky. Rather distinguished."

He stroked his beardless chin. "Yeah?"

Dawn slid a look at Kevin, who was staring at Callie. He had a goofy, pleased expression on his face. She tried not to gag. This was how all men reacted to Callie when she paid them some attention. And she was oblivious to her charms!

Kevin's goofy expression intensified. "I would've known you anywhere, Callie. You look . . . good. Really good."

Dawn felt an all-too-familiar coil heat in her belly. *No.* She would not nurture such immature, unfounded jealousy. She would let it go.

From where she was standing, she appraised Callie. She did look especially good today. Her big coat covered her thinness, and her cheeks were pink from the exercise. Her long blond hair was held back in a loose-fitting ponytail. "Callie can't help but look good," she said, and she meant it.

Kevin leaned back against the counter. "How do you like Cape Cod?"

Callie lifted a shoulder in a shrug. "What's not to like?"

"She hasn't seen much of it yet," Dawn said. "But we're working on that."

Kevin lifted his coffee mug. "Come and sit with us, Callie. Dawn just made a fresh pot of coffee."

Dawn pulled a coffee mug out of the cupboard. "You can tell us about the class. I'm curious about it."

Callie gave her a look. "Really? Because maybe you should have stayed."

Instead of ditching her, she meant. Dawn really hadn't intended to leave Callie alone for the class, but when she returned with the janitor, she saw that Callie was already sitting up front, there were no free seats next to her, and she was engaged in a conversation with a cute guy with long hair. Dawn didn't want to interrupt her progress at rejoining the world. So she decided to head home and come back later. Then she completely forgot about her.

Just as Dawn started to pour coffee into an empty mug, Callie interrupted her. "Thanks, but I need to go up and get some work done." And she was gone.

Kevin waited until he heard the upstairs bedroom door close. "That's a good sign, right? She's got work to do?"

Dawn shook her head. "There is no work. She just lies in bed all day, every day, staring at the ceiling."

"Oh." He paused, then lifted his mug. "Mind if I add some vanilla ice cream to my coffee?"

"Go right ahead."

Kevin was already looking through the freezer. "Hey, good job organizing the freezer so ordinary joes like me can find stuff."

That was a dig at Dawn's territorial attitude toward the kitchen. She had her own systems in place, excellent ones, but Mom and Kevin could never seem to figure them out.

"I didn't. Mom must've. She's come back from Ice Cream School with a new determination to get involved."

Then something flashed through Dawn's mind. Her eyes looked to the ceiling, where Callie was probably passed out on the air mattress. *Nah.* Couldn't be Callie's doing. Not in the sad shape she was in.

• • •

Sunday, February 6

Callie couldn't stop thinking about the sunrise on the ocean. Bruno Bianco had described it almost poetically. And the look on his face— like he'd had a supernatural encounter. A rapturous experience, a mountaintop high. Whatever it was, she wanted it for herself.

So yesterday afternoon, she searched on her phone for a route to get to the ocean from the Creamery. She also googled the time of the sunrise over Chatham, and the temperature . . . and that was when she nearly abandoned her plan. But she was desperate for that sense of wonder, of well-being, that filled Bruno Bianco's face as he described the sunrise. She wanted to feel something other than panic and worry and problems. She was tired of feeling bad, all the time. Tired of only thinking about herself and her problems.

Most mornings, her aunt went out on an early dog walk with that Lincoln guy. But today was Sunday, and she knew Marnie was a churchgoer. Still, she decided that if Marnie did leave early for her walk with Lincoln, and if Dawn slept in, then Callie would go to the ocean and find that sunrise and see if she could capture some of that good feeling.

Part of her hoped Marnie might not go. Part of her hoped she would.

Callie waited in bed, listening for sounds of her aunt on the rise. After a few minutes, she heard Marnie's bedroom door open and shut and her footfalls on the stairs.

Okay, Callie. You made yourself a promise. Get up and go. She sighed, squeezed her eyes shut, and forced herself to get out of the bed. It took every ounce of willpower she could muster, because every fiber of her being wanted to crawl back to bed and shut the world out.

But . . . that *feeling*. As Bruno Bianco described the way the morning sunlight glittered on the ocean, she felt herself drawn to that vision. She wanted to see it. Desperately. She longed to be someplace beautiful, to fill her mind with something majestic.

As much as she wanted to stay in bed, she wanted that feeling of euphoria even more. She tiptoed downstairs and bundled up, scarf and mittens and coat, thick socks and tall boots. Hanging on a peg by the door was a flashlight, so she grabbed that too. She was as prepared as she could be for the elements.

She opened the door and felt a knife-like blast of cold hit her in the face, making her eyes water. Thoughts of a warm bed called to her.

She wavered.

No!

She was going to find that sunrise feeling if it killed her.

● ● ●

Linc
If you haven't left yet, bring your niece along.
Should be a beautiful sunrise today.

Marnie
Nice thought but I'm halfway to the lighthouse.
And yesterday's outing wiped Callie out. It didn't
go the way Dawn expected. Will fill you in.

OK. See u soon.

Chapter
ELEVEN

Without ice cream there would be darkness and chaos.
—Don Kardong, Olympic marathon runner

Twenty minutes later, Callie had made it down to the empty beach. She crossed the clean-washed sand to head close to the water. No orb of sun on the far horizon yet, but when she swung around to look behind her, she saw only pitch black. In front of her, the sky over the ocean was just starting to lighten. The great expanse of sea was shimmering. She noticed a big log that had drifted up on the beach, and she sat down, cross-legged, with her back against it, to wait for this apparently wonderful moment.

Just then a gust of wind blew in from the water, clutching icily at her face, snatching her breath away so that she turned involuntarily to one side. "Whoa! Make it snappy, sun!"

To her surprise, a voice behind her answered back. "Have patience."

She startled, but not entirely. She recognized that deep rumbly voice. "It's you." The author guy. Bruno Bianco. Though she could barely make him out in the dark.

"It's me." He eased down beside her. He wore a Chatham Anglers baseball cap, a thick puffy down coat, and work boots. He seemed completely different from the serious-minded professor in yesterday's class. He seemed like a regular guy. "So you came to see the sunrise."

"I did." She tucked her hands into the pockets of her coat. Actually, Dawn's down coat. "But it's so cold!"

"The temperature always drops right before dawn."

Her teeth were chattering. "Why is that?"

"Something about weak solar radiation."

She glanced at him. "And you do this every day?"

"Try to. As often as I can." He gave her a nudge with his elbow. "Just watch. It's worth hanging around for the show."

She stared out at the horizon, waiting for the sun to appear. Somewhere on the long ribbon of beach, a dog barked. The sky was starting to brighten to a pink light of dawn. But if the sun didn't make its appearance soon, she was leaving. Her cheeks were so cold they felt frozen. She was shivering.

"So you never really said what made you come to Chatham."

"I did say." She'd told him twice now. "My cousin. She lives here." She said all that through chattering teeth. He seemed unconcerned.

"I'm starting to wonder about your cousin. Seems a little odd to think that people who love you would invite you to come here in the dead of winter."

Well, no one actually invited her, but she didn't feel the need to volunteer that information.

"As you've probably already noticed," he said, turning to jut his chin behind him, "Chatham is a ghost town in the winter."

She felt as if she had to say something. Explain herself in some way. "The timing worked. I'm, uh, between jobs."

He nodded, like he got it. She braced herself, expecting him to ask her about what kind of work she did, and why she was in between jobs, and what she wanted to do, and on and on. But he didn't ask her anything else.

Was there more? Nope. He seemed utterly still, and completely content with being still.

She couldn't leave it alone. There was something about his . . . quietness . . . that made her feel compelled to fill the silence with rambling words. "I've never seen a sunrise on the ocean before. You'd think that living in Boston, I would've grown up going to the seashore. But there was never time. Mom was sick, of course. She had multiple sclerosis. So there was that." *Stop talking, Callie! Apply your verbal brakes!* But no. It was like someone turned on a spigot and left the water running at full blast. She couldn't stop yammering away. "And then after Mom died, Dad packed me off to summer camps with my cousin. This same cousin who lives here in Chatham. But they weren't really camps, in case you were wondering. More like school for overachieving kids. Or, more truthfully, overachieving parents. Anyway, so that's what I did, all those years. And suddenly, here I am, twenty-eight years old, unemployed, with a very, very bleak future, and it's only now that I'm finally seeing the sun rise on the ocean. That seems kind of a sad reason to see the sunrise, don't you think?" Kind of like, she thought, someone who might be having a complete mental breakdown?

When he didn't respond, she cast a furtive glance at him, but he wasn't looking at her. She thought that maybe he wasn't even listening to her! His entire focus was fixed straight ahead.

"Here it comes," he said in a whispered hush. "The holy moment."

She lifted her head, surprised to see how light had transformed the sky in the last few moments during her ramble. And then she saw what Bruno was gazing at: a sliver of sun rising low on the horizon. The water was calm, almost glasslike, the surf lapping gently. Right before her eyes, the sun rose, slowly and quietly, changing the entire atmosphere. So dramatic, so sensational, yet without fanfare. No trumpets blaring, no fireworks. It occurred to her that this had been going on every single morning of her life, yet she'd missed it.

"'Life is not measured by the breaths we take but by the moments that take our breath away.'" He glanced at her and added, "Maya Angelou."

She gave him a curious look. "The poet?"

"Yep." He pushed himself up. "I'll leave you to your own holy moment." And with that, he walked off toward the water.

She watched him go. Odd, odd guy. Kinda cute, but odd.

Right before her eyes, the sky kept changing into bursts of color: striated oranges and pinks and reds. Birdsong filled the air. She breathed in the fresh salty scent of the sea. She shifted in the cold sand underneath her. It was a sensory overload. And it was *wonderful*.

As she watched the sun continue to rise, as the sky turned a pearlescent pink, she thought this Bruno guy might be on to something about the power of awe. There was a feeling inside her that she couldn't quite describe—it seemed too intimate for words. She felt thoroughly insignificant before this nearest star, a sense that she was observing something powerful and mighty, yet that awareness didn't make her feel unimportant. She was surprised how soothing it was to be in the presence of things greater than herself. Something about her smallness as she faced something so vast . . . it just felt right, and good. Like she was flooded by a wonderful sense of well-being. The morning sunshine, despite the bone-chilling cold, was insistently, relentlessly cheery.

She stayed for a long time, until the sun had risen completely into the sky. Reluctantly, she got up and headed back to the road. She was glad she'd come. She felt, if not *good*, at least better than she had when she first got up this morning. She felt at peace for the first time in a long while.

• • •

Monday, February 7

Rain started in the night and kept up all morning long. Dawn and her mom had looked at four different wedding venues this morning—two in Harwich, one in Truro, and the last one in Chatham. Each place was nice, but none of them felt quite right. The problem was, Dawn didn't really know what she *was* looking for.

She still felt a little gun-shy after planning such an elaborate wedding last spring and Kevin calling it off two months prior. She had no concerns about Kevin getting cold feet again—they'd worked through the issues that came to the forefront last year and were better, stronger for them. But it still bothered her that she had spent so much time and energy and effort on creating the perfect wedding, overlooking some of the most important things. Like the groom's growing reluctance.

Maybe that was it. She was worried about caring too much about the wedding, all over again.

It was hard not to get swept away—the enthusiasm of each of the wedding planners was contagious. Overwhelming. They were creative types, with grandiose ideas. If Dawn and Kevin didn't have a clear vision of what the wedding should be, these wedding planners sure did. They seemed to recognize Dawn's insecurity and swooped in with brilliant suggestions, all over-the-top.

"You're awfully quiet," Mom said, on the drive back from Truro.

Dawn glanced at her. "Just thinking about those venues." She noticed what time it was. "The Creamery should've opened an hour ago."

"Dawn, no one is banging on the door for ice cream on a rainy day in February."

"Still, it's good business practice to be predictable." She sighed. "When is the baker coming back from Florida?"

"Not until late April."

Dawn let out an exasperated sigh. "I hate to bake."

"You're not so bad. I thought the last batch of pumpkin muffins were really good."

"They were an anomaly. Baking is frustrating. I follow the recipes exactly, but there's still an element of mystery that intrudes. The humidity in the air, the oven temperature can fluctuate, some eggs have more volume than others. Makes me crazy. I just want to make ice cream. That I understand. If you follow instructions, then what goes in comes out as ice cream."

"I could try to bake."

"You're a cook, not a baker. Baking requires precision."

"Maybe I could ask Callie to help out."

Dawn shook her head firmly. "You can't put that kind of pressure on her."

"You're already putting pressure on her to go to that class."

"That's different."

"How?"

"She only has to listen in the class. Just be a receiver. Not a giver."

"Or is it that you don't want Callie cooking in your kitchen?"

"Mom. I am doing all I can to get Callie back on her feet. I'm insulted you would think I would be so shallow a person." There was a tiny bit of truth in that, though. "I have high hopes for the Happiness Campaign. I'm sure we're going to see some improvement in her soon."

Mom lifted her eyebrows.

"What?"

"Have you ever thought of just asking her about what's made her feel so depressed? Just talking to her?"

"No need." Dawn shrugged. "I know what's made her depressed. Her failed career. I would feel depressed, too, if I poisoned two hundred people with my ice cream."

Mom went quiet, which meant Dawn had sounded too snarky.

"I know you feel sorry for Callie, Mom, but I just don't think pity is what she needs. Pity doesn't do anyone any good. Sometimes, you have to fake it 'til you make it."

"Sounds like something your dad would've said."

"Well, Dad was usually right. I think he would agree with me that Callie needs to get out of bed and fill her mind with something else. Volunteer work, maybe."

Mom gave her a sideways glance. "As long as she stays out of your kitchen."

That too. Oh, definitely that.

●　●　●

Tuesday, February 8

The skies cleared on Monday night, and the stars shone brightly, so Callie plotted her path to the sunrise for Tuesday morning. This time, she laid out her own clothes, coat, and boots by the back door. Flashlight too. She dozed off and on until six o'clock. Then, confident Dawn was sound asleep by her steady breathing—she'd been out late with Kevin the night before, which meant that she'd be sleeping in late—Callie quietly tiptoed out of the room, down the stairs, dressed, and slipped out the back door. It was quieter than the front door, which had to be pulled hard to shut tight.

She had memorized a map of Chatham she'd found on her phone, and had figured out a shortcut to the beach. She walked straight down Main Street a few blocks, then turned left and walked briskly a few more blocks, crossed Shore Road, and there it was. The vast Atlantic Ocean. She could hear it and smell it before she could see it in the dark. This morning, there were a few people walking along the beach, their dogs crisscrossing the sand in happy abandon. Callie walked halfway toward the water and sat down. She wiggled her bottom into the sand. Behind her, the sky was coal black. She waited, watching for that first light to arrive, and as she waited, she felt her whole self settle. Peace filled her. This sunrise moment was the only thing that kept her from falling into a yawning hole of despair.

"Morning."

Callie startled. Bruno Bianco! *For Pete's sake.* "What are you doing here?"

"Same thing as you." He dropped down beside her on the sand, uninvited.

Why did he have to be here? Chatham had six separate beaches. Plenty to go around! The ocean was enormous. Why here? He was ruining her special moment. She started to feel a tightening in her chest. A long, red blush seared up her neck. No. Not the MS hug. Please no! Not here. Not now. When they hit, she could hardly breathe. A flush started in her neck and the flame shot upward. Her chest would literally hurt. She couldn't talk, couldn't think straight. If she got up and walked away, she'd probably trip and do a face-plant. The MS hug took over her entire body.

At least it was still dark, she thought. *He can't see me looking like*

I'm about to explode. She took in a deep breath and held it, slowly releasing it. *Don't think about it. Think about something else.*

"See what I mean?"

She let her breath out slowly, through pursed lips. "About what?" She took in another deep breath. Had he noticed how weird she was acting? She hoped not. It was still pretty dark, after all. Breathing in and out, holding her knees tightly against her like she was freezing. But each time she stole a glance at him, she found he wasn't even looking at her. Maybe he wasn't the noticing type. Slowly, as casually as possible, she released her breath, and inhaled again oh-so-slowly.

"About awe. Every single day, I try to experience awe."

"Awe?"

"Yes. Awe."

She blew out a long breath. "Is this the same thing"—she paused to inhale slowly—"as the finding-good-things-in-a-day habit?" As soon as she asked, she regretted it. She was in no condition for a long conversation. But she was desperate to distract herself from the effects of the MS hug, and so far Bruno was helping. Hopefully, unaware.

He shifted a little in the sand to look at her. "Different habit. That habit is meant to rewire our brains."

And then he was gazing at her so intently that she forgot what he had just said. Oh! Brain rewiring. "How so?" Her breath was coming more easily now.

"By paying attention to things that bring joy, your brain starts to notice joy and connects it to memory. The more you register good things, the more you'll think about and remember moments of joy. Circumstances aren't necessarily different, but how you feel, how you think, is different."

She pulled her eyes away from his, after noticing they were kind of sad, puppy dog eyes. Almond shaped, droopy at the corner. "And that's not the same thing as experiencing awe?"

"No. Experiencing awe helps us get out of our heads. It reminds us that the universe doesn't revolve around us. The good-things habit is just about feeling happier. The things don't have to be a big-deal thing. Just little things. A moment you enjoyed. First sip of coffee every day, for example. That's a good thing, in my book."

"Mine too." Okay. She could agree on a daily good thing. "So that's the secret to happiness? Awe?"

He cocked his head to look at her. "It's part of it."

"There's more?" She'd been hoping for a clear, straight path. Point A to point B.

He nodded. "Come to class next Saturday to find out." The tiniest sliver of sun appeared. Like last time, he said, "I'll leave you to your holy moment," and off he went.

She sat and watched the sun rise. Today, a large cloud floated in front of it, so the sun limned the cloud, outlining it with radiance. It was different than the striated colors of the first sunrise she saw, but every bit as breathtaking.

Ten minutes later, she was nearly halfway back to the Creamery when she realized the MS hug had indeed subsided without going into a full-blown boa constrictor squeeze, pressing the air right out of her lungs. She wondered why, and if it might have had something to do with awe.

● ● ●

Callie
Do you think much about being "in awe"?

Jesse
Huh?

This author guy I met calls awe the ability to marvel.

Cool! We should all do more marveling.

I marvel. I marvel at how low I've sunk.

Chapter
TWELVE

My love for ice cream emerged at an early age and has never left.

—Ginger Rogers

Wednesday, February 9

Rain pelted the roof of the Creamery. Aunt Marnie and Dawn had gone to look at some wedding venues and wouldn't be back until the shop opened at one o'clock. As soon as they left, Callie went downstairs. She made herself some avocado toast and ate it, ate the whole thing, along with coffee she'd found left in the pot. The warm buttery lights in the front room made the patina of the scarred wooden floors gleam. It was a charming spot to breakfast on a winter day. Such an ordinary moment, but it made her feel good, and she decided that this would be her first good thing for today's good-things list.

Under a large glass cloche were muffins Dawn had made early this morning. She lifted the cloche and examined a muffin, split it in half, then sniffed. Morning Glory muffins, her favorite. She tasted a bite. Oh boy. Again, not enough cinnamon. Not enough cloves or nutmeg. There was crushed pineapple in it, but barely enough to keep it moist, and what was there had been macerated. A few chopped walnuts, but not enough. Besides being dry, they were missing the three most important parts of making a truly memorable muffin: bite, chew, crunch. Like Dawn's last batch of pumpkin muffins, these, too, were rubber muffins.

An inner battle started to wage.

This was why customers weren't coming into the Creamery. Dawn's coffee was good, but these overmixed, tasteless baked goods were hurting the Creamery's reputation. Maybe not hurting, but they sure weren't helping.

And while it was clear, even to Callie, that the majority of the homes in Chatham were empty, there were plenty of year-rounders left to coax into the shop. Lots of them. Just look at the size of the Saturday Happiness class. When food was excellent, customers found their way. That was the foundation of food service.

It pained Callie to think of the Creamery's missed opportunities. Imagine if the Creamery offered hot soup, a different variety each day. Or sandwiches. Imagine tomato-basil soup with a grilled sourdough panini, oozing with fontina cheese. So simple. Inexpensive to make yet with huge profit margins.

Still, she wasn't here to make over the Creamery. She wasn't here to make another colossal mistake that might end up poisoning innocent customers.

Thinking about this made her stomach clench, because she knew what she had to do.

She covered her face with her hands. One more time. One more exception to her no-cook/no-bake rule. For Marnie and Dawn, she had to swap out those awful muffins. Not just any muffins, but her oh-so-memorable Morning Glory muffins, known far and wide in Boston.

She rummaged around and found everything she needed but carrots, apples, cans of crushed pineapple, a bag of walnuts. If she was going to break her rule, she had to do it right. She exhaled a sigh of resolve, then headed to the back door, grabbing her coat off the hook. When she and Leo were walking home from the class last

Saturday, she had noticed a small store just a few blocks away. The sky was dark with threatening clouds, so she picked up her pace, wanting to get back to the Creamery before rain started up again.

Ten minutes later, she'd found the grocery store. She opened the door to a whoosh of warm air. She'd always found grocery stores to be calming, especially when they were empty like this one. She grabbed a cart and curved her way around the produce aisle, stopping to examine the imported Philippine mangoes (green, not ripe!), sniff the honey crisp apples (too long in the cold storage!), then up and down the aisles. She had managed to put only one thing in the cart when, suddenly, she steered around an endcap and saw him, sitting at a table stacked with books, with a long line of customers. Bruno Bianco.

Yep. Definitely him. Sitting there, with those books stacked around him, with adoring people waiting in that long line, he had a certain appeal. He was surprisingly good looking.

At that moment, he looked up. Their eyes met.

With that came a jolt of panic. She hadn't showered this morning. Or brushed her hair. Or applied a stitch of makeup. She had to get out of here.

She steered her cart around sharply and bumped into the cart of an elderly woman, who let out an unearthly shriek.

Oh no . . . of all people! She'd bumped carts with the *shusher*. Mrs. Nickerson-Eldredge! "I'm . . . so sorry! I just forgot something on another aisle and I swung my cart around and there you were." Callie could almost feel the woman's disapproval pinning her to the shelf.

"The carts go in one direction."

Good grief. This wasn't a highway. "I am sorry."

"Well, you should be mindful of the direction you're headed in, young lady."

Boy, wasn't that the truth? "You're right. My mistake."

Mrs. Nickerson-Eldredge glared at Callie as she pushed the cart around her. And suddenly in front of her cart was Bruno Bianco. The shock of his presence left her temporarily frozen.

"Hey there, Callie."

"Oh. Good morning." She looked behind her. How had he moved so fast? "Looks like you've got something going on."

"Signing books."

"Here? In a grocery store? That seems kinda weird."

He shrugged. "The bookstore had a leak in the roof from today's rain, so this is plan B." He held out a book to her. "I thought you might like to read it. My gift."

She looked at the title: *The Secret to Happiness* by Bruno Bianco. "I didn't realize the class was based on a book."

"You still need to go to class."

"I do? Why?" She hadn't decided yet if she was going back.

"Because I think it will help."

Help, how? she wanted to ask. But instead of that, instead of a normal question from a normal person, out of her mouth burst, "An owl. I heard it hooting."

He said nothing, but looked at her in that way of his, like he was studying her. Like she was a curiosity.

"Last night. I was lying in bed and heard its hoot. It was so haunting and lonely and lovely that it gave me a chill down my spine." She felt her face grow warm. What a weird thing to say. He must think she was a nut job. Maybe she was. "It's not like a pod of dolphins, but . . ."

"It gave you a sense of wonder," he said. "See? Doesn't have to be as splashy as a sunrise. It could be something like listening to Mozart. I encourage everyone to look for daily experiences of awe. I'm convinced that single habit can change peoples' lives. Those who seek awe just seem . . . happier."

"So, then, is *that* the secret to happiness?"

"Read and find out."

Suddenly a very attractive woman appeared beside him. She looked curiously at Callie before saying, "You're needed back at the table, Bruno." She placed a hand on his arm, a bit possessively.

He gave a nod to Callie and left with the woman.

Flustered, Callie tried to regroup, find the ingredients she needed, and leave the store as quickly as she could. On the way home, she pondered the curious look she received from that woman—almost amused. What was up with that? She glanced down at herself. Did she look so odd today? Her big down parka went all the way to her knees, followed by black boots. She looked like everybody else in the Northeast on a cold, rainy winter day.

That woman's look made her annoyed. That *woman* made her annoyed.

Why should she care?

She had definitely not come to Cape Cod in search of male companionship. Not even a fling. Not that she was the fling-y type. She wasn't. But still.

Back at the Creamery, happily alone in the kitchen, she listened to music on her iPhone and boogied around a little while she grated and chopped and mixed. The smell of baking filled the kitchen and she found herself feeling homesick for her old life. While the muffins were baking, she cleaned the dishes she'd used and left the kitchen exactly as she had found it. After the muffins cooled, she tried one and found it to be . . . in a word, spectacular. She tossed Dawn's muffins in a plastic bag and took them out to the trash can. Then she placed her muffins under the glass cloche in the front room.

Afterward, she felt tired, but not quite the same kind of exhaustion. Maybe Dad was right. There was nothing like activity to rid the mind of brooding. Lying on the air mattress, she picked up Bruno Bianco's book and opened to chapter one. "When Life Doesn't Turn Out the Way You Planned."

She wiggled to get more comfortable and started reading.

· · ·

Marnie ran as fast as she could from Dawn's car to the back door of the Creamery, trying to dodge heavy raindrops. Dawn had dropped her off and gone to meet Kevin for lunch to fill him in on the venue options they'd looked at today. She hurried to unlock the front door and turn over the closed sign, just as Linc happened to come up the path. She'd expected him, because he came to the Creamery each day after he finished his morning volunteer work.

Just to check in, he would say, but she knew he didn't want to go back to that big empty house of his.

She opened the door for him with a smile. "You're our first customer today!"

"And what a day." He left his umbrella outside and shook off his raincoat before hanging it on the hall tree. "How'd the wedding spots work out?"

"I don't think Dawn felt like any place hit the mark."

"Does she have a mark in mind?"

Marnie froze, then turned to him. "You know, I don't think she does. I think *that's* the problem." She grinned. "Lincoln Hayes, you have surprising insight into people."

He smiled, pleased. His cheeks were pink from the cold, and it struck Marnie that he was quite a handsome man. Had he always been so? Or was she just noticing it more lately?

Now it was her turn for a flush of color on her cheeks, but it wasn't from the cold. Horrible hot flashes! She spun around and flipped on the lights, then turned up the heat. Poor Callie. It was cold down here and she hoped the upstairs was a little warmer. A cinnamony smell filled the air and her gaze swept the room, looking for its source. Under the large glass cloche was a platter of muffins. "I'll get some coffee started to warm you up. Dawn made muffins this morning. Help yourself." She looked through the cloche. "They do look tempting." She went into the kitchen to make a fresh pot of coffee. As she was filling the container with water, Linc came into the kitchen, half a muffin in one hand.

"Marnie, this isn't just good. This is incredible." He held out the rest of the muffin to her.

Marnie stopped the faucet and took a bite of the muffin. Moist crumb, chewy texture, crunch on top with the chopped walnuts. "You're right. It's delicious." She took another bite before she finished filling the coffeepot with water.

"I could eat ten of these. What kind is it?"

"I think Dawn said she was trying a recipe for Morning Glory muffins. Kind of like a carrot cake without the icing." She took another bite from Linc. Carrots, pineapple, walnuts, cinnamon. Unbelievably satisfying. Sweet but not too sweet. "I'll have to tell Dawn to make them more often." Marnie scooped coffee into the coffee maker and turned it on.

"Tell her to make them every day."

Marnie closed the lid on the coffee container and set it back on the shelf. And that was when she noticed that the KitchenAid mixer was still plugged in. Dawn was a stickler about unplugging appliances when not in use. She tugged on the cord and an odd thought flitted through her mind. Could Callie be the baker behind these delicious muffins? Wow, wouldn't that be something?!

She looked around the kitchen for other signs of recent baking. Nothing. She opened the garbage bin to see if there might be any carrot peelings or a can or some recent evidence to point to Callie. But there was nothing in it but the coffee grounds from breakfast.

No. No way. There was no possible way.

● ● ●

Thursday, February 10

Toward the end of Callie's second week of self-imposed exile to Chatham, she felt her energy level rise. Just a skosh, but it was noticeable. She hadn't been to the beach to see the sunrise in a few days, not with the hard, icy rain pounding on the roof. But Thursday morning called for clear skies, and she had overheard Marnie making plans to meet Lincoln super early, and she knew Dawn was also going out on a run with Kevin. As soon as she heard them leave the Creamery the next morning, she slipped out of bed, dressed warmly, hurried downstairs, and out the door. She was eager to arrive at the ocean before the sun started its ascent.

On the walk down Main Street in the dark, it occurred to her that she hadn't had this much interest in anything in a few weeks, maybe months, and realizing that made her feel good. Her leg muscles were working, she was breathing hard. Her first good thing on the list for today.

She went to the beach and walked halfway to the water. She was going to sit down, but the sand was so wet from yesterday's rain that she knew she'd soak her pants, so she just stood. Then she waited, her eyes fixed on the glowing horizon. She wanted that good sunrise feeling again. She knew it didn't really change her life, but it made her forget her troubles, at least for a while. That was her second good thing of the day. And it wasn't even seven o'clock yet. She smiled. She was getting the hang of the good-things list.

Bruno Bianco was spot-on when he said the moment felt holy: the light starting to flood the sky, the gentle lapping of the waves at low tide, the tangy smell of the ocean.

Everything at this moment felt so sublime that Callie wished she had a magic wand that would make time stop. She wanted this moment to last forever.

But, of course, life didn't work that way. Low tide would soon ebb away, replaced by high tide with its relentless pounding of waves. Nothing could stop it from coming.

Reluctantly, she walked back toward the road.

The Creamery was still empty when she returned twenty minutes later. She started the coffeepot and waited for the sound of drips pinging into the pot. While she waited, she decided to take a quick shower. She had found that a daily shower lifted her spirit—such a simple thing but it did make a difference—and once she even had the wherewithal to style her hair. But today when she looked in the mirror, really looked, she wondered what the point was of trying to look her best when she had no plans. Even worse, no future. Then that familiar tightness in her middle started up and she felt heat rushing to her face . . . and she abandoned the idea of a shower and went to lie down on her bed to wait until it passed. Trying desperately to distract herself, she grabbed Bruno Bianco's book and picked up where she left off.

> Gratitude is powerful. It has a lot to do with holding on to a moment as strongly as possible. Gratitude can shift our perceptions of time and slow it down.

Okay, she liked that thought. That's what she wished she could've done on the beach this morning. Made time slow down.

> Gratitude is a discipline that needs to be practiced. Think of gratitude as an atrophied muscle that needs exercising. It doesn't always come naturally, even to those who consider themselves to be easily satisfied.

Did she consider herself to be easily satisfied? No. Not even close. She had a tendency to keep moving the goalpost on herself. On her staff too. It wasn't all bad, because it was the impetus that kept her constantly striving to improve performance and achieve goals. But it also made her critical, finicky, and fretful. Tough to please. It was the very reason she had ongoing, escalating conflicts with the event planner at the hotel's restaurant. They were way too much alike.

> The practice of gratitude brings many benefits. Scientists have found that gratitude improves overall well-being—both physical and psychological health. Gratitude increases happiness and decreases depression. It breaks unhealthy mental habits and improves resiliency. Those who rank high on the gratitude scale are less defensive, less resentful. More sensitive to others, more empathetic and supportive. Gratitude can even help people get better sleep.
>
> So cultivate gratitude throughout your day. Look for things to be thankful about. Start hunting for them throughout your day. Gratitude is a gamechanger.

Her bedroom door burst open and there was Leo.

She raised her head from the pillow to look at him. "Leo, you really need to learn to knock before you enter a room."

He lifted a book in the air. "You told me I should learn to read."

She pulled herself up, leaning on her elbows to look at him. She had said that, but she didn't think he would've listened to her. And she certainly didn't mean to insinuate that she could teach him to read. She had no idea how to teach a child to read. But he didn't seem concerned about that. Without an invitation, he climbed up on her bed and sat beside her, legs straight out. She looked at the cover and smiled. *Cowboy Small* by Lois Lenski. An old classic. "Where'd you get this book?"

"My dad." He crossed one boot over the other. "I told him you said cowboys needed to learn to read, so we went to the bookstore and he got me this."

"But, Leo, I'm not a teacher."

"I know. You're a bed sitter."

"Well . . . I'm more than a person who sits in bed all day." Not really. Not lately.

"You can still sit in bed and teach me to read."

"I have absolutely no experience with kids and reading." Worse than that! She had no experience with kids. None whatsoever. She certainly didn't know how to teach a child to read. This was a responsibility she hadn't signed up for. What if he had a learning disability? After all, he was in first grade and not reading yet. What if he had dyslexia? What if she ruined his love of reading? What if the rest of his life, he hated to read, and it was all her fault?

He opened the book. "Don't worry. I'll help."

"Leo, do you know your letters?"

"Most."

"Do you know the sounds letters make?"

"Some."

Okay, then start at the beginning. She pointed to the first word.

"Hi there," calls Cowboy Small.

They went through the book, word by word, with Callie pointing and pronouncing, and Leo repeating. He knew more than he let on. He recognized the names of all kinds of accoutrements in the book. Cactus, Cowboy Small's horse—saddle, bridle, stirrups. Cowboy Small's spurs and chaps.

"I'm starting," she said, "to see the magic of the cowboy's life."

"Maybe you could be a cowgirl."

"Yeah? Maybe we should change my name to Cowgirl Cal."

He grinned, and her heart melted.

"Let's read it again."

"This time, you try and I'll help when you get stuck on a word."

So he did. There were only a few words on each page that he needed to sound out.

She had a hunch that it wasn't so much that he couldn't read as he wasn't interested in the books at school. Then she decided that his dad might be pretty smart—waiting until Leo was ready, then finding a book that spoke to his heart.

Again, she wondered about Leo's parents. He only talked about his dad, and Callie was curious about him. Why would anybody in this day and age give a six-year-old so much freedom to roam?

So different from her childhood. Every moment was scheduled. If she wasn't in school, she was taking some kind of lesson—piano, gymnastics, soccer. There was not a single day of the week without a tightly structured plan.

When they came to the end of the book, Leo closed it, hopped off the bed, and said, "Okay. I gotta go to school."

So soon? Leo left as abruptly as he arrived. But after he'd gone, Callie took a long hot shower and washed her hair and even took the time to blow-dry it. She'd found her third good thing of the day and it was only eight thirty in the morning. Leo the Cowboy.

● ● ●

Dawn

Are you free on Saturday morning at 10 to look at a wedding venue over in Sandwich?

Kevin

Sure! But what about the Happiness class? Will Callie go if you don't make her go?

Oh shoot. I forgot about that class! Oh well. It's clearly not the magic cure I had hoped it would be.

No change in Callie?

None. Zero. Nada.

THIRTEEN

I eat many different ice creams. I'm not an ice cream snob, although I do think Ben & Jerry's is the best. But I'm happy to eat anybody's ice cream, really. As long as it's good.

—Jerry Greenfield

Friday, February 11

Ice Cream School for Marnie had been a wonderful experience. Unfortunately, she was so excited about the people in the class, about the ice cream experiments, about bumping into Callie there, that she didn't take notes.

She really did want to learn how to make ice cream the way Dawn did. Her daughter had set the bar high and it had paid off. Last summer, the Main Street Creamery had received all kinds of accolades and reviews for its small-batch, homemade ice cream—even a mention in the *Boston Globe* about how Dawn made the base from scratch. After Marnie read that review, she knew that she'd never be able to use a prepackaged base as a backup, like she'd originally planned. It was Dawn who had insisted on making the base from scratch. Marnie didn't have such strong feelings about the base, but that was because she hadn't bothered to learn how to make the real thing.

So as soon as Dawn and Kevin had gotten engaged and there was talk about an African safari honeymoon, Marnie knew the time had come to learn how to make ice cream. She had a pretty good hunch that Dawn wouldn't set a wedding date until she was confident Marnie wouldn't mess up the Creamery in her absence. She called Penn State's Ice Cream School, put her name on the waiting list, and within a day, someone dropped out. She was in!

Off she'd gone to State College, Pennsylvania, in January, and now all she had to do was to practice what she'd learned. That was three weeks ago.

Each day, Dawn asked her if she was ready to start, but making ice cream with her daughter hovering nearby was a recipe for disaster. Dawn prepared ingredients in a very exacting way, paying attention to the slightest details, and Marnie was very much the opposite. Dawn's precision was why she was so skilled at making delicious ice cream. Repeatable performances, she often said.

Marnie never made the same thing twice, and rarely consulted recipes. It's the reason she didn't bake. She cooked. She threw things together and they generally came out well, especially salads. Pastas. But ice cream? That was a different beast. And the expensive ice cream machine terrified her. The instructor at Penn State told a cautionary tale about a student who left a spoon in and destroyed the machine. The student had been banned for life from Ice Cream School.

That's just the kind of thing Marnie could see herself doing.

Still, she had to face her fears. She had to make a batch of decent ice cream before she forgot everything she'd learned from Ice Cream School.

Today was the day. Dawn was helping Kevin with some kind of school project he was working on and wouldn't be back until after dinner. Marnie took the milk and cream out of the refrigerator, pulled out bowls, sugar, the scale, and opened her notebook.

She had decided to start with Salted Caramel, for two reasons.

One, she'd seen the instructor make it, step by step. Two, the instructor said the taste of burned sugar would camouflage any mistakes. She opened her notebook and skimmed the recipe, then gathered all the ingredients on the counter—milk, cream, tapioca starch, sugar. *This isn't rocket science*, she reminded herself, though it felt like it was. She measured sugar into the bowl, then double-checked it by measuring it on the scale.

Hold it. Something had already gone wrong. It was the scale. Completely incorrect. Which meant her entire measuring wouldn't line up with the recipe.

She poured the sugar back into the bag and scooped it out again. Then measured the sugar in the bowl, just to be sure. Again, it was off. She turned the scale off and on again, but it was still wrong.

Irritated, she leaned on her hands on the counter. If she couldn't even measure sugar to an exacting degree, how could she make repeatable performances of ice cream while Dawn was on her honeymoon? And why did the honeymoon have to be in Africa, of all places? So far away!

Okay. Deep breath. She could do this. She redid the sugar for the third time, and when the scale said she'd added much more than she thought she had, she let out an unmentionable word.

"What's wrong?"

Marnie turned to see Callie at the edge of the kitchen. "Thank God! I need help." She turned back to her row of ingredients. "I'm trying to make ice cream and I've failed on the first step."

Callie came closer and looked at the recipe book. "Measuring sugar?"

"The scale. It's broken. It keeps saying I've poured twice as much sugar as I started out with."

Callie picked up the bowl, poured the sugar that was in it back into the sugar bag, set the bowl on the scale, then pressed a button. "You forgot to zero out the bowl."

Marnie squeezed her eyes shut. A novice mistake.

"Don't feel bad," Callie said. "Just write down notes as you go." She went back upstairs and quietly closed the door.

So Marnie started again. Into the saucepan went the measure of sugar. She stirred until it dissolved, then added cream. Suddenly, the sugar seized up into clumps and she took it off the heat.

Oh no. This hadn't happened to the Penn State Ice Cream School instructor.

She pulled out another saucepan and tried it again. When the sugar had dissolved, she added the cream, and again, the sugar seized up. Oh boy. She'd messed up and she didn't know why.

Marnie dashed up the stairs with the saucepan and went right into Dawn and Callie's bedroom. "I don't know what keeps going wrong."

Callie had been standing at the window, looking over Main Street. She turned to Marnie. "What are you trying to make?"

"Ice cream. Salted Caramel. Look." With a wooden spoon, she lifted some of the brown sugar clumps. "The sugar seized up when I added the cream."

Callie peered into the saucepan, then up at Marnie. "Follow me."

Downstairs, Callie turned the gas burner on and set the saucepan back on top. Slowly, she stirred and stirred with the wooden spoon. Finally, she turned off the burner. "All fixed." She started toward the stairs.

"Wait! What did you do?"

"It's not what I did. It's what you didn't do. As the cold cream warms up, the sugar will melt again. Just keep an eye on it so it doesn't burn. That taste of burnt sugar is acrid on the tongue."

Marnie peered into the saucepan, full of smooth brown cream. The kitchen smelled like a candy shop. She smiled. "Callie, would you mind staying and helping me make it? Dawn wants me to get good at this and I've never made ice cream before."

Callie's eyebrows shot up. "But you run an ice cream shop. You went to Ice Cream School!"

"Dawn is the ice cream maker around here. Normally, she doesn't let me in the kitchen. But she wants to get married and go on a honeymoon, and she's terrified I'll ruin the reputation of the Creamery while she's gone."

"When is the date for the wedding?"

"No idea. I think she's waiting until she knows I can make decent ice cream first." Marnie lifted a finger in the air. "Not just decent, but a consistent and repeatable product."

"She's right," Callie said. "Consistency is what makes a restaurant successful." Her eyes swept the kitchen.

Marnie had a weird feeling that she was just itching to get in there. But then she surprised Marnie.

"How about if I sit on a chair, right here, and coach you through it? That way, we can be truthful to Dawn that you made it with your own two hands."

Marnie smiled. "Deal."

"What flavor?"

"Salted Caramel."

Callie's eyes flicked to the melting sugar on the stovetop. "Pull it off the flame. It's just about to burn."

It was? Really? Marnie thought it smelled heavenly. Like a candy shop. And then suddenly, it went sharp. She'd burnt it. She grabbed the pot and held it in the air. "How'd you sense it was going to burn?" Callie's eyes brightened when she posed the question, just a bit, but Marnie noticed.

"Instincts. Intuition."

"Intuition? For cooking? I thought I needed to learn to follow the recipe."

Callie smiled. "Attention to detail is good too. Intuition and attention. Both are needed, but both need to be balanced."

Marnie set the pan in the sink. "What flavor do you think I should make?"

She didn't hesitate. "Mocha. If this is the first time you've ever made ice cream, chocolate and coffee together will cover most sins."

"Let's do it." Marnie smiled. "Me, I mean. Under your supervision."

* * *

It occurred to Callie, as she coached her aunt through making ice cream, that she really hadn't known Marnie very well up to now.

She'd only known her as a warm and caring aunt. She'd never thought about her as an individual, not about her character traits, or about the qualities that made her unique. Callie sat and watched Marnie at work, the way she would've watched a potential hire create a meal in the restaurant . . . and she was floored. Not in a good way. It pained Callie to watch Marnie's slapdash style. Pained her.

A classical culinary school education had drilled into Callie the critical importance of precision in all things, of tidiness as one worked, of careful attention to detail. Aunt Marnie skimmed the recipe and threw herself into the project. She tossed ingredients into the bowl (not bothering with the recipe's order), was careless about measuring liquids (Callie cringed when Marnie tipped the bottle of vanilla extract and said to herself, "That's about a teaspoon, isn't it?"), and didn't even taste the espresso coffee before dumping it (yes, dumping, not stirring) into the base. Callie sat on her hands through nearly every step, but when Marnie microwaved the expensive chocolate instead of melting it slowly over a double boiler, she couldn't bear it any longer.

"Hold it!" She leapt off the stool, grabbed a spoon, and tasted the base. Just as she thought. Way too much vanilla—it left a bitter aftertaste. You could almost always fix a dish in a kitchen. An oversalted dish could be fixed by adding honey or sugar. Too fat or rich? Add a splash of vinegar or citrus juice. But ice cream was an altogether different beast. Fussy, it needed precision. "I take it back about trusting your instincts. That'll come later. For now, I think you need to pay a little more attention to the recipe. There's a right way and a wrong to do things."

Marnie's eyebrows lifted in surprise. "What am I doing wrong?"

Everything. Just . . . everything. "You can't mess around with ice cream." Callie took Marnie's base and set it aside. She grabbed Dawn's apron off the hook and slipped it over her head. She dipped her head in the refrigerator and took out more containers of milk and cream. "Let's start again. Everything comes down to fundamentals."

She took Marnie through each step, taking care to complete one thing before starting another. She had been appalled at Marnie's hummingbird behavior in the kitchen. It wasn't new behavior to her. Many cooks drawn to the kitchen had ADHD. But she hadn't realized that her aunt probably had it too.

When Callie had become the executive chef, she developed a plan for cooks who had ADHD tendencies. She took them off line work, where they'd have to jump from one thing to the next—and where bad habits made things difficult for everyone else—and put them on prepping. One task at a time. After new habits took shape and became engrained, she'd add on responsibilities, little by little. Success on top of success. And it had worked! As the saying went, they had the skills to pay the bills. She'd seen the difference it made in the cooks who were willing to adjust to Callie's rules—they had a better awareness of body space, of teamwork, of completing tasks. Take Jesse, for example. He had been as distractable as Marnie when he first started working for Callie. Worse, even. And look at him now! Helping to run the kitchen at Penn State's Creamery.

But Marnie? Callie wasn't sure what would motivate her aunt to comply to higher standards. After making the second batch step by step, trying to teach Marnie basic things like all ingredients begin on the left and are moved to the right after being used, she poured it into the machine and set it to churn.

Marnie looked at her curiously. "How do you know how to use it?"

"Well, uh, it's not my first rodeo." Then something dawned on her. "Have you not used the machine at all on your own?"

"Dawn hasn't let anyone touch it. She considers it her baby."

"I get it," Callie said with a laugh. "I felt that way about my first KitchenAid stand mixer." She put her hands in the apron pockets. "Tell you what. After this is finished, let's churn your base. I'll teach you how to use the machine." That way, her aunt could also taste the difference between the two styles of base-making. Marnie had done all the work for both bases, but the second one had been mixed Callie-style.

After the first batch had been poured into containers, labeled, and whisked into the freezer, Callie showed Marnie how to clean out the machine so there was no residue remaining to contaminate another flavor.

"But if you're just making the same recipe, would it really matter to clean it out?"

What Callie wanted to say was, "Just wait seven minutes and you'll discover that these two ice creams are as far apart as lemon and chocolate." But she didn't say that. Instead, she said, "It's a good habit. And the kitchen is all about good habits."

She coached Marnie through each step of using the machine: closing the gate, pouring the base into the machine, turning on the refrigeration, setting the timer. She told her how to listen for the slosh, then a few minutes later, she asked Marnie to listen again. "Still sloshing?"

"No." Marnie tipped her head. "It's more like a wool ball in the dryer."

"Good description. That means the ice cream is freezing. You need your ears as well as your taste buds to know when it's done."

She heard the bang of a door, turned, and there was Leo, standing in the kitchen. "I hear ice cream."

Marnie laughed. "Dawn's convinced there's a bug planted in the kitchen that alerts certain people to ice cream readiness." She pulled out six bowls and six spoons. "Okay, Leo. We need your tasting skills."

Callie let Marnie handle pouring the ice cream from the gate into a container, while she took the second batch out of the freezer. "It's still a little soft," she said, handing Leo a bowl and spoon from her batch.

He took a bite, then another, then another. "It's good," he said, wiping his mouth with his sleeve. "Chocolate-y. Can I have more?"

"Try this batch next." Marnie gave him a scoop from the first batch. "This is even softer." She seemed pleased.

Eagerly, he took a bite. Then his face changed. Then he dropped his spoon and pushed the bowl away. "It's too . . ."

Marnie looked at the container in her hands. "Too what?"

"I don't know. There's just too much . . . of something."

Marnie picked up a spoon and tried it. "I think it's just fine." Then she took a fresh spoon and dipped it in the container that Callie held. She took a bite and paused as she let the ice cream melt in her mouth, hitting every taste bud. Then she set her spoon down. "I believe you're right, Leo."

Too much vanilla, too much espresso. It was too much of everything. Leo was right. It was exactly as Callie had expected it to turn out. A flavor bomb. Callie felt a little sorry for Marnie, but she hoped her next attempt would benefit.

Marnie took the container of the first batch, the too-much batch, and tossed it in the garbage with a sigh.

As they were cleaning up the kitchen, the door opened and in came Marnie's very good friend Lincoln, followed by Nanette. Callie knew them by their voices, but it was nice to meet them, face-to-face. Lincoln looked similar to what she'd imagined—fit, energetic, full of purpose. He shook her hand like a proper gentleman. But Nanette—whose thin black hair was piled high on her head like a bird's nest—took one look at Callie and dragged her close for a tight hug, squishing her against her small body, rocking her back and forth. This woman was not at all deterred by Callie's stiffness. She felt enveloped by an overwhelming scent of rose perfume . . . and curiosity. "So you're the long-lost cousin we've all been so worried about. Ooh honey, you've come to the right place. Chatham'll cure what ails you."

Callie wasn't really surprised by Nanette's nosiness, but she was appalled by her lack of respect for personal space.

She finally released Callie only to hold onto her upper arms, digging into them with her fingers. "It's a small town. Everyone knows everyone."

Marnie rescued Callie from Nanette's grip by holding up two bowls of ice cream. "Linc and Nanette, you are about to eat my very first batch of ice cream." The one supervised by Callie.

True to her word, Marnie assumed full credit and that was just fine with Callie. But she did stick around to see their reaction. She felt like she was back with her staff in what was called the family meal, when they sampled the day's special and gave feedback. It felt pretty good.

As they sat at the table, they oohed and aahed over every bite, especially Nanette. Very effusive, that Nanette. But they weren't doing it for effect. At least, definitely not Lincoln. Callie could already tell he was the genuine type.

When Linc finished his last bite, he said, "Outstanding. Every bit as good as Dawn's. Don't tell her I said so," he said with a wink, "but maybe even a tiny bit better."

Callie thought so too.

•   •   •

Marnie
I have to confess something.

Linc
What's up?

Callie coached me through each step of making that delicious ice cream.

Really? So she's getting more engaged?

I had to plead for her help. She told me something interesting: Cooking requires both intuition and attention. A balance of both.

I like that.

She says I have the intuition part down pat. It's the attention part I need to work on.

☺

Chapter
FOURTEEN

You can't make everyone happy. You are not ice cream.

—Unknown

On Friday afternoon, Callie was upstairs, looking at a blank Word document to start her résumé after receiving daily texts from her father to do so, along with his texts demanding updates on the pending lawsuit (for which she'd had no recent updates from the hotel's legal department). She was coming to the conclusion that a pending lawsuit felt like a heavy storm cloud on the horizon. Visible enough to make everyone uneasy.

Suddenly sweet Leo appeared at her door. He hopped on the air mattress like he owned the place, opened the book *Cowboy Small*, and started to read. He hadn't just memorized it, he was actually reading the words. Sounding out, putting the letters together, and comprehending. Clearly comprehending.

"Leo, you're going to need to get more books."

"Yep. Dad got me a library card yesterday."

"He did, did he?"

"The librarian found more cowboy books for me. I'll bring one tomorrow. You might want to read it."

Callie swallowed a smile. She'd never thought much about cowboys. "I'll definitely read it." She swiveled on the mattress to look at Leo. "Leo, tell me about your dad. What's his job?"

"He types on a computer a lot."

Yep. Just what she thought. A computer geek. A coder, she'd bet. Maybe working remotely.

"What about your mom?"

"She's in Heaven. She looks down on us a lot. But she's really happy. She misses us but not too much. Dad says we miss her more than she misses us."

Oh. Oh my goodness. Callie didn't know what to say. Leo sounded so matter-of-fact. He could have been talking about a distant grandmother.

He looked up at her. "Dad and I are saving up to buy a pony like Cactus."

"Yeah? Your dad wants you to be a cowboy?"

"If I want to. He says I can be whatever I want to be."

Mentally, she added a check in the pro column for Leo's dad. He had plenty of checks in the con column, given for things like letting Leo wander unsupervised in town, for not helping his son learn to read when all the other kids were learning to read. But encouraging his son to be whatever he wanted to be when he grew up was a big plus, and it was only right to be fair. In her mental list, she underlined that check on the pro side for Leo's dad. Double points. "Now *that* is a refreshing perspective for a father to have about his son."

"Dad wants a horse too."

"So he's a computer guy, but he wants to be a cowboy?"

"A farmer, maybe. He has trouble growing plants, so we just have plastic flowers. But he says farmers are happier because they make friends with nature instead of fighting it."

Interesting. Callie was growing intrigued. "Leo, what kinds of things do you do with your dad?"

"We go to the playground a lot and swing on the swings. We make sandcastles on the beach. Dad likes to play with me. He thinks grown-ups aren't silly enough. He says that's why they're so grouchy all the time."

"Is that why?" She'd always wondered.

"Yeah."

"So how does your dad act silly?"

Leo looked up at the ceiling to ponder a memory. "Yesterday we were picking out little oranges at the grocery store and he put the oranges on his eyes. Under his glasses."

"You mean, like making googly eyes?"

Leo nodded.

Oh wow. Now she had a clear image in mind of Leo's dad. A typical computer geek, with poor social skills. Thick coke-bottle glasses. Short and chubby, like Leo. She pictured a happy-go-lucky portly man with a round, doughy face, wearing a Hawaiian shirt, laughing all the time.

"Then Mrs. Nickerson-Eldredge saw us and scolded him. She said he was being a bad influence on me."

Callie bit her lip to stop from laughing. "What did your dad say to Mrs. Nickerson-Eldredge?"

"He told her that sometimes it was good for grown-ups to be ridi . . . ridik . . ." He looked to Callie.

"Ridiculous?"

He nodded.

"Let me take a wild guess." Callie crossed her arms. "I'll bet you don't have a television in your home."

Leo shook his head. "Dad says it makes people sit inside too much."

Like Callie with her computer. She closed it. "Let's go downstairs. You look hungry." He was always hungry. Perhaps his father didn't feed him enough. A check in the con column.

Downstairs, Callie made a peanut butter and jelly sandwich for Leo and sliced some apples. "Let's go sit in the front room." They sat by Callie's favorite window, the one with the sun streaming through.

Callie watched as Leo ate his sandwich with enthusiasm, then munched the apples. Between bites, he kept rubbing his cheeks. "Do you have a toothache?"

"No. My dad's friend keeps pinching my cheeks." He rubbed his cheeks.

Such chubby cheeks! Callie wanted to kiss them. "A lady friend?"

Leo nodded. "But Dad says we both get to vote on a new mom. If I vote no, he won't marry her."

"Do you want your dad to find a new mom for you?"

He shrugged. "Dad says that when the time is right, it'll happen."

"Sounds like that's the way your dad thinks about a lot of things." Like Leo's reading. She took a slice of apple and chewed thoughtfully. "So you're not a fan of the cheek pincher?"

Leo made a face, like *Nope.* He cocked his head and looked at her. "Do you want to go out on a date with my dad?"

She practically choked on the apple slice. "What? No!" SO NO.

"You said you don't have a boyfriend."

"That doesn't mean I'm looking for one. I'm not. I only asked because I want to make sure someone's taking good care of you."

"Dad and I, we take care of each other." He swallowed the last bite of apple. "I could ask him if he'd take you out on a date."

"Absolutely, positively *not.* Don't even think about it." She gave him a look. "I mean it, Leo, Chatham's one and only cowboy. Do. Not. Ask."

He grinned.

● ● ●

Saturday, February 12

Dawn had such high hopes for this morning's wedding venue. For sure, she thought as she pulled up to the yacht club in Hyannis, this would be the one. She wished Kevin had been able to come with her, but something came up at work that needed his attention. He was a draftsman for a preservation architect, and had the opportunity to climb an iconic bell tower over in Plymouth this morning that needed some beams to be replaced. Or replicated? Dawn couldn't remember. Kevin's boss had found the original hand-drawn plans for the bell tower and needed Kevin's help to examine the documents against the tower's current condition. He apologized to Dawn for missing this meeting, but he didn't sound too terribly sorry. She understood. His work required a certain passion, which he had. It was the way she felt about making ice cream.

And he'd given her his proxy. "If you like it," he'd said, "book it. Nail it down."

So that was her plan as she walked through the yacht club, a gorgeous setting, especially as she sensed an instant connection with the event planner, a very sophisticated woman named Jayne Andrews. She had gorgeous thick gray hair, cut in a sleek bob. Jayne took notes on everything Dawn said, something she appreciated. Finally! A wedding planner who listened to her client. She felt they were on the same wavelength—a wedding of simple elegance.

"We don't want a large wedding," Dawn said. "Seventy-five guests, max."

Jayne scribbled down 75+. She opened the door to a large room, full of windows that faced the harbor. "Picture white chairs lined up on each side, with a wide aisle ending at an altar. Your groom, so handsome in his tuxedo, will stand below a white arched trellis dripping with roses."

Roses? Dawn wondered when roses would be blooming on the Cape. Their flower budget was pretty tight.

And Kevin wouldn't be caught dead in a tuxedo.

"Over here," Jayne said, her arm extended with a flourish, "imagine a quartet."

"A quartet?" Dawn's voice rose an octave.

"Perhaps a trumpeter. Oh, and a harpist. Don't you just adore harps at weddings?"

A harp? Was Jayne serious? Whenever Dawn heard harp strings, she wondered if she might've passed in the night. "Remember that we're trying to aim for simp—"

Jayne Andrews had stopped listening. She stood by the window that overlooked the harbor. "And over there, the two of you will sail off from the reception, amidst twinkling sparklers."

"Sail away? In what? To where? We aren't going anywhere."

Jayne turned to her. "Darling, it's all about staging."

Staging. Dawn's jaw dropped. "Hold it. Hold it right there. This is getting complicated. I said I wanted a wedding of simple elegance."

Jayne Andrews peered at Dawn over the top of her glasses. "My dear, just because a wedding is simple doesn't mean it's uncomplicated."

Wait. What?

As soon as she could make an exit, Dawn left the yacht club, discouraged. On the drive back to Chatham, stuck in heavy traffic because of construction work, she wondered why she had thought a yacht club would be a good idea for a wedding, anyway. She didn't even know how to sail.

· · ·

Last night, Callie had settled into bed with a small reading flashlight to read more of Bruno Bianco's *Secret to Happiness* book. It was far more readable and enjoyable than she would've expected after those few awkward encounters with Bruno. The whole notion of such a serious, rather reticent man writing—and teaching!—about happiness struck her as some kind of cosmic joke. But the more she read, the deeper she dove.

> To quote Chinese philosopher Lao Tzu: "If you are depressed, you are living in the past. If you are anxious, you are living in the future. If you are at peace, you are living in the present."

She set the book down. So peace came from living in the present? But if so, wasn't that what she'd been doing these last few weeks?

She began to ruminate on the fact that Bruno's book must be wrong, because she *was* living in the present these last few weeks. Stuck in the present. Paralyzed.

She grabbed a pen off Dawn's night table and started to scribble notes in the margins. She must have fallen asleep, because when she woke, sun was streaming through the edges of the window blind, and Dawn's bed was empty. Callie looked at the alarm clock, threw off the covers, and jumped out of bed. She showered, dressed, and went downstairs for breakfast.

Aunt Marnie looked up in surprise when she saw her. "Are you going out?"

"The class. Dawn wants me to go." She looked around the doorjamb into the front room. "Where is Dawn?"

"Last night she got a tip on a possible wedding venue in Hyannis, so she took off an hour ago to check it out." Marnie took a mug from the cupboard and filled it with coffee, handing it to Callie. "You know, you don't have to go to that class."

Callie took a sip of coffee. Such good coffee. Her first on the good things of the day list. No, the second. A hot shower was the first. The more she looked for good things, the easier they were to find. She realized now that it was hard to appreciate things when you were speeding through life, fixing your attention only on what comes next. Slowing down had an advantage. She was starting to notice more. "It's okay. I don't mind."

"Really. You don't have to. Dawn's trying to help, but she doesn't have any idea of all you're dealing with."

"I'll go. It's kind of . . . interesting." Besides, she had underlined parts in red in Bruno's book that made her mad. She wanted to confront him, to hear his explanations.

An hour later, she sat in the front row—because she *was* a front-row kind of girl—and then she noticed when Bruno Bianco started to speak, the room fell silent. He had the kind of voice that didn't really need a microphone, but it was on anyway, which made him sound ever so slightly like the voice of Charlton Heston playing the role of Moses. She didn't think anybody even scratched an itch or coughed the whole time. Considering he was teaching a class on happiness, it struck her as almost funny that he rarely cracked a smile. No jokes at all.

Or maybe she was just in a mood. His topic today was harnessing the power of mindfulness. Stay in the moment. Stay present.

The topic irked her, because she'd always prided herself on being one who paid attention. She never allowed multitasking in her kitchen. If a prep cook was cutting an onion, she wanted him to dissect that onion like it was made of spun sugar. If he was watching a pot boil, she made him stay by the stove. Mishaps and accidents were a result of multitasking. It pulled one's attention away from the work that was most important. Multitasking caused distractions. She *knew* that.

So how in the world had she left that sauce for the chicken out on the counter overnight? She, of all people? Mortifying.

"This week," Bruno Bianco told the class as he wrapped things up, "your homework is to find time to just be still."

Was it just her imagination, or did he look directly at Callie when he said the words "be still"?

She was plenty still! Hadn't she spent the last two weeks in bed?

"Pause to look," Bruno continued, "at the world around you. We are especially blessed here in Chatham. It's an easy place to become focused and observant. The sea is right here, the sky is full of clouds."

"Gray ones!" shouted the man with those spiky eyebrows. "Full of cold rain!"

Bruno didn't miss a beat. Possibly, Callie thought, as a professor at a community college, he was accustomed to hecklers.

"Pay attention to ordinary sights and sounds that make up your day. Slow down. Don't be in a hurry. Drive the speed limit. You'll be surprised by the results. All of these efforts help to nourish the right brain, the creative side." He paused. "That's all for today. See you next Saturday."

As the class wound up, people stuck around to chat with each other, some to talk to Bruno Bianco. There was a small line forming for him, so she stood at the end, intentionally, patiently waiting until everyone left. She was practicing being still. When her turn finally came, she opened his book to page 32 to read, "'Life's biggest fallacy: I'll be happy if I get what I want.'"

His eyebrows lifted. "I take it you disagree."

"You'd better believe it. I had everything I wanted and I *was* happy."

He gazed back at her steadily. "Past tense?"

She looked away. "Things changed."

"And you can't get it back?"

Slowly, she shook her head.

"Sometimes," he said, "that can happen."

His voice was so tender that she glanced at him, surprised, but he wasn't looking at her. His head was turned away as he put papers into a file folder and she couldn't read his expression. Then again, that was nothing new, because he had always seemed hard for her to read. Lifting his head, he said, "Then think about what made you happy. Are you cut off from some of those feelings now? Is there a way to bring them back into your life?"

She looked away.

"Life is constantly changing. If you had truly found happiness, I don't think change would be able to wipe it completely away."

Oh yeah? Try a life-threatening diagnosis.

He paused from packing up his notes to peer at her in that serious way of his. "Maybe it's time to rethink what happiness really means for you, instead of letting other people define it for you. For example, maybe you want to ask yourself why you need everyone in the class to like you."

"What?!" She practically coughed the word. "That's not true."

"Why did you bring flowers today for Mrs. Nickerson-Eldredge?"

"Well, you see," she said, stalling, "I bumped into her in the grocery store and . . ."

"You're worried she doesn't like you."

True. But she *was* Aunt Marnie's friend. "She seems like the kind of person who is slow to warm up."

"Good instincts. She is. And what about the janitor?"

"The janitor?" Did this guy have spies everywhere? She had brought two muffins from the Creamery for the janitor. "Last week, my cousin sent him on a wild-goose chase to find chairs, and it seemed only right to thank him."

"Even though that's his job." Bruno pointed to his book in her hands. "And if you don't like what the book has to say, why bother reading it?"

"I just . . ."

"You just want everyone to like you. The problem with being a people pleaser is that it's a thin substitute for the kind of self-respect that comes from trusting your own values and speaking your own mind."

For once, she had nothing to say.

"When you try to live up to others' expectations, there comes a point when it's like trying to fly a kite with no wind."

She barely stifled a gasp. How dare this man—a virtual stranger to her—act like he knew her so well?

His eyes were fixed on her, concerned. "You never told me why your cousin thinks you're depressed."

"I'm not depressed." She made her voice sound overly certain. She had a feeling that if she didn't put this to rest, he'd never stop hounding her.

"So everything is fine?"

Callie knew he was waiting to see if she hesitated, so she didn't. "Absolutely," she said. "Perfectly fine."

"Callie, I have a hunch you're a better actress than you realize. You've even convinced yourself."

By now, she was offended and it actually felt good. It gave her a little spunk. A little detachment from his spot-on analysis, which felt a little searing. Who did he think he was, anyway? A psychiatrist? Well, yes, she remembered. There were a bunch of intimidating initials after his name on the book.

"Let's back up a little. Why would your cousin think you're depressed if you're absolutely, perfectly fine?"

"Because"—Callie stood a little straighter—"she discovered that I was fired from my executive chef job at a very fancy hotel in a very public and deeply humiliating way." There, she said it. It wasn't fatal to admit it. It felt a little good, in fact. Freeing.

"I see."

Did he? She didn't think so. "And my cousin knows that I loved my job."

"Being wrenched away from something you loved would make most anyone feel depressed."

"It was the right decision. I made a mistake."

His eyebrows knit. "One mistake?"

"A pretty serious one. I poisoned two hundred people. Accidentally. But I would've fired me too." She tried not to sound terribly noble, but she couldn't hide a noble note.

"So, was this the first time you experienced failure?"

Was it? She supposed, in a way, it was. "Yes."

"I don't know much about the chef world, but it seems you were pretty young to have become an executive chef at a fancy hotel."

"I was."

"A lot of stress, I would think."

Slowly, she nodded. Finally, a little empathy was cracking through this guy's shell.

"Think it's possible that achieving so much, so early in life, might've ended up being a handicap?"

"How so?"

"Most people need time to make a few mistakes along the way. Some trial and error. And in the process, they learn a lot about themselves. About what it takes to get back up when you're knocked down. Failure can be fun, you know."

She squinted, as if to say, *You're kidding, right?*

"I admit it takes a little work to embrace the benefits of failure, but there are some. Failure can be a wonderful teacher."

"It's hard to get my head around the idea of failure as fun." She looked around, wondering what had happened to everyone else in the room. Had they left? She'd come to show him the parts of his book that she didn't like, and he had taken charge of the conversation to point out things she would rather not think about. She should leave, quick. She took a step back and he noticed.

"Then what *do* you consider to be fun?" Bruno said. He stopped packing up his messenger bag to look right at her. He seemed to genuinely want to know her answer.

She looked right back at him. "Work."

He was quiet for a long while, so long that it made her start to get nervous again.

"What?" she finally said.

"Feelings always have a cause. There's always a reason why you're feeling what you do."

She smirked. "Next you're going to tell me that I had some deep-down desire to be fired." He didn't correct her. He actually didn't correct her! "You've got to be kidding me. Why would I want to get fired?"

"Maybe you needed a pause more than you needed to work."

She shook her head firmly. "That makes no sense."

"There are times in life when we need an enforced pause."

"If that were true, then why didn't I just quit?"

"You tell me."

She lifted her palms in the air. "I don't know."

His eyes drilled into hers. "I think you do."

She didn't like this conversation—nope, not one bit. She took another step back. She'd had enough. "I've got to go," she said.

"Callie, dig deep."

Where was all this emotional jabbing coming from? Wasn't a happiness teacher supposed to be nice? She felt the sting in her chest that comes right before you start to cry. She. Did. Not. Cry.

"Think, Callie. Why didn't you just quit?"

Before she could stop the words from coming, they blurted out. "So I didn't have to make the decision myself."

He lifted his eyebrows, then dropped them, as if to say *Now we're getting somewhere*. But he didn't say as much. Instead, he tapped the book she held in her hands. "Keep reading."

● ● ●

Jesse
How's everything going?

> **Callie**
> Bruno asked me if I had a subconscious need to get fired. He wondered if I needed a break. An enforced pause, he called it. Crazy, right?

140

Who's Bruno?

> The author guy. The one who teaches the
> Secret to Happiness class. The class that's
> making me very unhappy.

Maybe it's not such a crazy idea. You worked
seven days a week. You had no life. And the
insane event planner made work miserable for
you.

When she didn't respond, he texted once more.

Jesse
Bruno, huh? ;)

She turned off her phone.

Chapter
FIFTEEN

Popsicle lovers have no age limit.
—Callie Dixon

Dawn was in the Creamery's kitchen on Saturday afternoon, stirring a pot of melting chocolate to be used for mint chocolate chip ice cream. She had looked for fresh mint in the grocery store, but there was none to be found in February, so she was trying to decide if she should tint the base with green food coloring or just leave it as is. She didn't like using artificial flavoring, so she decided to stick with the natural creamy color. She heard the front door open and assumed a customer had come in. "Be right there!"

Kevin walked into the kitchen, an exasperated look on his face. "I can't do it anymore."

"Can't do what?"

"Can't live with Nanette. I caught her making my bed while I was in the shower."

Dawn swallowed a smile. Nanette's intrusiveness had been an ongoing irritation to Kevin. "Is that so bad?"

"I don't need another mother. My own mother is plenty. Dawn,

I'm serious. We need to set a wedding date. We need to find a place to live."

Dawn turned off the burner and carefully poured a thin layer of the chocolate over the silicone mat to cool and harden. Later, she would break it into chips and add it to the mint-flavored base.

"Hey, are you even listening to me?"

"I am. I am also working with extremely hot chocolate." She finished pouring and set the pan on the stovetop. "Kevin, I'm trying to find a venue. Once I settle on one, everything will fall into place. I promise." She went over to him and put her arms around him, pulling him close to her. "Just give me a little more time."

He gave her a skeptical look. "What about this morning's venue? How'd that go?"

"Not an option. At all."

"How bad?"

"The wedding planner had us sailing off into the sunset. It was all about staging. All about photo ops." She made a face. "Next week, I have appointments to look at three more venues. Come with me to see them." She stood on her tiptoes to kiss him.

The front door opened. "Yoo-hoo! Kevin!" A familiarly screechy voice rang through the Creamery.

They broke apart, turning to see Nanette at the end of the kitchen, holding up a sock. "There you are! I found your sock that went missing. It was under your bed."

Kevin forced a smile. "Thank you, Nanette." He gave Dawn the side-eye.

Nanette sniffed the air. "Is that chocolate I smell?" That woman had an uncanny sense for arriving when Dawn had just finished making ice cream. Uncanny.

• • •

Sunday, February 13

Early the next morning, Callie went straight to the beach, sat by what she thought of as her driftwood log, and waited for the sunrise. She still felt unsettled from the conversation she'd had with Bruno

Bianco at the end of yesterday's class. Enough so that she nearly didn't come this morning, just in the slight chance that he might come to this beach too. But then she decided she wasn't going to let him spoil this special moment for her. He might have introduced the holy moment to her, but he didn't own it. The sunrise was there for everyone.

And suddenly, Bruno Bianco plopped down in the sand beside her. She thought about getting up and leaving, about heading down to find another beach that gave her more privacy, but he'd brought a thermos full of hot coffee and two cups—the kind of thermos and cups you'd take on a camping trip. "I brought a peace offering," he said, unscrewing the top, "just in case you felt I was too hard on you yesterday."

The warm scent was divine. "You were too hard on me, but I do love coffee, so I accept your apology." She wondered why he had such a thermos, because she couldn't imagine him roughing it in the wild. He struck her as the type who would be more at home in the British Museum. As she sipped the coffee, she thought it might be the best cup of coffee she'd ever had. It wasn't, not technically. But the entire ambiance—hot coffee on a cold beach at dawn, Bruno's thoughtfulness in bringing it—made that first sip of coffee taste like nectar from the gods. "You keep talking about a secret to happiness. A key. I want to know what it is."

"You mean, like a formula?"

"Yes. Yes, that's exactly what I mean."

"Callie, true happiness isn't something you can rush. It's a gradual process. A journey. It's not like you can flip a switch and suddenly be happy. No such thing as a happy pill."

Frustrating! "Maybe your whole happiness thing is overrated."

He turned back to her, that amused look had returned to his eyes. "*My* happiness thing?"

"Aren't you considered the guru of happiness?" She'd googled him.

Bruno lifted his eyebrows. "So what makes you think it's overrated?"

Oh no. No, no, no. She'd already had a generous dose of this—his turning questions around on her. This morning, she had a question for Bruno. One she wanted an answer to. "Are you truly happy all the time?" He had a kind of brooding, aloof vibe.

"Am I happy all the time?" He took a sip of coffee, then another. It seemed as if he was really thinking through how to answer her. "No. Nor do I think I should be. But content with my life, that I am. I think contentment is better than happiness."

"How so?"

"Because contentment is not dependent on circumstances." He finished off his coffee. "One thing I've learned in life, when you focus too much on a certain goal, even happiness, you're missing the present."

With that, he picked up his thermos, took the cup right out of her hand—she hadn't finished!—emptied it on the sand, and bid her a good day. He was off to his holy moment.

●　●　●

Early Sunday afternoon, after Dawn and Kevin had headed to Needham for the day to visit his folks, Marnie sat in the front room to work on her Bible study lesson while the house was quiet. The pastor at her church had started a new class on Sunday nights and she hadn't gotten around to doing the study yet. She had just dug into the first question when Callie poked her head around the doorframe.

"Hi there!"

Marnie was delighted to see her. She'd started appearing more often downstairs, but then, after returning from yesterday's Happiness class, she withdrew back into her shell. Like the outing had caused a setback.

"I didn't think anyone was home. It was so quiet."

"Just me! Come and sit."

Callie drew back a bit.

Too cheerful? Too enthusiastic? Marnie toned it down. "I'm working on my Bible study lesson."

Callie took a tentative step into the front room. "Is that a requirement for your church?"

Marnie smiled. "No, not a requirement, though the pastor would probably like everyone to take the Bible that seriously." She patted her notebook. "There's a class on Sunday evenings that Lincoln and I attend. That's what this lesson is for. You're always welcome to join us if you'd like."

"Maybe. Sometime."

In other words, Marnie thought, thanks but no thanks.

"I appreciate the invite, but I think . . . one self-help class is enough for me right now."

Marnie coughed a laugh. She put down her pen and sat back in her chair. Self-help? Callie's mother had had a very deep faith. "The Bible isn't a self-help book. It's a story. One long story, about God and his relentless love." She leaned forward. "Callie, your mom took her faith very seriously. I remember visiting her in the nursing home and her Bible was always open. Don't you remember?"

"Once she went to that nursing facility, Dad never let me visit her. He didn't want me to remember her as an invalid."

Richard had said the same thing to Marnie and Philip, but Marnie visited Beth anyway. Not enough, though. She felt a spiral of guilt, one that was becoming more familiar. Why hadn't she done more for Beth? For Callie?

Callie filled a mug with hot coffee in the kitchen and returned to stand at the doorjamb that separated the shop from the kitchen. "Valentine's Day is tomorrow, isn't it?"

Marnie sat back in her chair. "Is it? I'd completely forgotten."

"So what are you doing for it?"

"Doing?"

"The Creamery. Aren't you planning something special?"

Marnie paused. They were still in the first calendar year at the Creamery, still learning about the ebb and flow of customers. "I just assumed . . . there wouldn't be an uptick in customers."

Callie's eyes went wide. "There won't be any if you don't give customers a reason to come in."

"I guess we could offer chocolates and . . . maybe flowers?"

Callie's gaze swept the room. "You couldn't go wrong with adding sweets. I guess I was thinking more . . ."

When her voice fizzled, Marnie looked up. Of course. "You're thinking we should offer a unique flavor of ice cream?"

Callie whipped her head around. "Definitely."

Marnie wasn't sure Dawn would have time to make a Valentine's Day customized ice cream tonight after a long day with Kevin's parents. Maybe this was her moment. She could create a novelty ice cream. "Something pink, maybe? Cherry ice cream? Though it's hard to find cherries in February. Maybe cherry extract and pink food coloring could help . . ." Her enthusiasm came to an abrupt stop as she saw the horrified look on Callie's face. "What would you do?"

"I'm sure whatever you and Dawn come up with will be perfect." She turned to head upstairs. "I'll leave you to your brainstorming."

"Hold it! I want to know more. What would you do?"

Callie paused, one foot on the stairs. "At the restaurant, one Valentine's Day, we made frozen bars. They were a huge hit."

"Frozen bars? As in popsicles?"

"Yes, like popsicles, but for grown-ups."

Marnie squinted. "I'm picturing a Dreamsicle."

Callie cringed. "Nothing like that." She stepped down and leaned against the wall, arms folded against her middle. "It all started when I was cleaning out the refrigerator and realized I had a ridiculous amount of perishable raspberries that were close to spoiling. And just at that moment, my sous-chef Jesse walked in eating a popsicle. Something about the happy, goofy look on his face made me think of creating a bar for grown-ups. Giving them a little bit of their childhood back, but in a very luscious frozen dessert. I wanted it to be churned, like ice cream, full of fruit, and then I dipped the top of it in white chocolate, tinted a pale pink, then rolled in dried raspberries. The kitchen staff went crazy over them." She lifted her palms in the air. "I know it sounds funny, but the customers loved them. Frozen dessert bars became a staple on the dessert menu. Not just on Valentine's Day. They're a great opportunity to create seasonal offerings."

Marnie watched her, noticing how a sparkle lit her eyes. She had trouble envisioning this frozen bar, but she sensed a crack of light had just broken through. "Show me. Show me how to make them."

Callie furrowed her eyebrows. "You learned how to make them at Ice Cream School."

Had she? She couldn't remember. "I didn't pay attention."

"There's loads of recipes on the internet."

Marnie wasn't going to accept that. "Trust me. I will mess them up. I'm not a detail person. I need your help. I need you to walk me through them. Teach me how to make your famous popsicles."

"Frozen dessert bars."

"Exactly."

Still, Callie hesitated. "Why don't you ask Dawn? I'm sure she can come up with something."

"Can't." Marnie shook her head. "Dawn resists new things. You can't believe how hard it was to get her off of making vanilla ice cream."

Callie nodded, like she completely understood Dawn's logic. "Vanilla can be challenging. Getting it just right . . . it's hard."

"Fifty-nine tries to get vanilla right. So you can imagine what it would be like for her to try and make a frozen dessert for Valentine's Day . . . which is tomorrow." Marnie went straight past Callie to the freezer and pulled out a bag of frozen raspberries. She turned and held them up in the air. "Look!"

"But . . . Dawn seems a tiny bit territorial about her kitchen."

"True. But Dawn's gone all day today. The kitchen is ours. Let's get cooking. Or freezing. Or whatever it is we need to do." She clapped her hands together, giddy with excitement.

"Aunt Marnie, I just can't." Callie looked down at her slippers.

"Then teach me. Just like you taught me how to make mocha ice cream. You can supervise. Be my coach." She walked up to Callie and put her hands on her shoulders. "We've got nothing to lose, Callie. If they don't turn out to be salesworthy, we'll save them for Leo. But if they do, Dawn's confidence in my abilities will skyrocket. Maybe she'll finally set a wedding date."

Callie gave that some thought. "You promise to take full credit?"

"Absolutely."

"And Dawn doesn't even need to know I'm involved."

"If that's what you want." Marnie thought Callie was being a little too sensitive to Dawn, which was odd, because in the past, it was always Dawn who was too sensitive to Callie. But right now, all she wanted was to get this girl back in the kitchen. She'd do whatever it took, because she had a bone-deep feeling that the kitchen was key to her recovery. "I need you, Callie Dixon. The Creamery needs you."

Callie started to cave. "But there are things you'll need."

"I'll start a list." She grabbed a pad of paper and a pencil.

"Silicone molds, for one."

"I think I have plastic ones somewhere."

"Nope. Only silicone molds. They're pliable. You'll never get them out of those plastic molds. Sticks too. And then whole milk plain Greek yogurt."

"There's yogurt in the fridge."

"It's not the right kind. Greek yogurt has a lower water content than regular yogurt."

"Why would that matter?"

"Lower water content means fewer water crystals to make the bars icy." She looked at the ceiling. "White chocolate. Honey or agave."

"There's both in the cupboard and lots of sugar. Aren't the raspberries sweet enough?"

"Keep in mind that when food freezes, the taste becomes less intense, so you have to make it slightly sweeter than you think." She lifted a finger in the air. "And dried raspberries."

Marnie stopped writing. "Dried raspberries? Is there such a thing?"

"Yes. You can make a crushed dust out of them. Isn't there a gourmet grocery store in Chatham? There's got to be one."

"There's the Chatham Village Market. They have a lot of specialty products . . . but I've never heard of dried raspberries."

Callie took the list out of Marnie's hands. "I'll go."

"You'll go shopping?"

"It'll be quicker."

My oh my, Marnie thought. She didn't expect such a big step forward for Callie. "Want me to come?"

"I think it'll go faster if I go and have you start prepping the kitchen."

Marnie knew what Callie meant by that. The kitchen sink was full of breakfast dishes. Dawn had made Kevin a spinach, mushroom, and ham omelet when he stopped by before work, then they both had to rush off.

"Time is of the essence if you want these ready to sell by tomorrow. The frozen dessert bars will need four to eight hours to freeze." She grabbed her coat and put it on. "Also, crank up the freezer as cold as you can get it."

"Will do." Marnie tried to hold back a beaming smile.

"While I'm gone"—Callie clapped her hands—"meesen plahtz."

Marnie stared at her, baffled. "We're missing plates?"

Callie's eyes went wide. "Mise en place. Everything in its place." Then she laughed. An honest-to-goodness laugh. The first true laugh since she'd arrived.

The sound of it warmed Marnie's heart.

• • •

Monday, February 14
Valentine's Day

The raspberry frozen dessert bars were a smashing success. Linc, who had sampled one last night, hand delivered one over to Nanette. That was all it took. Nanette let everyone in town know that the Main Street Creamery had something special, a Valentine's Day–only surprise, and by three o'clock, they had sold out of every bar Marnie and Callie had made—over sixty popsicles. Fancy pops, Marnie called them.

"Callie," Marnie said, in a state of besotted admiration, "you are a wonder."

The look on Callie's face! Priceless. Embarrassed. Pleased.

And it wasn't just the fancy pops that were a success. Marnie had heated up a ridiculous amount of white chocolate to dip the pops fully. She didn't want to waste it, so Callie had suggested pouring it out on a silicone mat, sprinkling it with leftover dried raspberries, and popping it into the refrigerator to set. A few hours later, raspberry white chocolate bark was ready to sell, broken into pieces and put in cellophane bags with a pink ribbon. Those bags sold out nearly as quickly as the fancy pops. A steady stream of customers poured through the Creamery all Valentine's Day long, which was a thrill in itself after six long, quiet weeks.

Even better, Marnie thought, was Dawn's reaction. Highly profitable, the bars were inexpensive to make and had an appeal to all ages. "And they really aren't difficult to make?" she asked Marnie, more than a few times.

"They weren't," Marnie insisted. Especially when you had an expert looking over your shoulder, leading you through each step of the process. But she didn't share that part with Dawn. Marnie couldn't shake the feeling that she was deceiving her, especially when Dawn gave her a hug at the end of Valentine's Day and said, "Mom, you should've gone to Ice Cream School years ago."

Marnie almost broke down at that point and told the truth.

But at the same time, keeping Callie's participation a secret did serve a purpose. Dawn believed that Marnie had brought all this kitchen goodness back from Ice Cream School and, in a way, she had. Marnie was trying. She wanted to be the kind of kitchen support that Dawn's high standards required. She wanted Dawn and Kevin to set a wedding date and go on their African safari, and not worry that Marnie would resort to using a prepackaged base for the ice cream.

And then there was the lift that being in the kitchen seemed to give to Callie. It was so fun to see her tackle a project with all her chefiness. The fog around her seemed to burn off at the prospect of helping Marnie. She was able to help without any pressure.

That was it. The pressure. If Dawn knew what Callie was up to—teaching Marnie how to make ice cream, how to make fancy pops, and now that Marnie was thinking about it, she was absolutely sure it was Callie who had baked those muffins and scones during the night—then the pressure would start. Dawn would be convinced that she had set Callie on the road to recovery with that Saturday class, and she would expect her to pull her weight at the Creamery.

Marnie had a sense that any pressure placed on Callie would only set her back. She couldn't let that happen, because there were little signs of recovery in her niece. But they were little, and fragile. She worried that pressure might cause Callie to shatter like a teacup.

She loved Dawn dearly, but that girl had a lot of Philip's and his brother Richard's "Buck up, private" attitude about life. Empathy wasn't her strong suit.

A familiar knocking on the door broke her reverie and she crossed the room to open it. There was Linc, holding a bouquet of red roses.

"Come in, come in!"

"For you." He held the flowers to her.

"Where on earth did you find red roses in February?"

"Over in Hyannis Port. Just flown in from South America, or so I was told."

Marnie inhaled the clean, sweet scent of the roses. "Lincoln, they are stunning." She went to the kitchen to find a vase large enough to hold this bouquet. She opened a few cupboards and then called to Lincoln. "Can you reach? It's in that top cupboard."

Linc pulled the vase down and set it in the sink to fill with water. She walked to the sink, set the flowers in the vase, lifted the faucet to get the water filling it, all while standing right next to Linc—who did not budge. She could feel his breath just tickling her face. They were *that* close.

And she got this crazy feeling that he wasn't watching the flower vase fill with water, as she was, but, instead, was watching her. She was being studied and it made her feel nervous.

He seemed a little nervous, she could tell, from standing so close. Her hair had been tucked behind her ear, and then it fell forward against her cheek. She didn't want to reach up to push it back. Didn't want to break this intimate moment, which she suddenly wanted to last as long as possible. And then he reached up and pushed the tuft of hair back behind her ear, brushing the pads of his long fingers along her cheekbone. "Marnie," he started, "I'm hoping—"

And just then Dawn and Kevin came through the door, laughing over something, and the moment was over.

Later that night, she thought about those red roses. Red roses on Valentine's Day. She suddenly wondered if Linc was hinting for their relationship to change from friendship to . . . something more.

She wasn't sure she was ready.

● ● ●

Marnie
When did your friendship with Paul make a shift to a romance?

Maeve
It happened gradually. I was hardly aware of the transition. One day, we were friends. The next day, we knew we loved each other. Why?

No reason. Just wondering.

Chapter
SIXTEEN

A balanced diet is a popsicle in both hands.
—Unknown

Wednesday, February 16

Three days in a row the weather in Chatham was picture perfect. Sunny, brisk, chilly but not too cold. Callie rose early, walked down to the beach, and stood on the shore to watch the sunrise, and each time something quickened within her, a little spark. An awareness of the immensity of the world and her own smallness in it, and somehow, that feeling felt good. Really, really good. It seemed odd that she could experience such a good feeling, especially knowing it wouldn't last. Still, she couldn't get enough of it. It lingered like steam from a shower. She was addicted to it. But when it faded, as she could guarantee it would, it took her energy and mood along with it.

Twice, Bruno Bianco found her on the beach. She worried he thought she was stalking him—she wasn't! Not long after she arrived for the sunrise, he would appear and plop down beside her on the beach, uninvited. With a normal person, there might have been the start of some kind of conversation, but not with Bruno. Every attempt at talking fizzled out like a spark going dark. He would just let it die. She'd say, on the whole, he seemed about as excited to talk to her as she felt talking to Mrs. Nickerson-Eldredge.

She should've just left it alone like a normal person would've. But she'd never been good at silence with others, especially ones she didn't know very well. She had to try to stir up a conversation—whether they wanted to or not.

This morning, she tried, "Have you written other books?" though she knew this one was his first. She'd googled.

"No."

"Do you plan to write more books?"

"Only if I have something to say that's worth reading."

She waited for more. Was there more? Nope.

Nothing.

Uncomfortable pause.

"Hobbies? Things you do for fun?"

Another pause so long she thought he wasn't going to even answer at all. This was conversationally agonizing. Finally, he said, "I read a lot."

"Comic books or cookbooks?"

When that didn't get a response, she peeked around at the side of his face to see if he was stifling a smile. He was! So, there *was* a smile in there.

But then, like other times, he had to go and ruin everything. "Callie, it's okay to be still, you know. Focused and present. Fully in the moment." And off he went to his holy moment.

That man! He had an amazing ability to pop her good feeling like a dart aimed at a balloon.

He made her very uncomfortable. No, that wasn't accurate. It was his stillness. His utterly calm countenance. *That's* what made her so very uncomfortable. Mainly, because she wanted to be more like him, rather than her typical inner feeling of trying to lasso a tornado.

The good feeling returned whenever Cowboy Leo popped into

the Creamery before school for a visit. Once Leo had become familiar with Callie, it was questions all the time.

"Did you know that cows have four stomachs?"

"Why do some camels have one hump and some have two?"

"Why do dolphins sleep one half brain at a time?"

Those odd questions made Callie laugh out loud. She loved wacky trivia! Jesse always said she knew one fact about everything in the world. At last she'd found someone else who loved trivia as much as she did. Six-year-old Cowboy Leo. "How do you know so much?"

"My dad reads to me a lot."

Okay. Another check in the pro column for that dad.

Leo was such a sweet boy. She'd never had a little boy in her life before, so she didn't know if all boys were like him or if he was just unusually wonderful. In just a few weeks, she had grown rather fond of him. And he was coming to visit her with clockwork regularity. He popped into the Creamery in the morning before school started and in the early afternoon when school let out. He didn't stay long, but those visits were the highlight of Callie's day.

This afternoon, the Creamery was empty but for Callie when Leo arrived after school. He held out a paper bag to her.

"What's this?" She opened it. "Water guns?"

"Dad said these are the only kinds of guns that I can play with."

"Your dad is right." She held the bright green plastic gun in her hand and squeezed the trigger. Man! This did seem like fun.

"Wanna play?"

Dawn had gone on another wedding-venue hunt. Marnie had a dentist appointment. She was thinking of canceling it, but Callie told her to go. "I can handle the shop. I'll take care of customers." Marnie seemed so pleased, though Callie doubted there'd be any customers on such a gray, cold afternoon other than Nosy Nanette, who never paid for anything, anyway.

She took the water guns to the sink and filled them with warm water, handed one to Leo, and smiled. "Here are the rules. Stay downstairs. If any customer comes in, the guns are put away. Immediately. Deal?"

He peered up at her. "Deal."

They shook hands. With that, he squirted her, right at her face, then ran off squealing into the front room. Callie went after him. They squirted each other until the guns emptied. Then they filled them again. It was like Callie was a kid again. She loved playing with him.

● ● ●

After her dentist appointment, Marnie did a few errands, then called her friend Maeve, who had moved to Three Sisters Island in Maine. The little island-off-an-island had gotten a cell phone tower, which made impromptu phone calls so much easier. "How's the weather in Maine?" she asked Maeve.

"Gray. Cold. Bleak. How's the weather on the Cape?"

Marnie smiled. "Same." It was so good to hear Maeve's solid, calming voice. They'd been friends for years, had raised their children together, had helped each other through widowhood, and now they were both facing a brand-new life stage. "How goes married life?" Maeve had married Paul Grayson last fall, a former sports radio announcer who had lost his voice in a severe case of laryngitis. He had three daughters, one of whom had ended up marrying Maeve's son, which was how Paul and Maeve got reacquainted.

"Married life is good," Maeve said. "Really good. There's certainly an adjustment in living with someone again, but it's worth it."

"What makes it worth it?" Marnie really wanted to know. Maeve had been widowed for a long time, and she had been content with her life. It still surprised Marnie that her friend had completely uprooted her life to move to Maine. Even though her son was there, and now her grandson, it was still quite an upheaval.

"I suppose it's a little bit like I felt being married to my first husband. I knew there was a very likely chance that he wouldn't have a long life because of his heart issues. I knew it, but I also knew I would regret letting fear of the future stop me from loving him."

A baby cried in the background and Maeve had to end their call abruptly, promising to get back to her soon. But that was okay. Marnie felt as if she'd gotten what she needed. Just hearing her friend's voice always made her feel good. And, like always, Maeve gave her something to think about.

• • •

Friday, February 18

It was getting to be a regular thing. Bruno Bianco would plop right down beside Callie on the sand about five minutes before the sun rose. Sometimes he would bring coffee, but not always. Like every other time, he didn't say much. But she did. She would start blathering on until the top of the sun started to light the horizon and he would rise, telling her he would leave her to her holy moment. She probably drove him away with her nonstop chatter.

Today, if he appeared on the beach, she promised herself she would be quiet. Not say anything unless he said something first. He came, he sat, and she didn't say a word. She held to her promise. It worked for about three minutes, until the tip of the sun crested the horizon and he told her, like he always did, that he would leave her to her holy moment. A switch flipped on in her head and words started spilling out.

"So, I had this idea for you." The thought had occurred to her in the middle of the night, and she thought it was a good idea. But now, in the cold morning light, she wasn't quite so sure. Was it a good idea? It actually seemed pretty risky. But once she'd thought it, she couldn't seem to unthink it.

He sat back down and glanced at her, mildly curious.

"Can I hire you as my therapist?"

His eyebrows shot up.

Too much.

Too soon.

Before he could answer, she was covering. "It's a terrible idea."

"For a terrible idea, it's not too bad."

She brightened.

"But no."

"No?"

He shook his head like, *Nope.*

158

She hadn't expected such a flat turndown. "Why not?"

"That's not why I'm teaching the class. I'm there only as a facilitator. Volunteer position only. Helping my community. If I'm honest, it's also because I buckled to pressure applied by Mrs. Nickerson-Eldredge. She believes everyone in Chatham owes the town something." He lifted his palms. "This is my something."

Ah. No wonder he never seemed terribly enthusiastic about teaching the Saturday class. "What if you acted as my life coach?"

"Because I'm not a life coach. I'm a professor at a community college." His gaze was fixed on the ocean. "But therapy, now that's a good idea. I wish others would consider it. Things happen. An unwanted phone call on a dark night. Or the boss lets you go. Or—"

"You poison two hundred people."

His chin lifted. "I meant everyone gets *those* moments. Everyone. I think it's wise to develop inner resources to prepare for those moments. Because they will come. The wheel will turn, for everyone."

Nice. "Now I'm *really* depressed."

He coughed a laugh. "I was trying to say that therapy is a good idea. I can give you some names."

She shook her head. The more he resisted, the more she wanted to work with him. "You've got the answers that I'm looking for."

"How do you know that?"

"Because I'm reading your book."

That stopped him short.

"I have a pretty open schedule. You can squeeze me in, whenever you've got time to spare."

"No time to spare. In fact, my days are full."

"Full," she repeated. She swiveled her bottom in the sand to face him. "Your days are full." With what? He never volunteered anything about his life. She really knew nothing about him, other than he liked to walk on the beach to see the sunrise.

He didn't meet her eyes. "Completely full."

"Seriously?"

"Seriously."

"Well, what about this sunrise time?"

His eyebrows lifted. "You want me to give up *my* holy moment for your pursuit of happiness? Isn't that a bit ironic?"

Put like that, it did sound selfish. "Not give it up. Just do what we've been doing. Talking for five or ten minutes about your book before you go to your holy moment. And it's not forever. Maybe just a few days. A week at most." Maybe two. "I'm not going to stay in Chatham much longer." She wasn't sure how long she was staying, but she thought that knowing she wasn't here permanently might tip the scales for him. "You did say you thought you could help me."

"I said my *book* could help you."

"Same thing. You wrote the book."

She waited for more.

Nothing.

Uncomfortable pause.

"Maybe we could try? You know, to start me on the right track. Help me find my way back to a happy life. I'm really . . . trying."

Another pause so long she thought he wasn't going to answer her at all.

He let out a sigh of defeat. "I would only do this in an unofficial capacity. And only when I text you that I'm available to meet. Not every day."

"Deal."

"So when I am available, I just happen to be on the beach at sunrise. As do you. We have a brief conversation and that's it. Nothing more."

"Just what I had in mind. Just two friends meeting on the beach."

"Not friends. Merely formal acquaintances."

"Got it."

"And anything you choose to reveal can be used in a future book."

Whoa. "Will you at least change me into someone exotic? A princess in exile? A KGB agent?"

"Maybe." He looked straight at her. "There's one more thing. And this one is nonnegotiable."

"What is it?" She suddenly knew this was going to be uncomfortable. She braced herself.

"No more pretending."

Her chin lifted. "What?"

"Pretending. It's a coping mechanism. Telling everyone that you're just fine. That you're always fine. Because you're not just fine, are you?"

She didn't look at him.

"If I take you on . . . you're going to have to work on telling the truth. Start being authentic with yourself."

"Me? I am authentic!"

He gave her a look. *Please.*

She didn't answer him for several long moments. She felt indignant, a little angry, but not because he was wrong. Because he was right. So right. He was right about a lot of things. Her righteous irritation drained away, like a stopper had been pulled in a sinkful of water.

"Fine," she said.

And then the conversation died. Which was probably a relief to him because he had used up his ration of words for the day. Sadly, the sun had risen and they hadn't even paid attention to it. He glanced at his watch, then tipped his head to motion that they should head out. He held a hand out to help her up, and when she took it, she noticed it was warmer than hers.

They just strolled along silently toward the road, listening to the waves reach the shore behind them. This time, she kept quiet.

● ● ●

Kevin and Dawn had run up along Shore Road to the Chatham Bars Inn and crossed over to the beach. Along the shore, they stopped, then slowly trudged south along the water's edge. The sun was just lifting off the horizon, lighting the sky behind clouds. The gray waves smacked the beach, but Kevin hardly noticed. He'd been going on and on and on about an old house that Mrs. Nickerson-Eldredge—who adored Kevin, absolutely adored him like the son she'd never had but always longed for—had brought to his attention. The owner was a man she'd known since grade school, and he was ready to sell, ready to move to an assisted living facility. "The location is amazing, but the house is in terrible condition. Someone's going to just come in and demolish it, scrape the land clean, and build a huge mansion. It's a crime to let something from the nineteenth century disappear. Once it's in the dumpster, it's gone. That building is a treasure. It should be saved."

She squinted a little, and ventured, "Can it be saved?"

"Sure, for the right price. Probably cheaper to just mow it down."

"These houses don't come along very often, do they?"

"Hardly ever. Usually a piece of property like this goes through private sales."

"Maybe we should try—"

"No, Dawn. Not an option at this time in our life." He changed the subject. "How's the Happiness Campaign going?"

"A complete fail. Very disappointing. Callie's gone twice to the class on Saturday, but that's it. Other than that, she's sequestered herself upstairs, doing who knows what. She says she's job hunting, but I think she just stares at the ceiling all day and all night. I hardly even go in my room anymore other than to sleep. I jammed my clothes into Mom's closet, and all my makeup and hair stuff into a bucket that I keep in the bathroom. I've got to do something more to light a fire under Callie."

"I thought we had decided that it wasn't your job to fix her."

"You're wrong. It is my job. It's what Dixons do. We fix things. We fix people."

"It's what you do. Your mom has the good sense to leave Callie alone."

"Sure, but Mom's part hippie. She has this 'live and let live' attitude. If I left Callie to Mom's care, she would remain a permanent fixture at the Creamery."

Kevin sighed. "So what do you have planned for poor Callie?"

"Working on that. But did I tell you that sending Mom to Ice Cream School was a brilliant idea? She seems to have picked up some kitchen organizational tricks while she was there. I'm very pleased. I'm starting to think we will be able to go on the African safari and not come back to a foreclosed sign on the Creamery door."

Kevin laughed. "Speaking of, any more thoughts about where we will be getting married?" He stopped and took her hands in his, tugged her close, and bent down to kiss her. "I want our own home. Just you and me."

"Me too! I'm working at it. It's hard to find the right venue."

He swept his hand over the beach. "What about here?"

Nope. No way. Not happening on the beach. "A little too rustic. And no privacy, either." She put her hands up around his neck. "I'll find the perfect spot."

He squeezed her close to him. "Doesn't have to be perfect."

"Noted. I'll find us the good-enough spot."

He was squinting behind her. "Isn't that your cousin Callie?"

Dawn turned to see who he was looking at. Far in the distance, a woman was walking away from the water, her back to Dawn and Kevin. A man was walking beside the woman. "No. Zero chance of Callie being on the beach at this hour, and walking with a man—considering she knows no one in Chatham other than us—makes it less than zero."

Dawn squinted. Could it be?

The woman was tall, like Callie, and she did have that long stride. Could it be?

Nope. Not a chance.

● ● ●

Callie couldn't stop thinking about Bruno. That was the thing about him—he had a way of startling her with his insights. She thought about his words to her: Stop pretending. Start telling the truth. Become authentic. What did that even mean?

Callie
Do you think I'm authentic?

Jesse
Interesting question. You do deflect a lot.

In what way?

So you don't have to talk about yourself.

Is that what it means to be authentic?

It's what it means to be real.

Being real. Her shoulders slumped. This was enough to shift her whole perception of herself.

Chapter
SEVENTEEN

Ice cream is worth melting for.

—Unknown

On Friday evening, Dawn and Kevin checked out Chatham Bars Inn as a possible wedding venue. Mom had been championing for it all along. First built in 1914, the Chatham Bars Inn was originally a hunting lodge for wealthy Bostonians. Over the century, it had evolved into a luxury hotel on a grand scale, now considered Chatham's finest address. When Dawn and Kevin had become engaged, the first time, they planned to honeymoon at the Chatham Bars Inn. When Kevin broke off their engagement, Dawn went anyway and took her mom.

Tonight, she and Kevin walked through the lobby and settled into chairs by the fire in the large living room to have a glass of wine. She looked around the room, with its thick Oriental carpets, soft upholstered armchairs. As elegant and luxurious as the furnishings were, it was also remarkably cozy. Mom had pointed that characteristic out frequently to Dawn when they were staying there for the groomless honeymoon—she'd enthused over the inn's interior decorating. She especially loved this antique-filled, enormous living room. It was true that the inn was lovely in every way—the grandeur, the classy ambiance, the setting on the ocean. But Dawn knew this wasn't the right place for the two of them to be married. It spoke to their past, not to their future together.

She explained all that to Kevin, and he understood. "We'll just keep looking," he said, reaching out to cover her hand with his.

"Thanks for being so patient. I know you're getting tired of rooming at Nanette's."

"I am. I really, really am." He picked up her hand and kissed it. "I'm ready to live with you and you alone."

"Same here." Which brought up another problem. Where to live after they married? So far, they hadn't been able to find a place they could afford. Or if they could, the lease ended at Memorial Day. Rents skyrocketed for the summer months. So frustrating to live in a tourist town. Dawn took a sip of wine.

"I'm kind of intrigued by this Happiness class," Kevin said. "Would you want to go with me sometime to hear this guy?"

Dawn's stomach tightened. "Aren't you happy?"

"Of course I am." He set his wine glass down. "Never been happier. Other than when Nanette barges into my room."

"Then why do you want to go to the class?"

"Just curious about it. Aren't you?"

"To be honest, I haven't thought about it. My mind's been occupied with wedding venues."

"Has it been helpful for Callie?"

"Not at all." Dawn's shoulders drooped. "Disappointing. Callie just seems glued to her room. My room. Twenty-four/seven."

"So the Happiness Campaign is a failure."

Dawn lifted a finger in the air. "No, not a failure. It's just been put on pause while I was working on the wedding. I'll get back to the campaign soon." She needed to brainstorm some ideas about what else to do for Callie.

"What does Callie say about the class?"

"Nothing. She doesn't say much about anything at all. It's so weird, Kevin. She used to be such a chatterbox. I had high hopes for the class."

Watching the fire, Kevin said, "Doesn't it seem supremely self-centered to focus on our own happiness all the time?"

"Well, I don't think it means giddy. Like . . . not every hour is billable, we all know that. But I think there's probably room for improvement. I complain too much. I get annoyed with people more than I should. I know that I'm definitely my best self when I'm happier. And when I'm my best self, I'm kinder and more patient and more understanding."

"And more fun."

"That's true too. I'm not exactly a fun seeker."

"But you're getting better at it."

"Ice cream helps."

He grinned. "In college, I took a philosophy class and had to read Aristotle. I've forgotten most of it, but the one thing I do remember is that he said that the whole aim and end of life was happiness."

"Really? What do you think of that?"

"Two thoughts." He lifted two fingers in the air. "One, it's interesting people think they have a God-given right to be happy. Like . . . it seems as though happiness is a birthright."

Sipping her wine, she pondered his insight. "And the other thought?"

"That people have been trying to find happiness for a very long time."

Later that night, as Dawn cleaned up the kitchen after making scones for tomorrow, she thought about Callie and the Happiness Campaign. She'd let the campaign falter this last week as she put so much energy into the wedding. She found a pad of paper and pencil and sat down at a table to list everything she could think of to help boost Callie's mood. Play Callie's favorite music. But then she realized she didn't know what kind of music Callie liked. Make Callie's favorite ice cream. Again, she had no idea what that was.

She really had no idea what she was doing. But she had to do something for poor Callie.

Poor, poor Callie.

• • •

Saturday, February 19

Callie arrived at the Secret to Happiness class early to get a seat up front. She didn't want to risk a seat in the middle or back. Bruno began the class right on time. After welcoming everyone in his mildly enthusiastic way, he stood in front of the whiteboard with a marker in his hand. "Let's talk about what can steal your joy. Throw out some suggestions."

A young woman raised her hand. "Comparisons."

Not a problem for Callie. Dawn, maybe, but not Callie.

"Absolutely right about comparisons." Bruno turned and copied the word on the board. "Here's another way of thinking about it. Are you using the right yardstick? The happiest people are neither unrealistically hard on themselves nor too easy on themselves." He lifted his marker. "What else?"

From the back of the room, someone shouted out, "Holding grudges."

Bruno nodded and copied it down.

Nope. Grudge holding was not a joy thief for Callie. She didn't really hold grudges, other than the one she had for the event planner at the hotel.

"Change," said the man with the bushy eyebrows. "I hate change."

"Good one," Bruno said. "Most people are okay with change if they initiate it. Not so much if they don't."

Boy, wasn't that the truth. Now Callie's interest was dialing in.

"Expecting too much from others."

Not for Callie. She didn't expect much from others. Zero expectations of her dad. Especially after he and his third wife had divorced. She didn't even try to get to know his new girlfriend. Or had they broken up?

"Yes, definitely true," Bruno said. "I would add, expecting things to happen that are out of your control."

Callie's hand shot up. "So . . . is the secret to happiness having low expectations?" Because lately she'd gotten very good at that.

"Well, yes and no," Bruno said. "It's all about accepting what you can change and what you can't, what you want and what you need. I think it's wise to reduce expectations in areas where you have little control. Hoping for rain in a drought, for example. Winning at Powerball. But in areas where you have some control, moderately higher expectations will motivate you to try a little harder, do a little more. And then you'll end up with greater satisfaction."

A few more things were added to the whiteboard list: Negativity. Anger. Being overly busy.

All good things, but they didn't really resonate with Callie.

"Brooding over past mistakes," said a young guy wearing a Boston Red Sox baseball cap.

OK. Now it was hitting a little closer to home for Callie.

"Excellent," Bruno said. "What else?"

A middle-aged woman raised her hand. "Greed. Wanting too much."

Bruno's head bobbed in agreement. "The easiest path to be rich is to have fewer wants."

Callie recognized that comment from Bruno's book. He had even mapped out a clever strategy to help people work on appreciating what they had: To imagine a historical figure from another century who popped into your modern home. William Shakespeare or Betsy Ross or perhaps a great-great-grandparent. Imagine how he or she would take in your modern conveniences. Imagine him opening your refrigerator, turning on a hot shower, flushing a toilet. Imagine him getting in an airplane and looking down through the window. The exercise was designed to help readers appreciate all that they had rather than all that they lacked.

It was wonderful advice, but even greed, as insidious as it could be, wasn't something that tangled Callie up in knots like it did to so many others. She had few wants. Her bank account was fat, fed by her paychecks. She didn't shop, didn't vacation. She just worked.

"Anything else?"

There was a long, quiet pause—something Callie was never good with—and out of her burst the one thing that had always stolen her joy. "Perfectionism."

"Yes!" Bruno pivoted toward her, and he was all surprise. He flashed a shocked smile for half a second before turning to write the word on the board.

Well, how about that, she thought to herself. Now that she knew he was actually capable of smiling, she wanted another one.

But Bruno was back to business. "Yes, exactly. When you set impossible goals for yourself, you'll never achieve them. Perfectionism is a sure route to misery."

"Why is perfectionism so bad?" the baseball cap guy asked. "Wouldn't you want your brain surgeon to be a perfectionist?"

"Good point," Bruno said. "Culturally, we value it, just like you said about wanting a perfectionist neurosurgeon. But there's a difference between someone who strives for high standards and someone whose best is never good enough." He drew a line down the board to divide it in two. On the left side was the list he'd been working on. On the right side he wrote the words *adaptive* and *maladaptive*. He pointed to the first word. "There's such a thing as adaptive perfectionism, or healthy perfectionism. And then there's maladaptive perfectionism, or unhealthy perfectionism. Setting yourself up to impossible expectations. Maladaptive perfectionism makes a person very vulnerable to all kinds of psychological disorders. Depression, eating disorders, even suicide." He put down the marker. "Okay, for the next ten minutes, break up into groups of two or three and discuss some of these joy thieves."

Callie had been on the aisle side, but when she turned to her left, her neighbor had already created a circle with two others. She looked behind her. Same thing.

Shoot. She hated these kinds of moments. Feeling left out. It reminded her of elementary school days when she was picked last for dodgeball.

Suddenly, Bruno was in front of her, pulling a chair out of a row to face her.

She smiled, grateful. A little nervous, because their conversations usually took place in the dim light of dawn, as they were both facing the ocean. Usually, she didn't have to look straight into those puppy dog eyes. She didn't have to think about how his hair seemed windblown—so uncool it looked cool. She hadn't noticed how his five o'clock shadow rimmed his face, or that he had a cleft in his chin. And suddenly her endless-chatter button switched on. "I think you're right about perfectionism. I'm glad you're pointing out its dangers. It's simply devastating. It's good to teach people about it. Really, really good."

"Oh?" He tilted his head slightly to the side. "You've had some experience with perfectionism, then?"

"A tiny bit."

When he waited for her to continue in that calm, unflappable way he had, she added, "My father's always had big plans for me."

"And how's that going?"

"What do you mean?"

He studied her, like he wasn't sure how to put it. "Didn't you get fired from your dream job?"

"Oh. That. My father didn't take it well. He expects me to get back in the saddle." She snapped her fingers. "Pronto."

He held her gaze just a second too long. "Sounds like a lot of work."

"You have no idea."

"Let me gander a guess. It's an exhausting roller coaster that you have no idea how to get off."

"Yes," she said, a little astounded by his insight. "Yes, exactly that."

When she had no answer, he leaned toward her. "Callie, when you finally realize that living up to other peoples' standards is simply not sustainable, it frees up a lot of energy to truly enjoy your life."

And before she could puzzle that out, he had risen and left, back up front as the cheerless facilitator.

* * *

Monday, February 21

True to his word, Bruno had texted Callie last night that he was heading to the sunrise and would be available for a very, very brief conversation. Two verys. Right after she'd received that text, her dad

171

called to badger her about job hunting and lawsuits, and as soon as she hung up with him, she'd had the worst MS hug to date. She hardly slept. She felt teary and emotional and fragile. She wouldn't have come, had she not told Bruno she'd meet him on the beach. He was there, waiting for her, with coffee in a thermos, and typical of Bruno, he didn't say much, as if he expected her to fill up the air with words. She did. About nothing important at all. Just words.

"Did you know that Queen Elizabeth owns all the swans in England?"

He lifted his eyebrows.

"I'll bet you didn't know that bumblebees can fly as high as Mt. Everest."

They settled down on the sand to watch for the sun. He handed her a cup of coffee. "So do you want to talk about it?"

"About *it*?" She was stalling.

"Whatever has you feeling so . . . brittle."

She looked at him in surprise. The man was perceptive, she'd give him that. He seemed to be reading her voice.

So she told him about her father's phone call, about his insistence that she be forced out of her comfort zone. "I'm not sure I need to be forced out of my comfort zone. He's convinced that failing at my job is the reason that I ended up in Chatham."

"So what is the reason?"

She blanched.

"Too personal?"

It was personal. Extremely personal.

"You did ask me to be your life coach."

True.

"How can I help if I don't know what's really going on with you?"

Maybe he could help. In a way, he was a stranger to her. He certainly never volunteered anything about himself.

Sometimes it was easier to talk to strangers than to someone she knew well. With a stranger, there was no obligation. No strings attached. She could just say what she needed to say. A stranger wouldn't react the way a father or cousin might react. She looked at him. Why not? Talking to Aunt Marnie had felt like a relief, though Callie felt as if she must have scared her. Her aunt had never brought up MS again.

Bruno was a good listener, and maybe he had some wisdom to share. If not, she had nothing to lose. If he responded in a completely lame and unhelpful way, she could always stop going to his class. Tell him she didn't need his life coaching. Find another beach to watch the sunrise.

Okay. She would tell him. But she was glad the sky was dark and her face couldn't be seen.

"The reason I came to Chatham is because I needed some time to figure out my life. The rest of my life, anyway, which probably won't last very long. I'm pretty sure I have multiple sclerosis. My mother had it. She got it right about my age, and it means a greater likelihood that I might get it too."

This seemed to floor him temporarily, because he remained silent for several seconds, more silent than usual. She cast a glance at him and noticed something in his expression, a crack in the aloof, distant façade.

"I see," he said, nodding, like it was taking a minute to sink in.

Then something seemed to click. He cleared his throat. The professor was back on the beach. "You have symptoms?"

"I do."

"You've seen a doctor?"

"I have. The tests were inconclusive. That's the thing about MS. No tests can pinpoint if you have it."

"So you're just waiting until it starts to kill you."

"That's one way of putting it." A little cold, perhaps.

"Let me take a guess here about what's really got you depressed."

She looked at him, waiting for him to say all the wrong things. All the things her dad had said. Think positive! Mind over matter! Fake it till you make it!

"You're trying to figure out how to live with the uncertainty. How to make a life that's full of meaning and fulfillment, even if you don't know how much time you might have left."

Slowly, she took a deep breath and then pivoted to face him in the sand. The sun was just starting to rise, lightening all around them, so she could see his sincere expression. "Yes. Yes, that's it exactly." She hadn't even realized what he had just stated so eloquently, and yet he just precisely defined the weight she felt.

He gazed back at her steadily. "That's quite a burden to bear alone."

And with that, from deep inside her, rose tears. An endless well of tears.

• • •

All afternoon, Callie felt as if she had a terrible hangover, despite the fact that she hadn't had anything to drink. She couldn't even remember the last time she'd had any alcohol. The cause of this hangover was oversharing, a result of being oddly emotional with Bruno Bianco. She had said way too much and was paying the price for it today. As she rolled the conversation around in her mind, her feelings of dread worsened. She felt appalled at herself for the amount of talking she'd done, the things she'd shared with him. After all, she certainly didn't go around *chatting* about MS.

And then she had cried! Callie never cried. Never, ever, ever.

His tender response made her cry even harder. She would've expected him to bolt off down the beach, to run for dear life. Instead, he stayed. He handed her a tissue, and patted her gently on the back, whispering, "It's okay, Callie. You don't have to fake it anymore."

She hadn't asked him to be her life coach because she was needy. She was taught early on to avoid being needy. Avoid being anyone's responsibility or obligation.

She decided she wouldn't go back to the Saturday Happiness class ever again. She wouldn't go to the beach again. She wouldn't see Bruno Bianco again. As an author of the kind of book he wrote, he'd probably witnessed the breakdown of plenty of people. Seeing her in such a messy state was nothing special to him. Not like it felt to her, like she was exposed to the world in her underwear.

But then she couldn't stop thinking about the last thing he said to her, after wiping away her tears with a fresh tissue. "So, Callie, you're angry, and aching, and lost, and lonely. And scared."

When she nodded, he added, "So let's start there."

● ● ●

Later that night, Callie received a text.

Bruno
Doing okay?

Callie
I'm fine!

Long pause.

Maybe not so fine.

Now . . . you're finally on your way to being fine.

EIGHTEEN

It's harder to hate someone when they like the same ice cream as you.

—Shannon Wiersbitzky, author

Thursday, February 24

Marnie hadn't asked, but she was pretty sure Callie hadn't told her father of her suspicions about multiple sclerosis and she implicitly understood why. Without any conclusive tests to determine a firm diagnosis, Richard would be at a complete loss of knowing how to handle uncertainty. Like Philip, he would make the whole situation more difficult. He'd either raise the alarm and start treating her like an invalid, or he'd dismiss it, telling her it was all in her head.

Today, Marnie and Linc stopped for lunch at their favorite Harwich spot after volunteering at the food bank. They got in line and ordered their sandwiches. Lincoln ordered smoked turkey, provolone, and olive tapenade on herb bread. Each week, he tried something new. It was a quality she appreciated about him—he was not a man afraid of change. Marnie ordered soup again, but this time she chose butternut squash.

While they waited for their lunch, she asked him a question that had been niggling at her as she tried to put herself in Callie's shoes. "How do you manage the uncertainty of living with the possibility of a recurrence of your cancer?" Long before she'd met him, he'd been treated for thyroid cancer. It was the defining moment in his life, because it was then he'd realized that he had no one to put down for an emergency contact. He said he was *that* focused on his work—nothing and no one else mattered. After he recovered from his surgery, he radically changed his life's focus. He retired, moved to Chatham, spent his days volunteering at nonprofits. Best of all, he said, he had made friends.

"I don't think about cancer much. I used to, but not anymore. I'm doing all I can to live a healthy, full life, pleasing to the Lord. What's the point of worrying?" He offered her a bite of his sandwich and she took it. "How about you? It hasn't been that long ago for you. Does recurrence still weigh heavy on your mind?"

"At first, it was right in my face." She held her hand against her nose. "Now it's moving away." She held her hand out about a foot from her face. "It's there, but not constantly present. After that one-year mark, when I had an all-clear mammogram, I started to feel like my old self."

"Oh? Is there a difference? I'm rather fond of your new self."

She looked up in surprise and her breath caught with the tenderness of his gaze. He was looking at her in a way that she never even looked at herself. Here it was again . . . that sense that Lincoln, in his gentle way, was nudging them toward something more. How to respond? Before she could say anything, the waitress interrupted them with coffee refills, and the moment had passed.

Linc took a sip of coffee. "What makes you ask about cancer recurrence? Are you worried about it?"

"No, not for me. It's Callie who I'm worried about." She had told Lincoln about Callie's concern for MS, knowing he would keep it confidential. "Imagine being twenty-eight years old and not knowing if you're going to become an invalid . . . or not. I guess that's why recurrence has been on my mind. We're both living with that reality."

"Marnie, have you ever told Callie about your breast cancer?"

"No."

"Maybe you should."

She nodded. Maybe she should. It just wasn't that easy to talk about.

• • •

Friday, February 25

There was a reason Dawn had always been Callie's favorite cousin. She was so . . . earnest. So determined. Callie relied on Dawn. Their fathers would drop them off at those summer camps, and Dawn would settle right in while Callie was still watching the taillights on her dad's car. Dawn would unpack, read through the activity list, memorize the campus map, and start making plans. Callie watched, and did whatever Dawn was doing.

So when Dawn came into the room this morning and announced she was ramping up the campaign to help Callie get back to her old self, she sat up in bed, curiosity piqued. "What's my old self?"

"Happy, happy, happy. You were happy all the time."

Dawn made it sound like poison ivy. Callie flopped back against the pillow. "I've been thinking lately that maybe happiness is overrated."

Dawn's brows furrowed. "Really? Is that possible?" Then her face relaxed. "No, that's not true. That kind of dour thinking is what happens when you stay in bed all day long. Happiness is a good goal to have. For everyone." She pulled the curtains back so the sunlight flooded the room, so bright that Callie had to blink at the brightness. Dawn clapped her hands together. "So, today, I'm taking you out for a run."

"Oh, I don't know, Dawn. I haven't run in a couple of weeks. Months, maybe."

"Well, that proves my case. Exercise is what you need." Dawn lifted an article in one hand. She'd torn it out from a magazine at the dentist's office. With the other hand, she started counting on her fingers. "One. Exercise reduces depression. Two. Decreases anxiety and stress. Three. Gives you better sleep. Four. Strengthens the immune system and reduces risk of diabetes."

Callie waved that last one off. "I'm not at risk for diabetes."

Dawn ignored her. "And five—" She leaned forward to rest her elbows on her knees.

Callie squeezed her eyes shut. She knew what was coming next.

"Exercise makes you happy." Dawn leaned back, satisfied with herself. "It's a scientifically proven mood booster. It releases oxytocin and dopamine and endorphins into your bloodstream . . . and those help make you happy. Exercise is good for you in just about every imaginable way. Haven't you ever heard this phrase? Move a muscle, change a thought."

"No, I haven't."

"Feelings follow actions and your body leads the way."

Callie squinted. Sounded a little like her dad. A lot like him.

"How about this one? Inside is not the same as outside."

Callie shook her head, like *Nope. Not that one, either.*

"Getting outside in the fresh air works wonders on your outlook. Trust me. It works. A long run is great therapy."

Callie had to smile. *My cousin: therapist and ice cream maker.* Dawn's concern . . . it was sweet. But still. "It's kind of you to think about me, but—"

"No buts. We're going. It's a beautiful, sunny day. The fresh air and sunshine will work wonders on you."

Callie shook her head. "Dawn, I just don't think I can be happy anymore."

"Well, I think you can. In fact, I *know* you can. Meet me downstairs in five minutes."

Callie rolled onto her side.

She glanced up at the window. The sun was shining brightly. It *was* a beautiful day. She hadn't even noticed. With that, she threw off the covers and let herself give in.

• • •

Dawn met Kevin after work for a glass of wine at the Chatham Bars Inn. It was becoming their go-to spot to find some time alone. They sat in the main room, right by the fire. There was hardly anyone else in the room—just two old men playing chess in the corner. But even the lovely, tasteful setting couldn't lift her crummy mood.

"Okay. What's wrong?"

She exhaled a sigh. "Callie. She just stays in bed. If she's not sleeping, she's staring at the ceiling or scrolling through her computer."

"Looking for jobs?"

"So she says. I called Brynn and she had an idea. She sent me links to all these scientific studies to convince Callie to get up and move. To come on a run with me. I had to drag her out of bed. It took a lot of persuading. Lots of protests. She hadn't run in ages, she said."

A smile started on Kevin's mouth. His eyes lit. "Let me guess. She outran you."

How did he know? "By a country mile. We were just supposed to go on a light run. To the beach and back. She took off like she was a gazelle."

Kevin started chuckling.

She looked at him, appalled. "Kevin, this is *not* funny."

"But it is! It really is." His chuckling turned to giggling, then to full-out laughing. Tears running down his cheeks, gasping for breath, uncontrollable belly laughs. So much that even the two old men stopped playing chess to look over at them.

Disgusted, Dawn sipped her wine and kept her gaze fixed on the crackling flames in the fireplace.

It took Kevin an absurd amount of time to pull himself together. Finally, he wiped tears from his eyes. "I'm sorry." He blew out a puff of air. "I know you meant well. It's just that somehow, everything turns into a race between the two of you."

"I'm trying to help her, Kevin."

"Why? Why do you keep pushing this Happiness Campaign?"

"Because Callie needs someone to get her up and going."

Kevin gave her a look that was part affection and part *Give me a break.*

She lifted her palms. "What?"

"Maybe you're the one who starts the race with Callie. This time, the stakes are depression."

"I don't get what you mean."

"Callie's shield has a crack in it. She's lost and sinking. It's like you think if you can knock out Callie's depression, you've finally won. At long last, you have outshined her in something."

Her mouth opened wide, then snapped shut. She wanted to be indignant, wanted to say she wasn't that kind of a person. But she couldn't lie. Kevin wasn't wrong.

Maybe this was what she'd been waiting for all these many years: a chance to swoop in and be the hero, the strong one. A chance to rescue Callie. Was she that shallow a person?

She squeezed her eyes shut. Yes, she was.

* * *

Dawn
Do you think I'm a competitive person?

Brynn
Eh, you're kidding, right?

No. Not kidding.

Remember our big idea to have regular Friday night board game parties at our apt for our friends?

Oh yeah! Those were fun! Whatever happened to those?

Those? Try once. We tried it one time.

Once?

Exactly. No one wanted to come after that first time. First party, last party.

Chapter
NINETEEN

A bad day eating popsicles is better than a good day
doing anything else.

—Dawn Dixon

Saturday, February 26

Bruno Bianco gave Callie a slight nod when she arrived at Saturday's
Secret to Happiness class—barely acknowledging her presence, the
same way he did with Mrs. Nickerson-Eldredge or the man with the
spiky eyebrows. Callie hadn't even seen Bruno since last Monday,
when she'd had her meltdown. He hadn't texted her to meet for the
sunrise, not once, though the weather had been pleasant. She'd gone
to the sunrise anyway, each day, for her own holy moments.

She knew that Bruno had been reluctant to be her life coach. She
wondered if he regretted saying yes. Probably. She thought about not
coming to class today, but she just couldn't resist it. She was getting so
much out of Bruno's book that even if he had quit as her life coach,
she was going to glean all she could out of the class.

Today's topic, he wrote on the whiteboard, was money and happiness. "If," Bruno said, "you ask most people what it would take to make them happier, they'd say they need more money."

The man with those spiky eyebrows waved his arm high in the air. "I sure do!"

Bruno ignored him. "But there's overwhelming evidence to prove that more money does not equate to more happiness."

Spiky eyebrow man stood up. "Couldn't we just try?"

That got a laugh out of most everyone, all except Mrs. Nickerson-Eldredge, seated next to Callie. She clucked to herself. She didn't like interruptions.

After the class quieted down, Bruno added, "Money can't make you happy unless you know what you want." His gaze swept the room and landed on Callie. "So what is it you really want?"

What did Callie want? First and foremost, to be healthy. To have a future.

But what else? What more did she want? She'd hit her goal of being an executive chef, and as much as she enjoyed her work, she couldn't deny there'd always been some vague feeling of emptiness that had kept nipping at her heels. Something like, *Is this all there is?*

She half listened to the rest of class, and this time, she left as soon as class ended. All the way back to the Creamery, she kept pondering the question, What do I want?

Dawn was making ice cream in the kitchen and barely looked up to nod a welcome to her as she came in the back door. Aunt Marnie was in the front room, serving customers, so Callie went upstairs. She was just opening up her computer as she settled onto the air mattress when the bedroom door swung open and there stood Leo, hands on his empty gun belt. "Dad and I are going away for a while," he said. "I won't be able to come see you."

"What?" She felt her face fall. "Where are you going?"

"I don't know."

Hoping he couldn't hear the letdown in her tone, she asked, "How long will you be gone?"

He held up his fingers. "Three sleeps." He jumped up on the air mattress and snuggled in beside her.

Three whole sleeps? Did that mean five days, if you included travel days? She had to force down her disappointment. "But . . . doesn't that mean you're missing school?"

"Maybe. I don't know. Dad and I are going on an adventure. We do that sometimes. He says that adventures are just as good as school."

Callie was floored. A check in the con column for Leo's dad. You didn't take kids out of school! Everybody knew that.

But then again, Leo's childhood sounded like it held almost zero stress. True, his mom had passed away, but it seemed to Callie that she must have died when Leo was very little. Even the way Leo described her, having fun in Heaven, gave him this clear image that she was well, she wasn't missing anything, and that they'd be together again. And from what she could tell, Leo's computer geek dad was doing a pretty good job filling in the gap she must have left in their lives. His pro column was filling up with checks.

She couldn't help but think of her own childhood, of growing up without a mom, of how her dad tried to fill in the gaps. Her dad was a firm believer in the idea that idle hands were the devil's playground. A day off school without being deathly ill? Not a chance.

"What kinds of things do you do on these adventures?"

"Different things. Last time, we went fishing."

Fishing. A sport that required an infinite amount of patience, quiet, stillness. Something she'd never done, not once. It was not a sport suited to her father's temperament. She put another check in the pro column for Leo's dad.

As Leo chatted away about his day, Callie suddenly had a glimpse of what it might feel like to be a mom, to have your child come home from school, to listen to all the small things that made up his day. Losing his ball at recess. A boy throwing up in class and being sent home. A girl having a birthday and bringing in pink cupcakes. Even though Leo hated the color pink, he ate the cupcake so the girl didn't feel bad.

It suddenly became clear to Callie what she truly wanted, what she'd always wanted, what had always been missing. Which meant— and this was big news—she wanted *that*. To be a mom. To be part of a family. To have a little boy just like Leo.

Later that day, when Dawn popped upstairs to change her clothes, she asked her what she knew about Leo.

Dawn had been digging through her closet for something and popped her head out to look over at Callie. "Is he still bothering you? I'll tell him to stay downstairs."

"No! Please don't. He's not a bother at all. I just wondered . . . what do you know about him?"

"Not much," Dawn said, sitting back on her heels. "You know all about his dream to become a cowboy. Everybody knows that. He stops by all the time. And he loves ice cream."

"What about his home life?"

She shrugged. "Sounds odd, but I don't know. I never really thought about his parents. He always knows when to go home, so I assume his mom or babysitter has that drilled into him."

"When I asked about his mom, he said he didn't have one. He only talks about his dad a lot."

"I can ask Nanette. She knows everything about everyone."

"No! I mean, no, that's okay." As much as Callie would like to know more about Leo and his dad, the few interactions she'd had with Nanette made her nervous. That woman knew no boundaries. Callie was taking a shower the other day and Nanette had barged right into the bathroom with a cheery, "Yoo-hoo! Don't mind me! We ran out of TP so I came to borrow a roll."

No, she thought. Definitely do not ask Nanette. She'd sleuth out more about Leo's homelife when the time was right.

● ● ●

Wednesday, March 2

On Sunday morning, the weather made an abrupt shift back to winter. Hard, cold, pelting rain battered the Cape for the next few days. No sunrise holy moments occurred.

But then on Tuesday night, Bruno had texted:

I'll be at the beach at 5:30 am. Come if you want.

Earlier than last week, Callie noted. The earth's axis was tilting toward spring, even if it didn't feel much like spring. The wind cut like a knife through her winter coat, but she wasn't going to miss this appointment.

A few minutes before five thirty, Callie was at the log, shivering. Bruno arrived, bundled up in jeans, boots, an Irish fisherman sweater under a peacoat, a hat and gloves, looking the part of a Cape Cod fisherman. Before he sat down, the wind knocked his hat right off his head. In the dim light of morning, she squinted, watching him bolt after the hat as it danced along the beach. Something was different. He'd gotten a haircut! Short. Super short! And he was clean shaven. So maybe there was a woman in his life, after all. Thermos in hand, he plopped on the sand beside her and poured her a cup.

"Do you bring coffee so I won't start spewing out endless facts about nothing?"

He handed her the cup. "I bring coffee because it's my first good thing of the day."

She smiled and sipped the coffee in the dark, listening to the waves. It was a good thing—the warmth of the cup in her hands, the taste of the coffee, the soft light starting to fill the sky. There was a calm about this time that settled her soul.

"So I was wondering about something."

She turned to him in surprise. He never asked her questions on these mornings. He never had to. Usually, she was the one bombarding him with verbal assaults. "Ask away."

"What would happen if you took this spinal fluid test? Would that be conclusive?"

Her eyebrows lifted. "How do you know about that test?" Had he been looking into MS?

He peered at her, something gentle on his face. "I know stuff."

"You and Mr. Google?"

A slight grin lit his face. So, he *had* been googling MS. The thought pleased her. So did his smile. She wanted more of those. "The test would be conclusive if it found lesions." She tilted her head. "So you think I should get that test?"

He shrugged. "I'd never tell you what you should do."

Not sure about *that.* She thought he told her what to do a lot. *Read this book. Come to class.*

"Let me ask you a question. Would an absence of lesions convince you that you didn't have MS? That it wasn't lurking somewhere in your body, waiting to pounce?"

"Yes, of course it would." Then, "Maybe." And then, "I don't know." She'd never given it any thought, but maybe that was the subconscious reason she'd refused the test. She wasn't sure she would believe the results. "I suppose . . . it's hard to forget that it could strike at any time."

His eyes went soft around the edges. "And there's the heart of the matter. Fears don't totally go away."

"Hold it. What's the point, then?" She was thoroughly confused. This wasn't helpful! Not at all.

"Callie, the goal is to make fear more manageable, but it doesn't disappear. People have to face their fears in real life, and that's when they start to feel real relief. That's when they can start to change their life. That's when fears and doubts lose their ability to cripple you."

She stared at him, at a complete loss for words. Several long moments passed.

And then the tip of the sun started to appear and he swallowed the last of his coffee, put the lid back on the thermos, took her cup, tossed out her coffee (!), put the cups back on the thermos, rose to his feet, and said he would leave her to her holy moment. She looked up at him. "Why do you call the sunrise that?"

"Why do I call it a holy moment?" He looked out at the ocean. "Because it feels holy. Transcendent. A moment of sacredness."

"So then, you're religious."

The hazel eyes lit, amused. "So then," he repeated, "I believe in *God.* My faith has gotten me through some very tough moments." He looked down at her. "What about you? Do you have some kind of faith?"

Faith? Callie hadn't gone to church in years. There simply wasn't time. "I haven't really given it much thought."

"Seems like now might be a good time to consider it."

She shrugged. "Like . . . there's no atheists in a foxhole?"

"Are you an atheist?"

"Oh no." She knew that for sure. "I believe in God."

"Do you talk to God? Pray?"

"Seems to me . . . God's email box must be cluttered enough. Doesn't sound very noble to suddenly grasp on to faith because you think you're dying."

"I guess I was thinking more about the living you're doing." And off he went, to his holy moment. To his appointment with God.

It was the first personal thing Bruno Bianco had shared with her.

• • •

Jesse
How's the week going?

Callie
Do you ever think much about God?

Whaaaa?

Chapter
TWENTY

It was the color of someone buying you an ice cream cone for no reason at all.

—Lemony Snicket, American novelist

Kevin held up a bag for Dawn to see as he arrived at the Creamery. "I brought Chinese food." They were having an impromptu lunch date before the shop opened for the day.

She reached into the bag and pulled out to-go containers, then chopsticks and napkins. She opened a container of fried rice. "Good choice." As she tore the paper wrapping off her chopsticks, she said, "I looked at a venue yesterday in Brewster. It might be a possibility."

Kevin went to the kitchen and came back with two forks. "I've never been good with chopsticks."

She took one fork from him. "It wasn't great, but it wasn't awful, either."

"The fried rice?"

"The wedding venue in Brewster."

"Oh." He took a bite of the fried rice. "Kinda far away." He opened a packet of soy sauce and poured it over his rice.

Dawn felt an odd hitch spiral through her gut. Not even a week ago, all Kevin could talk about was nailing down the wedding date. He said he didn't care about the venue, not at all. But since then, he seemed distracted. Disinterested. Whenever Dawn asked him what was on his mind, he insisted it was nothing.

There was a niggling part of her that had started to feel anxious about his preoccupation, because it reminded her of how he'd been during the planning of their first wedding. There, but not really there. And it turned out, he really *wasn't* there. When the time came to mail out the wedding invitations, he said he'd changed his mind.

Was it just her imagination? Was she just suffering from jilted-bride PTSD? Or was it more than that? She had to find out. "Kevin, maybe we should hold off on any wedding plans. Put everything on pause."

His head jerked up. "What? Why would you say that?"

"Well, frankly," she said, setting down her fork, "I just don't think you're terribly interested in having a wedding."

His eyes widened. "I am! I'm ready to get married today! You're the one who keeps dragging your heels on finding a venue."

"That's because nothing seems quite right."

He gave her an exasperated look. "What does seem right?"

"Someplace that has meaning to us."

"Dawn, we both moved to Chatham less than a year ago. You might be looking for something that isn't there to be found. Not yet, anyway." He got up out of the chair and came around the back of hers to put his arms around her. "I'm sorry I haven't been more helpful. It's just . . ."

"What?"

"This old house. The one that's going up for sale."

She swiveled in the chair to look up at him. Oh wow. Wow. Wow. Wow. How had she missed *that*? "You want to buy that old dinosaur, don't you?"

"I want . . ." He searched for the words. "I want to preserve it. To protect it from demolition." He kissed the top of her head and went back to his chair. "And if that means buying it, then yes. I suppose that's what I'm struggling with. I would like to buy it. I would love to, in fact."

"Can we afford it?"

He patted his pockets with a slight grin. "Not a chance."

"Even with the honeymoon fund as a deposit?"

"Still doesn't come close."

"I have my savings account." Not much of one, but she still had a little nest egg. She loved her nest egg.

He shook his head. "I know you. You need that savings account to feel comfortable about the future. Besides, we agreed. You use what you want from your savings for the wedding. And I'm saving for our honeymoon." They'd created a budget and were both contributing equal amounts.

A throat cleared and they both turned to see who was there. Lincoln stood at the open door that led to the kitchen.

"I don't mean to be eavesdropping," Linc said. "I'm waiting for Marnie to come down for a walk." He walked over to them and rested his hands on the table. "What if I became your investor? Your silent partner?"

Kevin had a look on his face like he had trouble understanding Linc, like he'd been talking in a foreign language. Then he got it. "Oh, Lincoln, I can't ask—"

"But you're not asking. I'm offering." Lincoln pulled out a chair and sat down. "I know just the house you're talking about, and I've had the same feeling about it each time I drive by. It shouldn't be torn down." He folded his hands together. "So here's what I've been thinking. I fund the project, you act as architect and contractor. You manage the whole project. When it's done, I get back everything I put into it. But anything above that point, we split. Fifty-fifty."

Kevin looked astounded. "It's too generous."

"Well, hold on. You'll be working on the project without a salary. You're going to be putting in plenty of hours and handle all the headaches of working with subs. And then there's navigating permits with the town of Chatham. That's all yours, buddy."

"Why?" Kevin asked. "Why would you want to do this?"

"For the town of Chatham. For you, for Dawn."

And for Mom. He didn't say as much, but Dawn could tell how

Lincoln felt about her mom. The way he looked at her! Like she was the Queen of Sheba.

Kevin's mind was elsewhere. "What if something goes wrong?"

Linc only smiled. "I think *that* can be guaranteed. But I've never felt problems were a sign that things shouldn't be moving forward." He rose at the sound of Mom's footsteps coming down the stairs. "Think it over. Pray on it. Let me know."

Mom popped her head around the corner of the stairs. "Ready to go?" He lifted his hand in a wave and joined her to head out the back door. "We'll be back in an hour or so. Callie's upstairs."

Of course she is, Dawn thought. *Where else would she be?*

Kevin watched them go, then turned to Dawn. "Whoa. I sure didn't expect that."

Nor did she. Immediately, her CPA brain started mentally listing all the problems with it: Did Lincoln understand how costly those renovations could be? How time consuming? How frustrating it was to work with the town of Chatham's permitting policies? He seemed to have plenty of money, and he'd always been generous to them, but things could go terribly wrong. She was fond of Lincoln Hayes. He'd been a good friend to them as they remodeled the Creamery. What if things went sour? She didn't want to lose his friendship. She didn't want to mess things up for Mom.

Dawn watched Kevin for a long moment, wondering what was running through his mind. Most likely, all the same worries that she was gathering. He was as practical as she was. "So . . . what do you think?"

"Risky," he said.

"Totally."

"Old houses are land mines of problems. Money pits."

She nodded.

"And everybody knows you should never mix friendship with money. A cardinal rule."

"So true." Exactly what she'd been thinking.

He lifted his head and met her eyes with a steady gaze. "I want to do it."

She smiled. "Me too."

● ● ●

That afternoon, Leo appeared at Callie's bedroom door. "Hi, Cowgirl."

"Leo!" She beamed. "Hi, Cowboy. Glad you're back! How was your trip?"

"It was okay."

"Where'd you go, anyway?"

He scrunched up his face. "I don't know. We took a train ride."

"You had fun?"

"I liked the train ride. But when Dad had to work, it was boring."

She was so intrigued by this mysterious dad. "Where did your dad work?"

"In a room full of people."

Hmm, Callie thought. Sounded like some kind of meeting. "What did you do when your dad worked?"

"I colored at a table with Dad's friend."

"Your dad's friend?"

"The lady who pinches my cheeks."

Oh. Callie felt . . . stung. Why? How was this possible? How could she feel a stab of jealousy? She had no claim on Leo's dad. Her possessiveness, she told herself, had nothing to do with Leo's dad. Only for Leo's sake. She had fallen so completely, irrevocably in love with this little boy. It bothered her that this lady pinched Leo's cheeks when he didn't like it. Someone needed to tell that woman to knock it off. Keep her hands to herself. Someone needed to remind Leo's dad that this lady did not get his son's vote as a potential stepmother.

"She gave me some crayons and paper." He held up a folded paper.

Callie closed her computer and set it carefully on the ground. "Let's see what you drew."

He jumped up on the air mattress and handed the paper to Callie. She opened it to find a drawing of three stick figures, all bald. One big, one medium, one little. All in a row holding stick hands with each other. "What's this?"

Wiggling close to Callie, Leo pointed to each figure. "That's me. That's my dad."

"Who's this?"

He pointed to the earrings on the middle figure. "That's you."

Oh. My. Goodness. She felt a squeeze in her throat like she might cry.

Leo the Cowboy was the best thing in her life. The very best thing.

After he left to go home, she thought about Leo, about his mom, who was missing from his life. A woman who, for whatever reason, wasn't able to raise her son, to know him and love him and enjoy him. The thought made her start to cry, and soon she was sobbing. Big, gasping sobs. She never used to cry. Never. No exaggeration.

It was that one time, that Monday meltdown, that morning on the beach with Bruno Bianco, that opened the floodgate. Ever since, she'd been crying every day.

● ● ●

It was the strangest thing. Callie had a dream that night about Leo's father, whom she had never met, never laid eyes on. She couldn't make out his face in the dream, but she knew it was him. Or rather, she sensed it was him. And she knew, in her dream, that she felt irresistibly drawn to him. She lay in bed trying to puzzle out that dream, and all she could figure out was that the way Leo talked about his dad had given her subconscious some kind of attraction to him. Bizarre! Dreams were bizarre.

Besides, what did she even know about Leo's dad? Not much. Here were the facts she had patched together about him: He was a pretty relaxed, worry-free dad. He did some kind of work that didn't require too much of him. He took his son along on business trips that doubled as adventure trips.

All that was vague conjecture, patched together with tidbits Leo dropped. She wanted to find out everything about this man, yet a six-year-old boy was a terrible source of information. Most questions were answered with, "I don't know."

Was Leo's dad conservative or liberal? An early bird or a night owl? A baseball person or a football person? A cat person or a dog person? Coffee or tea or both? Did he pay attention to the news or did he have his head in the sand?

Just silly trivia, she knew. But that's what it felt like to have a crush—curious enough about someone to want to find out what made them tick. Maybe that was all there was to it, just a silly crush on a perfect-but-imaginary man.

Or maybe it had something to do with the reality that Leo's dad was unavailable to her. But the *idea* of him. The kind of man she could fall in love with.

● ● ●

Thursday, March 3

It had always seemed to Dawn that Mrs. Nickerson-Eldredge was blessed with a remarkable ability to never show any emotion that might be construed as enthusiasm. Even when offered a bowl of ice cream, her stern face registered nothing.

But it was Mrs. Nickerson-Eldredge who had brought the old dinosaur of a house to the attention of Kevin, before the owner met with a hungry realtor. And it was she who arranged a tour of the house on a moment's notice.

Dawn and Kevin and Lincoln and Mrs. Nickerson-Eldredge stood in front of the old house, silently evaluating it. Dawn wasn't sure if she could even describe it. She wasn't sure she could do it justice. Words were just a little thin.

One thing she could say: Seeing this big, old, neglected house knocked the wind out of her. The welcoming front porch. The wavy glass in the double-hung windows. The cedar shingles that had seen so many storms. Kevin was right. It held a story, this old house.

That said, it did need substantial work. The paint was peeling, the gutters were sagging, the porch steps were rotting, shingles were missing off its siding. And that was just the exterior. While the location was impressive—in a commercial zone—its condition was worse than the Main Street Creamery had been, and that was saying a lot.

Inside, the owner—an elderly man who walked slowly with a cane—showed them little quirks and idiosyncrasies about the house. Hidden delights too. One set of shelves spun around into a secret door. A closet housed a stairway up to the widow's walk. Even Mrs. Nickerson-Eldredge climbed the steps to get up to the widow's walk.

Kevin was like a kid in a candy store. He explained the architectural principles that made the building what it was. How the shapes and angles all played off each other and made relationships that were pleasing to the eye.

After prowling around in the attic and the basement, Kevin and Linc proclaimed the house to be in "fairly good shape for its age." At this point, the two were so gung-ho on the project that Dawn knew that their semi-professional inspection had no bearing on the outcome. This ancient, crumbling house was meant for them.

● ● ●

Friday, March 4

After receiving a brief "I'll be at the beach at 5:20 am. Come if you want" text from Bruno last evening, Callie met him by the driftwood log the next morning. He brought coffee, plus a blanket to sit on, which was quite thoughtful because the sand was really cold. As she sat down on crossed legs, she said, "Last evening I read your chapter about goals." In the book, he pointed out that most people were happier while progressing toward their goals. As soon as they reached a goal, happiness faded. Meeting goals didn't make for long-lasting satisfaction.

"And . . ." He flicked a glance at her.

She turned back to face the water. "My father. He's very . . . goal oriented."

"Goals can be good. Some more than others."

"As soon as he climbs one mountain, he's looking around for the next one to climb."

Bruno nodded. "Very common among driven people. They might get a temporary high when they hit the mark, but it's not long before the feeling fades. Happiness rarely syncs to achievement. People assume it does, but it doesn't."

"So what does?"

"You're still looking for the switch to flip, aren't you?"

"Yes! The title of your book promised there was a key."

"Did it?"

"Yes! Your book promised there was a key."

"Then," he said, giving her a nudge with his elbow, "keep reading."

• • •

Saturday, March 5

Callie had another dream about Leo's father. She tried to dismiss it as nothing more than a dream, but the sweet feeling she had after waking kept returning to her. She finally decided that the dream had more to do with Leo than his father. She didn't even know how much she wanted to have a little boy of her own until she met Leo. She'd always assumed that getting married and having a family was out in the distance, something she'd get to after reaching her career goals. A someday thing.

But then she had started to experience MS symptoms and she knew that marriage was out for her. Having a family was out. She knew what MS looked like. She knew what MS did to love. More to the heart of the matter: Who could love her now?

Maybe the dream had more to do with Leo than with her fictitious version of his father. She had definitely fallen head over heels for Leo. He stopped by after school each day, often before school too. Sometimes Dawn and Marnie were home, but often they were out on errands. Those were Callie's favorite moments of the day. Leo and Callie would work on reading together, and then have ice cream in the kitchen. And they would talk. There was something about that little boy that made her heart melt. She wondered if part of her pull to him was discovering what kind of childhood he was having. It was a lovely childhood, full of simple pleasures.

And that brought her back to his father, a single dad, who was somehow able to give his son all that he needed to make his life feel complete, his value and worth intact, with none of the pressure that Callie had felt from her own father. Not only did she admire Leo's dad—she even stopped trying to assess him with pros and cons because the pros column was so full of checks—but she also soaked up every single tidbit that Leo dropped about him. She was fascinated by this round-faced, chubby computer geek. She wanted to find out everything about him. Yesterday, Leo told her a story about how he and his dad had just made an elaborate sandcastle, surrounded by a moat, only to have a rogue wave wash it away.

"That's a bummer," Callie said.

"Not so bad. Dad said it was a good life lesson."

"How so?" Callie asked.

"Dad says stuff happens," Leo said. "He says you have to start over again a lot." His little face peered at her. "So we did. Bigger and better than the first one."

Before she knew it, she had tears in her eyes. She wiped them away quickly so Leo wouldn't notice.

What touched Callie was not just the life lesson part of it, and that *was* noteworthy, but that a dad would spend time making a sandcastle with his son. Two sandcastles. She couldn't remember a single time when her dad just . . . played with her.

She knew it was weird. She knew she was starting to obsess. Those dreams about Leo's dad—in which she didn't even see his face but somehow knew it was him and knew she loved him—they were nothing more than her vivid imagination. She'd had crushes on some guys, but she'd never truly been in love. Not like this feeling. For a man she'd never even met! Only one she imagined. She decided she should add crazy to her list of character flaws. She was going certifiably crazy.

That was the discouraged mood she was in as she walked down Main Street to head to the Happiness class. She hoped Bruno would finally reveal the secret, or secrets, to happiness. She thought he seemed to skirt the topic a lot. Like he wanted people to figure this whole thing out for themselves. *Frustrating.* If he had the answer, why didn't he just say so?

Bruno started off today's class on a completely different kind of topic. "One of the most important things a person can do," he said, "is to decide who is telling their story. We let other people tell our stories. We let them decide our worth, our value. Maybe even make decisions about our future." His gaze swept the room. "Who is telling your story? Who are you allowing to decide your life for you?"

Her phone rang in her purse, and Mrs. Nickerson-Eldredge turned to frown at her over the top of her glasses. It rang again. Callie reached into her purse to grab her phone before it rang a third time. She tried to silence it but accidentally answered. Immediately, her dad's voice boomed out, as loud as if he was sitting right next to her. "Callie, did you follow up on those leads I sent you?"

Oh great. Not even a hello. The badgering started immediately. "Dad, can I call you back—"

"Any interviews?"

"This isn't a good time to talk."

Naturally, he ignored her. "Callie, your whole life—everything you've worked for—hangs in the balance here. This is not the time to lose focus."

Mrs. Nickerson-Eldredge shushed her. The room quieted. Bruno watched her. Embarrassed, Callie rose and quickly walked toward the door, her father's loud voice yapping away in the silence. "Don't you want to get a job?" her father bellowed. "Do you really plan to just hang out in a crummy beach town for the rest of your life?"

She could feel a roomful of eyes drilled on her back as she fumbled to turn down the volume.

She hustled out the door and straight to the building's exit. "I can't believe you would even ask me that."

He just kept blasting away. "Because right now it doesn't seem like you do. It seems to me that you're acting like someone who's defeated by life."

Callie barely swallowed an audible gasp. He wasn't wrong. She leaned against a cold brick wall.

Who are you letting tell your story?

She'd never framed her life in such a way, but she suddenly saw something very clearly. The answer was so obvious. Her father had been telling her story for as long as she could remember. *"Make your mother proud. Make her life count. Do what she couldn't do."*

Strive. Strive. Strive.

So that's what she always did. All through school, she funneled her energy into achievement. She always had. The harder life got at home, the more productive she became. It's why she graduated at the top of her class and received all kinds of college scholarships, and why culinary school had been entirely paid for. Her nonexistent personal life was the reason the hotel's restaurant had been driven to one of the top convention hotels in Boston.

She had always done what her dad told her to do. Every time. Even as a child, she had somehow realized that achievement was the only means to get his attention. She'd never wavered, until this last year.

Who was she? What was she good at, besides working hard at work? What did she like? What was she passionate about? What would it feel like to do what she wanted instead of what was expected?

She had no idea. No earthly idea.

But in that moment—possibly for the first time ever—she realized that her dad didn't know everything. He didn't have it all figured out. And he couldn't help her now. Not at all. The rest of her life was up to her—and only her.

"Callie?" he shouted. "Are you still there?"

"Dad," she said, her voice shaky, "I have to go." And she hung up on him.

A sob burst from her mouth and she doubled over, hands on her knees. She felt cold and quivery. Her heart started racing. She sucked in air but felt like she couldn't fill her lungs with enough of it. She sat down on the cold concrete steps, trying to distract herself from her father's browbeating, trying to ignore the familiar coil of the MS hug starting to heat up her chest.

Distraction, distraction! Her mind shifted through all the things she'd learned from the Happiness class. *Think of three good things. Fill your mind with awe. Be grateful,* she reminded herself. *Be grateful.*

For what? This was AWFUL. Truly terrible. Slowly debilitating. She wondered if her mother's MS had started this way. Nibbling away at a person's life.

Despite her attempts to focus her mind on something else, her body wasn't having it. She felt as if she was in the midst of a raging storm. For a second, she thought she might pass out and topple over, right down the steps to the sidewalk. She squeezed her eyes shut and grasped her elbows.

"Callie."

She opened her eyes, and there was Bruno, crouched right in front of her. *Oh great.* Had he witnessed the whole, humiliating conversation with her father? Enough of it, anyway. The boa constrictor squeeze ratcheted up a few notches. She could feel red-hot heat climb her throat. Could sense her face turn splotchy.

He reached out to firmly grip her upper arms, his face just a few inches away from hers. "Slow everything down," he said. "Breathe through your nose. In through your nose, out through your lips."

She did as he said.

"Take it slow and easy. Slow and easy. Count to four going out. That's it. Now four going in. Good."

She took a few labored breaths. Better. The tight hold Bruno had on her almost felt like he was absorbing her distress, making her calm down. As if she'd been rowing against the wind, and suddenly the gust stopped.

"You're going to be all right now," he said. "Everything is okay."

"Thank you," she whispered when it felt safe to speak.

"Can I do anything for you?" Bruno asked her then, his voice as tender as she'd ever heard it.

She shook her head.

He glanced at his watch. "Stick around. I'll end class early today. There's something at the beach that I'd like to show you." When she hesitated, he said, "It won't take long."

Callie's first inclination was to say no. She'd started the day feeling off-balance, moody, and tearful, and it had only gone south from there. She was a mess. Plus, the MS hug always took a toll. Wiped her out. She should just go home and lie down.

But home seemed a little extra crowded today. Kevin and Lincoln were going over plans for that old house they had their eye on, Dawn was experimenting with a new flavor of ice cream called Positively Providential to celebrate Provincetown, Aunt Marnie was refinishing a side table she'd lugged home from a tag sale. If Callie went home, she'd be listening to the sounds of people making bright and cheerful plans, chatting and laughing, all day long. She knew if she went home, she'd sink into despair. "Okay," she said. "I'll wait."

Twenty minutes later, Bruno returned to her. "Ready?" His eyes behind his glasses were wide with concern. So embarrassing! She couldn't handle anyone's pity.

"Ready," she said.

As they crossed the street and walked toward the beach, Callie maintained her end of a one-sided conversation, telling him all she knew about eyes. Why she chose that topic, she had no idea. Maybe because she had been thinking about Bruno's concerned eyes. She was rambling. He had that effect on her. "Did you know that in complete darkness, the human eye can detect the light of a single candle fourteen miles away? Isn't that astounding?" Either he pretended to listen or he completely tuned her out—she couldn't tell, but it didn't stop her monologue. His eyes flicked over in her direction. "Should I try and ration my expressed thoughts?"

"I don't mind so much." A classic Bruno-style silence followed that remark. "The Hebrew word for rest is *nuach*. It means to be quiet. I find when I am at peace, living in the present, then I am quiet."

But he was always quiet. There was a calmness about him that Callie found to be almost disturbing.

"Sometimes, excessive talking can be a means of avoidance."

"What would I be avoiding?"

He gave her a look.

She coughed, then wrinkled her nose. "What?"

"Callie, it's okay to be upset with your father."

Was it? It didn't feel okay. She wondered how her dad had re-

202

sponded to getting hung up on. She didn't want to know. While waiting for Bruno after class, she had turned off her phone.

"Your father seems to have a strong personality."

She scoffed a laugh. "You can say that again." It struck her how little she knew about her dad. She knew he was dedicated to his work in a way that eclipsed all else, that he had a wall full of sales awards. She knew something was missing from his life that he kept searching for—with new wives, mostly. But a daughter's point of view was narrow. One small angle, not the full picture.

As they reached the beach, he shielded his eyes from the bright sun and scanned the ocean. "There. You can see their fins."

"Sharks?"

"Dolphins. I noticed them on the way to class." He pointed to the left. "See? Almost looks like a flock of ducks in the water."

"Those? They're dolphins?"

"Let's sit down. They should be passing in front of us soon, and you'll get a better look." They settled in the sand and sat for a long moment, taking in the blue sea. Bruno pointed. "See the pod? They've been hanging around all morning."

"Is that typical?"

"Sometimes. The Atlantic's battering surf is constantly changing the coastline, which can bring a change in sealife too. That's the fun of nature. You never know what you're going to discover." After a long moment, he turned to her. "Callie, since this is the unofficial version of class, there's something else I want you to know. Something that has made a difference for me. While it's important to stop letting other people tell our story, to me, it's even more important to let God tell our story. Then the story changes completely."

She felt that tight feeling in her throat like she was about to cry. Not again! A tear escaped before she could stop it and she quickly brushed it away, but Bruno noticed. He pulled a tissue from his coat pocket and handed it to her.

"Something weird is happening," she said, dabbing her eyes. "I cry. All the time. I never used to cry at all." Those deep, from-the-gut emotions were so foreign to her that she didn't quite know how to process them—so she just cried them out.

Typical of him, he didn't respond. At least, not in a way that seemed to relate to what she had said. "Tide's coming in."

"So it is." She assumed that meant that he would rise and leave her, like he did when the sun started its morning ascent. But he didn't seem in any particular hurry to go. He just kept his eyes on the dolphins out in the ocean.

"I wonder," he said at last, "if all the feelings you've spent your life avoiding have come flooding back in, just like the tide."

She stared at him. "So I'm having a breakdown?"

He *nearly* smiled at that. "Not a breakdown. A breakthrough."

That gave her pause.

• • •

Jesse
How's everything going?

Callie
Honestly? I'm a mess. I cry all the time.

You? You never cry! Even when the Dragon
Lady chewed you out in front of the staff, you
never shed a tear.

I know. It's strange. Even more strange . . . I
kind of like it.

Chapter

TWENTY-ONE

It's always popsicle o'clock somewhere!

—Unknown

Monday, March 7

It wasn't that easy to have a quiet, private conversation in the Creamery. Friends or customers were often coming through the door. Dawn's ice cream machine was swirling. Marnie had been looking for a chance to talk to Callie about her bout with breast cancer, but that moment didn't come until a drizzly, gray Monday. Dawn had gone to meet Kevin for lunch, the shop wasn't open yet, and Callie was sitting at a table in the front room, looking through Marnie's photo album that held pictures of Beth, her mom, as a young woman.

Marnie scooped up two bowls of Dawn's latest experiment with ice cream—Dawn called this one Providentially Provincetown, but it was really just vanilla and macadamia nuts. She sat down across from Callie and pushed the bowl to her.

Thoughtfully, Callie examined the appearance of the ice cream, even going as far as sniffing it, before scooping a bite. She lifted the spoon in the air for a moment, as if weighing it in her mind. Then she held the spoonful in her mouth, evaluating it, before she finally swallowed. "Dense. Nice firmness and texture. Coats the tongue as it melts. No iciness. Good viscosity."

"And it tastes good!"

Callie took another spoonful. "And there's that."

"Ever consider becoming a professional ice cream taster?"

"Sadly," Callie said solemnly, "that would require giving up coffee. It ruins your palate."

Oh. That would be a deal breaker. Marnie reached across the table to turn a page in the photo album to a picture of Beth. "How does it feel to look at pictures of your mom?"

"Honestly, it's like looking at a stranger. I never knew her when she was like this."

"No memories at all before she got really impaired?"

"Maybe a few. One of her laughing. She'd hidden Easter eggs in her wheelchair."

"That sounds like something your mom would've done." Marnie took a bite of the ice cream. "This tastes delicious . . . but I think it still needs something."

A sparkle lit Callie's eyes. "Well, since you asked . . . I'd consider adding semisweet chocolate shavings. Or maybe dip the chopped macadamia nuts in melted chocolate. Then sprinkle them with sea salt and let them freeze before mixing in. Something to contrast the sweet."

"Oh wow. That would be just the thing." Marnie finished off the bowl. "Callie, there's something I'd like to share with you." She explained the whole story—how she'd been diagnosed with breast cancer after a routine mammogram, how she'd had surgery, followed by six weeks of radiation.

Callie's brown eyes went wide with concern. "Are you all right now?"

"I am. I get regular checkups throughout the year. I have to admit—getting past that first mammogram was a very nice milestone."

"But this cancer could come back, couldn't it?"

"Hopefully not. But there's always a risk of recurrence."

Callie closed the photo album. "How do you live with that?"

"It's been an opportunity to strengthen my faith in trusting God. Like drawing from a deep well."

"But what does that really mean? After all, cancer must be scary."

"It is scary. But God is with us in those scary places. He doesn't leave us alone. Through the whole experience, I found that he was completely faithful. Completely present."

Callie glanced at the photo album. "Did my mom believe that?"

"She did. And it gave her the strength she needed to endure her illness. Not just endure, but to have a calm acceptance about it. Your mom used to say God always had a master plan."

"A master plan."

"She said it a lot."

Callie squinted. "Do you believe that too?"

Marnie nodded. "I'd bank my life on it." She'd said enough. She picked up the two empty bowls of ice cream. She was almost to the kitchen when she stopped. Turned around. *Hold it.* There was one more thing she needed to say. "Callie, there's something much worse than living with risk."

"What's that?"

The look in Callie's big brown eyes reminded Marnie of a doe. "Trying to live a life that avoids all risk."

• • •

Wednesday, March 9

It became a regular thing that week for Callie to meet up with Bruno for the sunrise. He didn't even text her anymore; it was just expected. Each morning, she'd find him waiting for her at the edge of the road and they'd walk down to the log together, sit and share coffee, and he would ask her a question or two, and she would talk.

On this Wednesday morning, he handed her the cup of coffee and said, "I want to throw something out there to you. Something about your MS symptoms. So hear me out."

She shrugged, like *Fair enough*, and tried to be open minded.

But there wasn't much she didn't know about MS. She'd become an expert on the topic.

"Tell me about your mother."

She didn't really know how to answer that question. The best she could do was to gather dusty memories and try to explain them. "My mother's life was pretty limited. I don't even remember a time when she wasn't in a wheelchair. I would sit on her lap and she would try and read books to me, until it became too difficult for her to talk. And then she started having seizures, probably a result of all the meds she was taking. Seizures were hard on her. There were a lot of paramedic visits to our house, and more than a few times, I watched her get taken out on a gurney to an ambulance. By the time I was five, she had to be in a nursing facility with full-time care. She died when I was nine." That was about it. *Sad.*

"And then? How did you and your father cope?"

"Cope?"

"Grieve."

"Grieve," she echoed.

"Grieving takes time," Bruno said.

"Dad always said it was best to get on with life. Not to look back. You only get one life, he says, and it only rolls forward."

"That kind of thinking leaves very little time to reflect."

Her dad? Time to reflect? She practically snorted a laugh.

"I'd like to hear more about your mother's death."

But that wasn't something she talked about—ever, if she could help it. "There's not much to tell. It was a blessing, Dad said. She'd been sick for so long that it was like she had already died."

"Did you spend much time with her as she became increasingly sick?"

"No. Dad said she wouldn't have wanted me to see her like that."

"So you never had a chance to say goodbye?"

"Not officially, I guess. She was cremated, so there was never a funeral." She stopped. "Why do you ask?" She wrapped her arms around her bent knees. "Don't tell me you think I'm depressed because I never said goodbye to my mother?" She barked an incredulous laugh. "You've got to be kidding. That sounds like something my father would say. This is all in my head."

"That's not what I said."

"Didn't you?"

He lifted his chin. "There are some losses that are so profound that they can put enormous strain on a person's systems—strain that gets expressed as emotional disturbance, physical symptoms, a reliance on pills." He spoke like he was reading straight out of a book.

"Translation, please."

"It's a direct quote by psychotherapist Richard O'Connor. It means that you've been masking feelings for a very long time, and now your body is trying to tell you that it just can't do it any longer."

She stared at him like he was going mad. "Isn't it bad enough that my body is making me sick? Now you're telling me my brain wants me to be miserable too?"

He gave a slight shake of his head. "Let me try another angle. What I wonder is . . . if your mind is trying to get you to pay attention to something that needs correcting."

"What? What needs correcting?" Besides the fact that she was both unemployed *and* unemployable, and facing a major health crisis. "Okay. So maybe I do have a few major issues. But you're saying that I am having a complete life meltdown because I've never grieved for my mother?"

"Avoiding or fearing feelings takes a toll. If you avoid the unpleasant feelings, you end up shutting down the good feelings too."

"My dad would say that the human being is wired to be adaptable."

"Maybe there are some things we shouldn't adapt to." He looked at her with such kindness in his droopy eyes. "Besides, ignoring isn't the same thing as adapting."

"Seriously? And don't give me any psychobabble."

His eyebrows lifted. "Psychobabble?"

"Don't answer my question with a question. I want to know. I want a direct answer. Do you think I'm having a meltdown because I have ignored my mother's death?"

"Ignoring the *impact* of her death."

She almost felt struck by his words.

"It's a sad thing for a child to lose a mother. Especially losing her little by little. I'm sure it was a very painful experience. Along with the pain, you've blocked out all memories of her. Even the good ones. There's beauty in those memories, Callie. Savor them."

When she didn't respond, he rose. The sun was starting its climb. He gave her a nod and went off to his holy moment.

But she was left feeling unnerved. Confused. Angry!

That said, *"There's beauty in those memories. Savor them"* really stuck in her head. She couldn't shake the thought. She didn't like this. At all. Because she was starting to think he was right.

Bruno Bianco was right about a lot of things.

That night, Callie lay awake for hours while Dawn slept, her mind drifting over to forgotten memories of her mother. She wished desperately that she could turn back the clock and have time with her mom again. Even just an hour. Just to let her mom know she was loved.

• • •

Thursday, March 10

Marnie had just finished cleaning up after the last few customers and took the dishes to the kitchen. Callie was there, putting dishes from the sink into the dishwasher. "Thanks for the help. It's been a busy afternoon."

"I noticed. Lots more traffic lately."

"Customers are loving Dawn's muffins. Especially the Morning Glory muffins. We sold out again."

Callie turned and gave her a smile, and Marnie was startled by how much she resembled her mother as a young woman. She said so aloud, and to her surprise, Callie closed the dishwasher and turned to her. She got the broom out of its closet and started to sweep a little. Then she stopped to look at her with a question that was almost a whisper. "Can I ask you something?"

"Of course."

"What was my mother like? I mean, before she was sick."

This was just the conversation Marnie had been waiting for since Callie arrived. "Lovely in every way. Warm, welcoming, caring."

"Peaceful?"

"Peaceful . . . as in, serene? Yes, I think you could say that. She had a kind of acceptance about life. Not in a passive way, more in a yielding way. I remember she would often say, 'Things happen for a reason.'"

Something flickered through Callie's brown eyes, like the spark of a memory.

"I always thought she balanced out your dad."

Callie coughed a laugh. "Who's not exactly the peaceful type."

Marnie smiled. "I suppose you could say your dad has other strengths." She leaned her hips against the stove and crossed her arms. "What makes you ask?"

"I wonder if you have to be born with a peaceful nature or if you could develop it."

She didn't hesitate. "Oh, the latter, I trust."

Callie tipped her head. "How so?"

"Because I believe peace comes with a deepening faith. That's how I would describe your mom's peace. She had it right to the end, Callie."

"But how? I mean, how do you get that peace?"

"Well, for me, it comes from resting my mind on God's presence. That's what gives me peace. A confident peace."

Callie's brow furrowed. "*Ruach.*"

"Pardon?"

"It's a Hebrew word for rest. Ruach means to be quiet. That notion of rest . . . I keep coming across it."

"Hebrew?" Of all languages! "Where did you come across that?"

"Just . . . from a friend."

What friend? Marnie wondered. Who could it be? Callie didn't seem to have any friends. Maybe it was Jesse. Though he didn't strike Marnie as the kind of guy who studied Hebrew in his spare time. More like the kind of guy who played video games.

"Callie?" she said, before her niece disappeared back up the stairs. "You can always pray. God always hears prayers. You can pray about everything."

Callie's brows knit together. "Is that in the Bible too?"

"It is," Marnie said. "It's all through the Bible." The very essence of it.

• • •

Friday, March 11

Callie knew she kept giving her aunt a lukewarm response to the topic of religion, but she did think about what she'd said. She did ponder their conversations. Religion made sense, for a small moment. If it were true, if things did happen for a reason—like her mother used to say—if God did hear our prayers, life and death made more sense. More purpose. It brought her comfort.

But holding on to that feeling was like trying to grasp steam from a teacup. It kept slipping away.

Her mind was a jumble of thoughts lately. A fast-paced Ping-Pong game of bouncing ideas. Something Bruno had written in his book kept circling around and around Callie's mind. She couldn't stop thinking about it:

The more you focus on something, the more you think about it. The more you think about it, the more your brain hones in on it. Eventually, what you focus on, you find. If it's something you've always feared, you will hunt for evidence to confirm you have reason to fear.

A terrible thought occurred to her. Could she have cued her mind to heighten her body's reactions to stress? She'd always been terrified of MS. Could such a phobia start mimicking its symptoms? And then this next part:

Minds and bodies are tightly linked. How does this work? Through one's emotions. When something is feared, it triggers a negative physiological response. The heart rate elevates and blood vessels constrict, increasing blood pressure and decreasing the efficiency of the cardiovascular system. The body's response to a perceived stress is not at all helpful and can be quite damaging.

She plopped back on the air mattress. Is that what Bruno meant when he said she'd been ignoring the impact of her mother's death? Did he mean to imply her mind was playing tricks on her? Fabricating symptoms? In which case, she really *was* going certifiably crazy.

But what did he know? A professor at a community college was *not* the same thing as a doctor who specialized in autoimmune diseases.

Later that morning, she ran this all by her aunt to get her input. "Could it be possible that I've conjured up MS symptoms?"

Marnie had been writing a birthday card to send to someone. Another niece or nephew? Callie wondered which one. But when asked the question, Marnie set down her pen and leaned back in her chair to give Callie her full attention. That was another quality she loved about her aunt. No matter what Marnie was in the middle of doing, she would stop for Callie.

She tipped her head to one side. "Describe the symptoms to me."

Callie told her about the latest MS hug that occurred during Saturday's class. "The worst one yet. Absolutely terrifying."

"And you said it came in the middle of your dad's call?"

She nodded. It had taken her a couple of days to turn her phone back on after she hung up on her dad. She had dreaded it, anticipating dozens of irate voice mails from him. Angry texts. But there were no voice mails. No text messages. No response from him at all.

She wasn't sure which was worse.

"From the way you've described those MS hugs . . . they do sound very similar to what I know of panic attacks. I remember a neighbor of mine in Needham suffered terribly from them."

"But why? What would make me panic? I wasn't experiencing any stress the first time I felt the MS hug. In fact, I was alone in my kitchen."

"Maybe," Marnie said, then paused, as if taking a moment to gather her thoughts. "Maybe . . . you were alone with your thoughts."

Callie fishmouthed. She *had* been thinking about her mom when she'd experienced that first MS hug. She remembered it vividly. She'd been riffling through a recipe box and come across one written in her mom's handwriting. Callie held the card up to the light to read. It was a recipe for a birthday cake—vanilla sponge with raspberry filling. Mom's favorite. Callie's twenty-eighth birthday was approaching, and it was at that moment she had realized her mom's disease had presented not long after she had turned twenty-eight.

"Thoughts can be powerful," Marnie said. "Good ones and bad ones. There's a verse in the Bible that my friend Maeve quotes a lot. 'Take every thought captive.' I used to think it sounded like war jargon, but I've come to see it means we should protect our minds."

"You seem to know a lot about the Bible," Callie said at last.

"Honey," Marnie said, getting up from her chair to put her arm around Callie's shoulders for a quick squeeze, "it's a long love letter from God that's written to us all."

Callie gave her a weak smile and went back upstairs. She plopped on the air mattress.

What if the squeeze that felt like it was robbing her very breath . . . what if it wasn't an MS hug but a panic attack? She grabbed her phone to google symptoms of panic attacks. The symptoms were endless.

Sweating. *No.*

Stomach pain or nausea. *No.*

Chills. *No.*

Trembling. *No.*

Then she slowed as she came to a few more symptoms of panic disorder.

Pounding or racing heart. *Yes.*

Dizziness. *Yes.*

Weakness. *Yes.*

Chest pain. *Yes.*

Difficulty breathing. *Yes.*

Sudden and repeated panic attacks of overwhelming anxiety and fear. *Yes.*

A feeling of being out of control, or a fear of death or impending doom during a panic attack. *Double yes.*

An intense worry about when the next panic attack will happen. *Definitely yes.*

A fear or avoidance of places where panic attacks have occurred in the past. *Totally yes.*

She lolled her head back against the bed pillow and squeezed her eyes shut. She could feel the color drain from her face. *Oh boy.* This kind of thinking put quite a spin on her self-perception.

What would Bruno have to say about that? She closed her eyes. What *would* he say?

● ● ●

Callie

What if my MS symptoms are actually panic attacks?

Bruno

There's only one way to find out.

How?

Read chapter nine.

Argh! So Bruno-ish. Why couldn't he just answer a simple question? Why did he always have to turn her searching questions into a "figure it out for yourself" moment? Irritated, she yanked the book off the nightstand and opened it to chapter nine.

Everyone, at some point, will come face-to-face with discomfort, disappointment, difficulty, adversity, grief. There's just no getting around it. Life doles out its share of battle scars. Pain is unavoidable.

Blah, blah, blah, she thought, skimming the first few paragraphs. *Yeah, sure. This isn't exactly new news, Bruno.* Then she came to this:

Thoughts can profoundly influence your response to life's struggles and setbacks. They can affect what you feel and why you feel the way you do. Fearful thoughts, especially. It's important to remember that fear, when given the chance, will step in and take control. Fear is the thing that makes you shrink back. Fear is what makes you feel insecure and weak. Fear is what sends your body into a full-blown fight-or-flight response.

So what fear is in your driver's seat?

Callie closed her eyes and let the book drop down on her chest. Bruno was right. She did know how to figure out if the hug was a symptom of MS or a panic attack.

She had to stop letting MS tell her story.

Chapter
TWENTY-TWO

Some things in life are like ice cream: They're only good for a while and then they melt.

   The trick is enjoying it and making the most of it while it's still ice cream.

—Unknown

Saturday, March 12

Marnie knew that Dawn didn't exactly pivot on a dime. She never had, even as a toddler. It was why she was so loyal, so steady and reliable. But it also made her slow to make a change, resistant to new plans. And then there was her streak of perfectionism. Combine all of those qualities . . . and no wonder she couldn't land on a wedding venue.

But this endless hunt for the ideal venue had crossed the line into ridiculous. Dawn was never going to find the perfect spot because there was none.

On Saturday morning, after Callie had left for the Happiness class, Marnie went straight to the kitchen. "Dawn, Lincoln asked me an interesting question and I couldn't give him an answer."

Dawn was measuring cream into a liquid container. "Shoot."

"What exactly do you have in mind for a wedding venue?"

Still pouring cream, Dawn said, almost mechanically, "I want a place that has meaning for both Kevin and me."

"So then, do you want to go up to Boston? Or Needham?"

"No. Our life is here." She put the cream back in the refrigerator. Grabbing a whisk out of a drawer, she added, "I just can't seem to find the right spot. Not yet."

Marnie went to the threshold between the kitchen, the stairwell, and the front room. She pointed to the front room. "So what about having the wedding and reception right here?"

Dawn spun around, whisk in hand. "The Creamery?"

Marnie clapped her hands together. "Yes! Right here. Hear me out," she said quickly, before Dawn rolled her eyes. "The Creamery is what brought the two of you back together in the first place. This is where your relationship with Kevin had its legendary reboot." She studied Dawn's reaction. *Oh my goodness*, she thought. *She's actually considering it.* "Imagine all the furniture moved out. This room could be transformed. I can turn it into a lovely setting for the ceremony. And for a dinner afterward. After all, you said you didn't want a big guest list."

Dawn was pondering. "But once we turn the corner to April, there's no time. The Creamery has to be ready to be a full-time ice cream shop."

"So . . . get married in March."

"March?" Her eyes went wide. "But it's already mid-March!"

"I know you don't do spontaneity—"

Offended, Dawn interrupted. "I can be spontaneous."

Like when? Marnie swallowed a smirk. "You and Kevin are ready to get married. Why wait? It'll only make everything more complicated. The wedding, the reception, all the details that bogged you down the first go-round."

"Yes, but . . ." Dawn's forehead wrinkled. "But this month?"

Marnie was on a roll. "Kevin's father will officiate. Your Boston friends can come down for it."

"What about extended family?"

"That's one of the benefits of a small wedding. No relatives."

A look of mild relief passed over Dawn's face. It was Marnie who had kept insisting on including the extended family in the guest list. "Still," Dawn said, "there's so many things to figure out. And March . . . there's just a few weeks left in the month."

But she wasn't saying no. Marnie could tell they were on to something. The deal was nearly closed. She tried not to reveal how happy she felt. She tried to act nonchalant. "Don't forget I used to do this kind of thing for a living. It'll be wonderful, Dawn. Trust me on that. I can handle everything. The flowers, the decorations, the caterer, the cake." She ticked off boxes in the air.

"But there's so many things Kevin and I haven't decided on."

"Like what? You love each other and want to be married. That's the most important thing to decide."

"True. But where are we going to live after we're married?" Her eyes flipped to the ceiling. "Definitely not here." She sighed. "It's already crowded."

"Frankly, you need to figure that out sooner or later. Why not sooner?"

Dawn was quiet for a long moment. "Let me run this past Kevin."

She was actually considering it! Marnie was thrilled. She wanted to dance around the room, to do a cartwheel! But she held back. The slightest sign of glee might push Dawn in the wrong direction.

Still, Dawn read her mind. "Mom, don't do anything until I let you know what Kevin has to say about it. No instant-action stuff. Promise?"

Marnie lifted her hands. "It's your wedding, after all."

"Brynn will be my maid of honor, of course. And you can take the wedding cake off your list. I want Brynn to bake it."

Excellent, Marnie thought. *Now we're finally moving forward.* She made a check-off sign in the air. "Maid of honor. Done. Wedding cake. Done."

"What about Callie?"

"What about her?"

Dawn squinted. "Do you think she'll still be here in a few weeks?"

Marnie was pretty sure Callie had no plans to leave. And that was fine with her. She had something else in mind for Callie.

• • •

Sunday, March 13

Callie made a conscious decision to stop thinking about MS. Stop dwelling on it. She even closed her computer tabs from medical sites about it. Instead, she shifted her thinking to grateful thoughts. It wasn't her natural mindset, far from it, but she was giving it a shot, and little by little, it started to change the tone of her life.

She tried to "cultivate gratitude"—a phrase Bruno used in his book. She worked harder to appreciate ordinary moments. While she waited for the hot water to warm up for a shower, she thought about how thankful she was to have hot water, how so many people in the world didn't have that luxury. While waiting for the midnight muffins to finish baking last night, she thought of Marnie and Dawn, sleeping upstairs, and how fortunate she was to have extended family to lean on.

It felt good to feel better, so she started looking for other ways to ratchet it up. She was taking Marnie's suggestion to try believing in a God who cared, who paid attention to her life, who loved her. Why wouldn't there be a God? It made just as much sense as having no God. Otherwise, existence itself was just too random.

She felt better when she saw the world that way—her mind became clear, settled, still. So didn't that suggest something real was at work behind that thinking? Peace resulted from knowing God, Marnie had said. And Callie did feel more and more moments of deep-down peace. Moments that lingered.

She'd come to realize that she wasn't good at being authentic, at acknowledging feelings. She'd spent her life carefully avoiding them. In his book, Bruno wrote a phrase:

Revealing your feeling is the beginning of healing.

She'd underlined it. Twice.

So was she any happier? She certainly wasn't as down-and-out as she'd been. This week, she'd spent less time upstairs in the darkened bedroom and more time downstairs, helping Marnie and Dawn with customers. And oh boy. They really needed her help! A steady stream of customers had started coming, mostly asking for Morning Glory muffins. It gave Callie purpose. She had a reason to get up every morning, to get up at night and bake. She had a reason to take care of herself.

So yes, overall, Callie was happier. But it took deliberate attention to redirect mental habits. It took hard work. "Taking thoughts captive" wasn't easy—but, after all, this was war! When MS fretting did break through her defense, it didn't cause her shoulders to tighten up, her heart to start racing. That was progress.

She thought she had reached a place of acceptance, because she found she was okay not knowing what the future held. Things happened for a reason, her mother used to say. It was a good way to think.

It really was.

In yesterday's Secret to Happiness class, Bruno stood in front of the whiteboard with a marker. "Today, let's discuss simple pleasures."

Callie's hand shot up. "I'd say that spending time with children has to be in the top ten." Naturally, she was thinking of Cowboy Leo. "When you get to know a child, you can learn so much. Playing more, taking yourself less seriously, laughing more."

She looked over and saw Bruno across the room, watching her like he was spellbound. What was that about? Did he assume she didn't like kids? She did! Well, she liked Leo.

Yesterday, Leo had arrived at the Creamery with a lone daffodil in one hand and held it out to her. "Dad says daffodils are meant to remind us of Heaven."

She sniffed its fresh scent. "How so?"

"He says that it's a miracle something pretty like a daffodil comes out of something that looks like an onion."

She smiled. That dad of his. He was something else.

She put the daffodil in a bud vase and filled it with water. "Leo, do you and your dad ever go to church?"

"Yep. Then we go out for doughnuts with sprinkles on top. Sometimes I pick chocolate sprinkles and sometimes I pick rainbow."

"Yeah? I always go for chocolate sprinkles. A purist, I suppose. So do you go to the same church as Marnie and Dawn?" Maybe she would start to go. Maybe this could be the way to finally meet Leo's dad. She would love to meet him in person . . . yet in another way, she didn't want to. He was a mystery to her. Maybe it was better just to imagine him as the world's most perfect man.

Leo peered up at her. "Our church meets in a basketball gym."

Nope. Definitely not the same church.

● ● ●

Dawn
Clear your schedule on March 26th.

Brynn
Sure. Why?

BECAUSE KEVIN AND I ARE GETTING
MARRIED! And YOU are my maid of honor!!!!!

Chapter

TWENTY-THREE

I think the serving size of ice cream is when you hear the spoon hit the bottom of the container.

—Brian Regan, comedian

Thursday, March 17

Dawn kept having to pinch herself. She couldn't believe the wedding was actually going to happen. So many things could have derailed this fast-approaching day and yet everything came together smoothly. When she first told Kevin about Mom's idea to have the wedding in the Creamery, and to set the date for the end of March, he picked Dawn up and whirled her around.

"Done!" he shouted.

And so the wedding date, and the venue, was set.

When Lincoln heard the news, he offered them the pool house at his "cottage" to live in.

"We'll take it!" Kevin told him.

Life was pretty good for Kevin. He and Lincoln had become official business partners. They purchased the old house in town without any major problems—of course it helped that Lincoln paid the full price in cash, no contingencies. The owner, an elderly man who was moving to an assisted living facility, didn't want the house to be torn down, but he wasn't going to budge on his price tag. Lincoln didn't even counter.

Kevin did some digging at the Chatham Historical Association and found out all kinds of cool history about the house. "It was originally owned by a stonemason. The foundation is evidence of his craftmanship. It's rock solid. See what I mean, Dawn? Every house tells a story."

Dawn couldn't be happier about Kevin and Lincoln's project, but for one thing. The house's location. It was in the commercial zone. She wanted to have children someday and she couldn't imagine raising a family on such a busy street. "Kevin, I just don't know if this is the place for our home."

"Our home?" He spun around, a confused look on his face. "I wasn't thinking of this as our home."

"You weren't?"

"No. Just one to restore."

"Then sell it?"

"That's the plan."

"Then we buy a house of our own?"

"Maybe. Hopefully. Soon. But . . ."

"But what?"

"Lincoln said that if this house works like he hopes it will," Kevin said, "he'd like to consider doing it again. Starting a business together."

"Flipping houses?"

Kevin looked wounded. "Preserving and protecting the dignity of old homes that might otherwise be torn down and built over with a monstrosity."

Was that so different from flipping houses? Dawn didn't think so, but she did love seeing Kevin so excited about his work. He'd never been excited about his architectural work in Boston.

Then Kevin had asked Dawn if she would mind terribly if they postponed the African safari honeymoon until the remodel of the old house was completed, and he seemed so apologetic, so appreciative of her understanding, that she had to swallow a smile. She was thrilled to put it off as long as possible! Right now Dawn had only two priorities: marrying Kevin, and doing all she could so that the second season of the Main Street Creamery started strong, stayed strong, finished strong. The first year had gone better than expected, but they had the "shiny newest thing in town" factor going for them. There was no resting on laurels, not in the food service industry. This year, they had to step it up. Keep coming up with new flavors, new ideas. Like Mom's fancy pops. Brilliant.

The whole week leading up to the wedding, Dawn felt copacetic. Unflappable. Like she was floating on a cloud.

Then she asked Mom a question about the caterer.

Aaaand her happy feelings popped like a soap bubble. Mom faltered, spun around, her face started to turn red . . . and Dawn froze. Oh no! Everything had been going too smoothly. Too easily. Something had to give. She dropped into a chair. "Mom, you didn't get a caterer, did you?" She clapped a hand against her forehead. "We talked about it. I gave you a list of suggestions. Reputable caterers. You said you were on top of it."

"I said I would take care of it."

Dawn gasped. "Do you mean to tell me that we have nothing to offer the wedding guests besides the wedding cake Brynn is bringing down? That's it? We should just hold the wedding in the church basement. Lemonade and cake and be on your way."

"Don't worry. I said I would take care of it."

"But have you?"

Mom's eyes were fixed on the tips of her shoes. "Working on it."

Dawn should have anticipated this. This was nothing new! Marnie Dixon was great with the big picture, the flyover, the brainstorming. Terrible at finalizing details. Just terrible at them.

"Dawn, calm down. I have a plan."

"What?"

"Just . . . trust me."

"Why should I trust you? You've forgotten a critical component to a wedding reception!" She threw her hands in the air. "The entire reception!"

Mom held a finger in the air. "I haven't forgotten."

"Mom, this wedding is barely a week away!"

"I know. I've got it handled. You just concentrate on being the bride. I'll take full responsibility for the wedding reception."

Dawn bonked her head down on the tabletop. Then she lifted her head and smacked it down again with each word: "I! Should! Have! Known! Better!"

• • •

Marnie waited until Dawn had left for a final fitting of her wedding dress, went upstairs, knocked on the bedroom door, and told Callie she needed to see her in the kitchen. Right away.

Callie followed her downstairs with a curious look on her face. "Is something wrong?"

"Nothing's wrong. Not if I get your help to make it right." She motioned to a teapot sitting at a table in the front room. Beside it sat two cups and a plate with two Morning Glory muffins. "Let's sit down." She poured some tea for Callie and handed her a cup. "Callie, I don't have a caterer for Dawn's wedding."

Callie sipped her tea. "I'll make some calls. I'm sure we can find someone." She put her teacup down. "Jesse! I'll call him. He would appreciate the work. He's great in the kitchen. I trained him myself."

"Actually," Marnie said, "I was hoping you would do it."

Callie's eyes went wide, then she shook her head vigorously. "I can't," she breathed. "I just can't."

"You can. Callie, you're doing so much better since you've arrived. Surely you can do this for us. For Dawn."

"Aunt Marnie, I would do anything for you and Dawn, but I just can't be responsible for preparing food for others."

"But you can. You've done it."

Callie sat, with an increasingly uncomfortable look on her face, especially as Marnie passed her a muffin.

"They're delicious, aren't they?"

Callie lifted her eyebrows in agreement as she took a muffin and examined it. "Perhaps a tad overdone."

Marnie only smiled. "They're perfect. Every single day, they've been perfect. People call and put in orders for them. We sell out, every single day."

Callie picked up her cup and sipped her tea, her eyes remaining downcast.

"You've been baking these muffins, haven't you?"

A long moment passed, then Callie lifted her eyes. "I wanted to help."

"And you did. In an amazing way. When have you baked?"

"Usually, in the middle of the night. Sometimes, when you and Dawn were out doing something for the wedding. I try to leave everything the way Dawn wants it."

Except for leaving the KitchenAid stand mixer plugged in. That was the one thing Callie consistently overlooked. Each morning, Dawn would blame Marnie for it, and she didn't mind the accusation.

"Callie, I need your help. I'm asking you to cook for Dawn's reception."

Callie's eyes grew shiny. "You don't understand. I promised myself I would never cook again. I couldn't bear it if something happened again."

"Mistakes happen all the time. It's part of life. You have to forgive yourself."

"It's not just that. It's . . . why it happened. It could happen again. It probably will happen again."

Marnie took a minute before responding. "When you helped me make ice cream, and those fancy pops, I noticed how careful you were about ingredients. You taught me about mise en place. Everything in its place. You start everything on the left and end on the right. You wash up as you go. Callie, it's certainly possible that you might make another mistake, but your habits are such that mistakes would be rare. And no matter if you have MS or if you just slipped up . . . you are human. Just like the rest of us." She put her hand on top of Callie's. "I'm willing to take the risk on anything you make."

Callie nibbled on the corner of the muffin, stalling. Thinking. She let out a sigh. "I appreciate your confidence, Aunt Marnie, but I just can't face that risk." She rose. "I'll go call Jesse. He can drive up from Pennsylvania on Thursday, prep on Friday, cook on Saturday morning. So if Dawn has already decided on a menu, Jesse can put together a list of ingredients to buy. I can do the shopping ahead of time."

Marnie wasn't quite so ready to give up on Callie. She went to the kitchen and came back with a pad of paper and a pencil. "Dawn left the reception in my hands. If I ask her what food she wants served, everything will grind to a halt as she ponders all possibilities. So . . . could you at least plan the menu?"

Callie gave that some thought. "How many covers?"

"Covers?"

"Guests. You have a guest list all set, right?"

Marnie nodded. "Plan for around forty to fifty guests." The list had been trimmed way, way down.

"How does this sound? A lemon-thyme poached lobster tail followed by a wood-grilled sirloin."

"Oh, that sounds delicious! But expensive."

"Do I have a budget?"

"Yes. A very small budget."

"Oh. In that case, what about salmon grilled on a cedar plank?"

"Smaller."

Callie closed her eyes, as if she felt a little pained. Then she opened them. "In circumstances such as these, I do have a recipe for a wonderful roasted chicken over wild rice."

"Now we're talking."

"A spring greens salad dressed with a light mustard vinaigrette. And to tie it all together, the inner rim of the plate will be swirled with a reduced apricot compote."

"It sounds perfect." Marnie could almost smell the chicken roasting in the oven. She nudged the pad of paper toward Callie. "The wedding cake is taken care of. Dawn's friend Brynn is baking it."

"A home cook?"

"Brynn is a fabulous baker."

Callie bit her lip, deep in thought. "The wedding's a week away."

"I know."

Callie grabbed the pad of paper and pencil. "I'll go call Jesse."

* * *

Jesse was delighted to get the reception gig, and together, he and Callie brainstormed the menu for Dawn's wedding reception. "You'll be my sous-chef, right?"

"No. If you need help, could you bring someone with you?"

Silence. "Come on, Callie. Why not? It could be fun to work together again."

"Can't. I'm in the wedding. The maid of honor." Dawn hadn't asked Callie yet, but she didn't need to. It was implied.

More silence. "Fine. I get it. I think it's a crying shame that you have hung up your spatula."

She ignored the topic. "You'll come? Next Thursday?"

He let out a deep, long-suffering sigh. "Let's see. I work until three, and it's an eight-hour drive. I'll probably hit all the commuter traffic around New York. So count on nine hours. I'll get in after eleven Thursday night."

"I'll have all the ingredients bought for you. Ready to go."

"All the cooking needs to be done in one day?"

"Yes, but I've seen you cook under pressure. You'll do great."

"Callie, you'd do even better."

"Thanks, Jesse. You're a good friend. I'll see you next Thursday night. Bring a sleeping bag. Call if you have any questions." After they hung up, she went down and told Marnie that the wedding reception was in good hands.

"Whose?" Marnie asked.

"Jesse. He's the best."

"No," Marnie said. "He was taught by the best."

* * *

229

Monday, March 21

Everything was coming together. Dawn's wedding dress was altered and hanging in the closet. Brynn was bringing down the wedding cake on Friday morning. Dawn and Kevin's friends were planning to drive down Friday afternoon and stay at an Airbnb for the weekend. Kevin's parents were coming earlier in the week. Lincoln had offered them a place at his cottage.

And the Creamery! Mom had showed Dawn the plans to transform the front room, and even Dawn had to admit that she'd outdone herself. On Friday, a party rental company would deliver several long wooden farm tables, rustic chairs, gorgeous blue velvet linens, pewter plates, and an old colonial pattern for silverware. Mom had even found antique lanterns for the tabletops—a nod to the smithy who had originally built the Main Street Creamery. Mom wanted lots and lots of candles. "The whole room will be bathed in a buttery glow," she told Dawn. Like something out of the eighteenth century.

Mom had promised, promised, *promised* that the catering for the reception was covered. Dawn was well aware of her mother's dodge-the-question strategy, and she had tried to corner her from every which way, but Mom sounded supremely confident that the reception was covered. Dawn felt less confident, but she could let it go. She didn't care. If the guests ended up with a granola bar and juice box, that would be fine with her. She and Kevin were finally getting married! That's all that mattered.

● ● ●

Wednesday, March 23

Marnie was quietly panicking. Each time she tuned into the weather report, it had upgraded what was originally a mild spring storm into a cold ice storm. She tried to remain extremely calm and unconcerned around Dawn, who was in a state of wedding bliss, but her stomach tightened each time she checked her phone for updates.

On Wednesday evening, after Dawn and Kevin had left the

Creamery to take some luggage over to Linc's pool house, she hurried up the stairs to talk to Callie. "We've got a problem."

Callie looked up from her computer. "I know." Her eyes flicked back to the screen. "I just got off the phone with Jesse. I tried to get him to take tomorrow off work, but he says he'll get fired." She blew out a puff of air. "He promised to get on the road right at the end of his shift. With any luck, he'll be able to drive right in front of the storm."

All the nonperishable shopping for Jesse's long list had been taken care of. Marnie and Callie had hidden everything so Dawn wouldn't catch wind of anything. As far as Dawn was concerned, the caterer was bringing everything. Thursday, Callie planned to buy all the perishables. Dawn might start to be aware of the refrigerator's overflowing contents at that point, but most likely, she wouldn't even notice. She was in wedding la-la land. "What if . . . ?"

"The worst happens?" Callie said. "Then we move to plan B."

"And that would be . . ."

A deafening silence filled the room. Marnie studied Callie's face, her own squeezed into a worried frown. Her niece was so still, so stricken, that Marnie worried this conversation might have triggered one of those MS hugs. Oh no. What had she done to Callie? What had she done to Dawn's wedding? Heat flushed Marnie's face. She felt an anxiety attack of her own start up.

Then Callie let out a puff of air. "Plan B is me." She gave Marnie a look. "I can't let my favorite cousin down." She closed her computer. "But let's not tell Dawn. Even about Jesse's race with the ice storm. I don't want her worried about her wedding day."

Marnie felt a cool breeze of relief waft through her. She smiled and bent over to kiss her niece on top of her head. "You are a wonderful person, Callie Dixon."

● ● ●

Thursday, March 24

Dawn clicked off her phone and let out a bloodcurdling scream. "MOM!"

Her mom rushed into the kitchen from the front room. "What's wrong?"

"Not a single one of my Boston friends can drive down. They said Emergency Services wants everyone off the roads. The ice is wreaking havoc." She covered her face with her hands. "No Brynn," she mumbled. "No maid of honor." Then she dropped her hands and looked at her mom with wide eyes. "No cake! Your caterer!"

"My caterer?" It came out in an odd squeak.

Dawn's mind had switched into overdrive. "Yes. We have to call them. Immediately. The guest list just got cut by two-thirds." She covered her face with her hands, then dropped them. "I suppose it's too late to reduce the order." She rubbed her hands together. "Okay. Here's an idea. What if we invited everyone we know in Chatham? Leo and his dad, Nanette and Michael, Mrs. Eldredge-Nickerson."

Mom leaned against the doorjamb. She seemed pleased. "I like that idea. I like it very much."

"So what time does the caterer plan to arrive?"

Silence.

Something was off. It was written all over her mom's face. Dawn's stomach tightened into a knot. "You said you had it covered. You said not to worry. You showed me the menu. You sounded very pleased." She walked right up to her mom, almost nose to nose. "You're hiding something. What is it? What are you hiding?"

"Hiding?" Mom said it in a way that seemed very nonplussed.

Dawn wasn't having it. "What have you done? Or not done?"

"Slow down. Wait a minute before you go into a full-fledged panic." Mom cleared her throat. "There is something—"

Dawn lifted her hands like a stop sign. She took a deep, calming breath. "Mom, don't blame yourself. I shouldn't have given you so much to do." It was her own fault. How could she have let this slide? She should have been paying better attention. Her mom was great with design, bad with food. She knew better! Then she heard footsteps above her, a sound that usually annoyed her because it reminded her that Callie had taken over her room. This time, the sound seemed heaven sent. "I think I might have a solution." She bounded up the stairs, two at a time. She opened the door without knocking and stood at the threshold with her hands on her hips. "Callie, I need you to step in for my mother's flakiness."

Callie was in the middle of changing the sheets on her bed. "Flakiness?" She tucked the corners of the sheets under the air mattress.

"Yes. Mom forgot to get a caterer." She pointed at her. "I need you. Desperately."

Callie's eyes widened at Dawn's distress. "Me? But—"

"No buts." Dawn clapped her hands together. "You can do this, cousin. You're a master in the kitchen."

And yet hesitation was all over Callie's face. "But then I won't be able to be your maid of honor."

Aaaand that stopped Dawn short. An awkward silence followed. A very, very long awkward silence.

"Oh," Callie said, getting it. "Oh, I see. I wasn't going to be your maid of honor."

Her face. Crestfallen. Dawn felt terrible. She crossed the small room and sat on her bed, facing Callie. "I'm sorry. I asked my friend Brynn. We've been friends since college. We shared an apartment for years and years. You understand, don't you?"

"Brynn. Yes, you talk about her a lot." Callie sat down on Dawn's bed, a thoughtful look on her face. "Dawn, why haven't you ever liked me?"

Dawn was slow to answer. "I've always liked you." Sort of.

"No, not really. Not the way I've cared about you. There's always been something between us, something that's kept us from being friends."

What could Dawn say? She was right. Why *did* Callie like her so much? Why didn't she ever take a hint?

"I've tried so hard to be close to you. While we were growing up, whatever you were doing, I wanted to do too."

Now? Do we really need to do this now? My wedding is less than forty-eight hours away! Dawn leaned forward, resting her elbows on her knees. "That's why you copied me in everything?"

Callie nodded. "It started with Space Camp. I had no interest in outer space, but when Dad told me you were going, I signed up too."

Dawn took a moment to gather her words. "If you wanted to be close to me, why did you have to outshine me all the time? Even in Space Camp, you earned the Future Astronaut award." There was only one Future Astronaut award and Dawn had wanted it so badly.

Callie tilted her head. "I didn't go there to outshine you. I was just . . . participating."

Oh boy. And by just participating, Callie couldn't help outperforming everybody else. Including Dawn.

"So you thought I tagged along to make you feel . . . diminished?" When Dawn slowly nodded, Callie continued. "I was just trying to be your best cousin. You're the closest thing to a sister I have."

Oh boy, oh boy, oh boy. Dawn flopped down crossways on the bed and covered her face with her hands. Kevin was right! Once again, she had missed what was most important. "Kevin says I suffer from acute competitive-itis. He won't even play any kind of game with me. Not tennis. Not Monopoly. Nothing. He says I turn into a crazy person."

"Like our dads. They never stopped competing. I felt as if they were always pitting us against each other."

Dawn dropped her hands. "You were aware of that?"

"Of course. My dad loves to win, no matter the toll on others. And winning was the only way he noticed me."

Right then, Dawn knew exactly the pressure Callie had grown up with. She knew exactly what it meant to be in a race you hadn't signed up for. "I felt I was always in a competition with you, and always ending up the loser."

Callie let out a scoff. "You're no loser, Dawn. Look what you've done with your life."

That was a kind thing to say. And it was true. Dawn had found the life she truly wanted to live, the one she was meant to live. She wanted that for Callie. She lifted herself up onto her elbows. "Maybe Mom's flakiness is a blessing in disguise, because there's no one's food I'd rather eat than yours. I *truly* mean that. Please, Callie. Please be the caterer at my wedding. I'll sous-chef for you. Mom can do dishes."

Callie took two steps toward the window to look at the sky. She was perfectly still for several moments, her back to Dawn, frozen in indecision or refusal. Dawn didn't know which. She held her breath. *Please, please, please, please, please.*

"Okay," Callie said at last. "I'll do it."

"Perfect," Dawn said, delighted. Overjoyed. She wanted to jump up and down on the air mattress! "What could possibly go wrong?"

"Lots," Callie said, turning around to look right at Dawn. "I could poison everyone. Accidentally."

Oh, that. "Your food . . . is worth it." It really was.

Slowly, Callie smiled. "Preheat the oven to 350 degrees. I'll be down in five."

Dawn went down the stairs, two at a time. "She said yes." She went straight to the oven and turned it on.

Mom looked startled but, curiously, not overly so. "That's wonderful news!"

Dawn turned to her. "Haven't I been telling you, all along? This is the way to handle Callie. Get her working. Keep her busy."

"Busy?"

"Yep. Busy. It's the secret to happiness."

● ● ●

Callie
How soon can you get up here?

Jesse
I was just about to text you. Are you sitting down?

Don't tell me.

Roads are closed. I'm stuck here.

NOOOOOooooooo.

235

You can do this, Chef. You're the best.

In other words . . . there's no one else.

Funny, the twists and turns of life.

Not funny. More like terrifying.

Callie had barely begun to get her head above water, and it wouldn't take much to wash her back under. Could she do it? She thought just maybe she could.

Chapter
TWENTY-FOUR

It's never too cold for a popsicle.

—Kevin Collins

Friday, March 25

The weather on Friday was horrific all throughout New England. Cold, blasting rain that froze as soon as it hit the ground. Truly awful.

But Friday turned out to be a wonderful day for the three Dixon women. Callie cooked, Dawn sous-cheffed, Marnie washed dishes. Appetizers of pancetta-wrapped asparagus, miniature crab cakes, pea soup shooters. For the entrée: herb-roasted chicken and wild rice with apricot compote, mixed spring greens with raspberry-infused vinaigrette. These were her foolproof recipes, her go-tos in a pinch, and she knew them like the back of her hand. Nearly everything could be prepared the day before, heated or mixed at the last minute, and all presented beautifully.

To Callie, it was a dream day.

She was working in the kitchen with the women of her family. She felt as if she was living out a Norman Rockwell painting! It was like, all along, she'd been starving for this sense of belonging, but she'd just now figured out what had been missing in her life. The more she got, the more she wanted.

When Kevin called to see how things were going, Dawn went upstairs to talk privately. As soon as Callie heard the door shut, she whispered to Marnie, "Is there any chance the power could go out?"

Marnie glanced out a window and sighed. "An excellent chance."

"But you have a generator, of course."

Pause. "No."

Callie nearly gasped. "Aunt Marnie, you really should consider getting one for the Creamery."

"It never occurred to me. You're right, though."

Callie paced from the back door to the stairwell, back and forth. Then she stopped and pivoted. "Grill?"

"We do have a grill! Charcoal too."

"Just one?"

Marnie nodded.

"Then we're going to get it set up as an outdoor warming oven as a backup."

Just then Dawn came downstairs, an odd look on her face. "Kevin reminded me of something. We have no wedding cake."

Callie opened the refrigerator to see how many eggs were left in the carton. Eight. Enough, though just barely. She spun around. "I could bake one."

Dawn had a funny look on her face. Callie couldn't tell if she was about to cry . . . or laugh. "What?"

Dawn took a deep breath. "Callie, I appreciate all you've done. But Kevin and I . . ."

"Ice cream!" Marnie said. "Of course. You *are* getting married in an ice cream shop."

"Actually, no." Dawn looked like she had something else in mind. "We talked about having ice cream, but that means we need more dishes and spoons, and someone has to do all the scooping. So no ice cream, we decided."

"Then what?"

Dawn's eyes darted between Callie and Aunt Marnie. "We want Mom's fancy pops."

"My fancy pops?" Marnie said in a weak voice.

Dawn clasped her hands together and smiled. "Yes. They're perfect. You can hold them with one hand while you dance. And if they're anything like the Valentine's Day fancy pops, they're every bit as delicious as ice cream. They're unique, and fun, and memorable." She scrunched her face up. "Please, Mom?"

Suddenly the back door opened with a whoosh of cold air and there was Cowboy Leo, all bundled up in a snow jacket and boots.

Dawn hurried to shut it behind him. "Leo, you've got to learn to shut doors."

"My dad sent me. He wants me to ask if we need to wear fancy clothes. He says he hasn't been to a wedding in a long, long time."

Callie froze. "Your dad? He's coming to the wedding?"

Leo nodded.

"Nothing too fancy," Dawn said. "In fact, I insist that you wear your best cowboy clothes. I wouldn't even recognize you without your hat on."

Leo gave a thumbs-up and went back out the door, leaving it open again. Dawn went to shut it. "Back to Mom's fancy pops." She glanced at the wall clock. "Is there enough time to make them? I'm supposed to meet Kevin and his parents soon to go over a few things, and I need to get in the shower. I could tell them I'll be late."

Callie and Marnie exchanged a look. Marnie read her thoughts. "You go on ahead. Callie and I can manage the fancy pops."

Dawn's face lit up. "Thank you! I'll let you pick the flavors. Anything you like. I trust your judgment. What you did for Valentine's Day was out of this world." She gave them a thumbs-up and dashed upstairs. On the way up she called out, "Mom, I'll be back in a few hours to help set up the front room."

A few hours, Callie noted. Just enough time to get those fancy pops in the freezer.

Marnie leaned against the counter. "Oh Callie, I'm so sorry. One more thing to do."

But Callie wasn't sorry. She was thrilled! "They're so easy to make, and they're what Dawn and Kevin want." The look on Dawn's face! She'd asked for Callie's custom popsicles.

Marnie put her hands on Callie's shoulders. "I don't know how you are able to cook and bake like you do."

"It's just following intuition. Anyone can do it."

Marnie shook her head. "Not anyone. But if you could teach others to cook like you do, you'd be making the world a better place."

Hmm. Interesting. But no time to ponder that now.

Marnie squeezed her shoulders. "Thank you. You've rescued us."

"I think I could say the same." Callie meant it too. She felt like she'd been given a miracle drug—having something and someone other than herself to worry about. It had done wonders for her outlook. Maybe *that* was the secret to happiness.

Callie heard the shower turn on overhead and opened the freezer. "Here's what we're going to do."

Marnie joined her near the refrigerator. "Anything you say, Chef."

Callie started pulling frozen fruit out of the freezer and lined packages on the counter. To Marnie, she knew she seemed like the consummate professional. Inside, she was a mess. Jittery and energized at the same time. Half her mind was checking off the ingredients required to make two versions of fancy pops. She knew just what she wanted to make—two flavors that were a staple at the restaurant. One would be coconut milk and lime, dipped in dark chocolate, sprinkled with lime zest. The second one would be yogurt and blackberries, dipped in white chocolate, sprinkled with dried blackberry dust.

The other half of her mind kept up a steady thrumming in her ears: *Leo's dad is coming to the wedding!*

• • •

Dawn had to hand it to her mom. She had great taste. By the time Dawn returned to the Creamery in the late afternoon, the front room had been transformed. All the furniture had been moved out to create an open space. The party rental company had brought in two large tables and twenty wooden chairs, linens and dishware, and somehow, Mom restyled this room from a cozy ice cream shop to a storybook-perfect wedding venue. Decorated from the floorboards to the rafters, yet not over-the-top. The room looked tranquil and sophisticated while still charming and warm. It looked like a magazine.

Speaking of great taste, Callie had outdone herself. According to Mom, anyway. Callie was still paranoid about the tiniest risk that she might cause food poisoning, so she wouldn't let Dawn sample anything. But Mom did . . . and she oohed and aahed over each course.

As they were cleaning up the kitchen, Mom said, "Better together."

"What is?" Dawn was sweeping the floor and glanced up. "The wild rice and chicken?"

"Us," Marnie said. "We're better together. The three of us."

Scooping wild rice into a container, Callie paused. "That's sweet of you to say."

"I mean . . . for the benefit of the Main Street Creamery," Marnie said. "Dawn's ice cream. My interior design. Callie's baking."

Callie shot Mom a warning look.

Dawn caught something in that look. "Callie's baking?" She set the broom handle against the counter. Her gaze went back and forth between Callie and Marnie, back and forth. Something clicked into place. "It was you, wasn't it?" She pointed at Callie. "You baked those muffins. The ones that everyone kept coming back to the Creamery to buy. The ones they keep asking for. Begging for. I can't even walk downtown without someone asking me for the recipe." *Man!* She'd given out her recipe too. She'd been so pleased to be asked.

Callie bit her lip. Marnie whispered to her, "I'm sorry."

"Why didn't you just say something if you didn't think my muffins were good enough?" Dawn said, annoyed.

"I was trying to help," Callie said. "I redid them one time, and then the muffins sold out so quickly, so I . . . did it again. And again."

Dawn tipped her head. "So you've been sneaking into the kitchen, baking, replacing my muffins, cleaning up . . . right under my nose? And I've been oblivious to that fact?"

Slowly, Callie nodded.

"When?"

"During the night, mostly."

"So that's why the house always smelled heavenly in the morning." Dawn gave Marnie a suspicious look. "And you knew this?"

"Only because I figured it out. Callie never said anything."

"I'm so sorry," Callie said. "I just wanted to find a way to earn my keep. You've been so good to me. Both of you. The muffins you'd made weren't . . ."

She knew. "They weren't exactly bringing in the customers."

"The texture," Callie said. "It was too tight. The muffins bounced like a ball." Her eyes widened in alarm as she realized what she had just said aloud. "A common mistake! I could teach you how to correct that."

"It's okay," Dawn said, losing interest in stupid muffins. She glanced at the freezer. "You've been rearranging things, too, haven't you?"

Slowly, Callie nodded. "Kitchen systems need to be set up so that everyone can find what they're looking for. Not just the head chef."

Dawn needed a moment to compose herself. *This.* This was exactly what she was afraid of when Callie had come to stay with them. She would improve on everything Dawn did. But then it occurred to her that Callie had, indeed, improved the Creamery. Even without trying to! Sneaking around at night so she wouldn't be found out.

The girl just couldn't help herself.

Once again, Dawn had missed the most important thing. God had brought a gift to the Creamery in the form of Callie Dixon, and Dawn had completely missed it. She took a step forward and put her hands on Callie's shoulders. "Mom is right. We're better together."

"You're not mad?"

"Mad?" Dawn scoffed. "How could I be mad? You're the third leg on our stool. I didn't even realize we'd been missing a leg until you came here." She wiggled her eyebrows. "And now that I know . . . you can't leave."

Callie's eyes grew shiny with tears. "You want me to stay?" She looked to Marnie, as if she couldn't quite believe what Dawn had said.

"You heard Dawn," Marnie said. "You're the third leg on our stool."

● ● ●

Dawn
Guess what I found out today? Turns out Callie has been baking muffins in the middle of the night and swapping them for mine.

Kevin
No way! So that's why the Creamery's had such an uptick in customers this last month.

Thanks.

Don't be mad. I just meant . . . they're incredible muffins.

Why would I be mad? Callie and I can both be good at things at the same time. We're not children. We're not sharing one swing at the playground.

Is this Dawn Dixon, my fiancée? Or am I texting with a stranger?

Funny.

Chapter

TWENTY-FIVE

All you need is love and maybe a little ice cream.

—Marnie Dixon

Saturday, March 26

Early Saturday morning, Callie heard the shower go on. Dawn was up, getting ready. Her favorite cousin's wedding day. Ten minutes later, when Dawn came back into the room, Callie had made her bed, had finalized the to-do list, and had divided the entire day into segments of time. There was a lot to do today to put the finishing touches on the wedding dinner. Before she started in the kitchen, though, she wanted to pick out a dress to wear tonight.

"Shower's free," Dawn said.

Callie turned from the closet to meet Dawn's eyes. "Are you nervous?"

She wrinkled her nose. "Just a smidge." She toweled her long hair dry. "What are you looking for?"

"A dress to wear tonight." Callie took her two dresses out of the closet and laid them on the bed. "Which one do you like best?"

Dawn made a face. "They look like you're going to a job interview."

Exactly. That's why she had brought them to Chatham.

Dawn riffled through her side of the closet. "Here are a couple to try." She started pulling one dress after the other and tossed them on the bed.

They were nice, but not nice enough to meet Leo's father. Callie wanted to look her best today. You only had one chance to make a first impression, after all.

Dawn could tell she wasn't sold on the choices. "What do you have in mind?"

"Something . . ."

"Sexy?"

"Yes!" And then she slapped her hand over her mouth.

Dawn stared at Callie. She stared at Dawn.

Then Callie whispered, "Please tell me I didn't just say that out loud."

Dawn burst out laughing. "I have just the thing." She dove back into the closet and pulled out a beautiful, sleek, little black dress. "Not sure who you're hoping to impress who's coming to the wedding, but this dress is life-changing."

"Really?" Callie said. It looked a little . . . insubstantial. There didn't seem to be enough material to cover up her body. She was a lot taller than Dawn, after all.

"It's the perfect dress. It fits everyone. Trust me. Go try it on."

She hesitated.

"Go! I'm the bride. I get to call the shots today."

In the bathroom, Callie pulled the dress over her head and squeezed into it. She tried to see how it looked in the mirror over the sink, but she couldn't really tell. Her first impression was no. No way. Too tight. Too slinky. Too form fitting. Not her taste at all.

She'd have to reconsider her job interview outfits. Maybe a scarf could help soften the severity.

Quietly, she returned to the bedroom she shared with Dawn. Her cousin had her head upside down, combing out her long strawberry red hair.

She flipped it back and saw Callie standing at the door. "WHOA!!! MOM! Come see Callie!"

Marnie opened the door to her bedroom and did a double-take when she saw Callie. Then a big smile filled her face. "It's perfect."

Well, okay then. She'd found her dress.

* * *

Standing on the Creamery's small front stoop, Marnie looked for a place to tape the sign she'd made this morning:

PRIVATE EVENT.

THE ICE CREAM SHOP IS CLOSED TODAY.

COME BACK ON MONDAY!

She smiled. Her daughter Dawn was getting married today!

She wished Philip were here. He would've loved seeing his little girl get married. And he had cared deeply for Kevin. She looked up at the gray sky, full of heavy, low-lying clouds. Maybe Philip did know. Maybe that's what the author of Hebrews meant when he wrote that people were surrounded by a cloud of witnesses.

A gust of wind blew the sign right out of her hands.

"Got it!"

She turned and there was Linc, holding on to her sign. That man! He had a knack for turning up at the right time. "If you hold it down, I'll tape the corners."

As Linc pressed the sign against the door, he stood right next to her, so close she could get a whiff of him. He smelled soapy and clean, like he'd just stepped out of the shower.

She taped the last corner of the sign. "There."

"Ready? Big day."

"The biggest." She smiled, and he smiled, and they stood on the stoop, smiling at each other like silly, awkward middle schoolers.

"Marnie, there's something inside I want to show you."

She followed him in, closing the door against the cold behind them. She hadn't even realized how cold it was until she came back inside.

He looked around the room. "Wow, wow, wow." He took a few steps forward and looked around. "You've transformed it from an ice cream shop to a . . ." He lifted his hands with a laugh. "I don't even know how to describe it."

Marnie grinned. The room turned out even better than she could've imagined. The owner of the party rental company, one of Nanette's cousins, was kind enough to arrive yesterday afternoon despite the crummy weather, deliver everything, *and* store the Creamery's tables and chairs in his truck for the weekend. She hadn't even thought about where to store the furniture until the driver made that offer!

In one corner of the room were two wooden farm tables, decorated and set up for twenty people. The chairs, for now, were in the center of the room, facing the fireplace. The ceremony would take place in front of the fireplace. Bouquets of dried lavender hung from the rafters, adding to the ambiance. Marnie had to admit that it looked . . . lovely.

"There's only one thing," Linc said, as he walked across the room, "that could possibly improve this room." He crossed to the fireplace and flipped a switch. A little gurgling sound started, then the dark cavity burst into flames.

"What's going on?" Marnie bolted across the room. "How could this be happening?" The decorative wooden logs had been replaced with artificial logs. And there were flames coming out of them!

"It's my wedding gift to Dawn and Kevin," Linc said. "It's been in the works for a while now. Kevin helped me with the permits and with the details needed to get a gas line to the fireplace."

A gas line? A flip-the-switch fire? "But . . . when did you get the work done?"

"Whenever you've been gone with Dawn for more than a few hours. Callie was a help with that—tipping us off about your schedule."

Marnie felt . . . gobsmacked. She didn't know what to say. That fireplace was a significant feature for the Creamery, and the warmth of the glowing flames, especially on a cold, dark day like today, absolutely made the room hum. She looked at Linc, this wonderful, thoughtful man, and wrapped her arms around him. She probably hugged a little longer than was necessary, because someone interrupted them with a clearing of the throat.

"There's one more surprise," he whispered into her ear. "Turn around."

She did. Standing by the kitchen door was her best friend in the entire world, Maeve. And right beside her was Maeve's new husband, Paul Grayson. Marnie let out a squeal and ran to embrace Maeve. "Did you come all the way from Maine? How did you get here? The ice!"

"We came down on Thursday morning," Maeve said, "before things got really bad. We've been staying at Lincoln's house."

"More like a palace," Paul added in his gravelly voice.

Marnie gave Paul a hug too. "I'm so glad you're here." She grabbed Maeve's hands. "Both of you."

Maeve gave her hands a squeeze. "I wouldn't miss Dawn's wedding day for the world."

● ● ●

Callie went over her checklist one more time. Then once again. Marnie and Maeve were upstairs helping Dawn with her hair and her dress with its dozens of tiny buttons. The dinner meal was warming in the oven. She'd kept it refrigerated as long as possible just to avoid any possible chance of . . . well, you know.

Guests started trickling in around four o'clock. First were Kevin's parents, along with Mrs. Nickerson-Eldredge—who considered promptness to be a virtue, and then Nanette and Michael. Callie peeked around the doorjamb into the front room. Still no Leo. No Leo's dad. She checked on the dinner warming in the oven. Hot but not too hot. The salad was in the refrigerator, ready to be dressed, dinner rolls and butter were already on the table. Champagne and wine were near the back door, which felt like a refrigerator. The fancy pops were in the freezer. And even though Dawn had said no wedding cake, Callie had baked a single-layer vanilla sponge cake this morning, added a raspberry filling, and iced it with buttercream. Her mother's recipe.

She took off her chef's coat and smoothed her dress. Dawn's slinky black dress. She'd taken care with her hair—sweeping it up in a chignon. She applied her makeup with a deft hand. She wanted to look her best tonight.

But what if Leo's mystery dad didn't come? What if the weather was too icy? She peeked in the front room again. Seemed like they should have been here by now, if they were coming.

"Hi, Cowgirl."

Callie spun around to see Leo peer up at her. "I was afraid you weren't coming!" He'd left the back door wide open and a gust of cold wind and rain blew in. She didn't care! He was here.

"Dad bought me new stuff." He held up a shiny boot.

"Leo, you look amazing."

"Are you grilling hot dogs?"

"No. The hot grill is my backup. Just in case—"

The back door closed and she looked up. Someone was wrestling with an umbrella. Leo's dad. She held her breath. The umbrella closed and there was Bruno Bianco. He looked up and froze, staring at her. She stared back at him. "Bruno?"

He just kept staring at her. Did she look that different? she wondered. Or was it Dawn's life-changing dress? "Bruno, why are you here?"

He just kept staring at her. It was like he forgot everything—what he was saying, what he was doing. He held very still.

"The wedding," Leo volunteered. "Dawn said we were invited."

Callie's head turned to Leo, then back to Bruno, then back to Leo. Then back again to Bruno.

Bruno Bianco? *He* was Leo's mystery dad? Her eyes went wide, her mouth dropped open. Words failed her. She was *that* shocked.

"You're the cowgirl?" Bruno had the most confused look on his face. "You're the one who's been teaching Leo to read?" He glanced down at his son and then came back up with a smile that reached his eyes.

Bruno?! Bruno Bianco was Leo's dad?

She felt a little tickle in her chest, the way she used to feel when a celebrity ate at her restaurant—a mixture of surprise and delight and self-consciousness. And shock!

Bruno was Leo's dad!

Dumbstruck. Utterly astonished. Astounded. That's how she felt. How had she missed it? All this time, she'd never uncovered a single shred of evidence that Bruno was Leo's dad. It had never even dawned on her that Bruno was the man who kept invading her dreams. All this time, she never knew.

Marnie's friend Maeve appeared at the bottom of the stairwell. "I think we're ready."

No one moved. Bruno and Callie just kept staring at each other in disbelief.

"Uh, Callie?" Marnie moved in a little closer to get her attention, then took one more step until she nearly stood between them. Her eyes darted from Callie to Leo to Bruno, before returning to Callie. "Dawn said to cue the music."

And with that, the moment shifted. Action. Bruno and Leo went into the front room to find a seat.

Pull it together, Callie! She gave a slight shake of her head. *Keep your head in the cockpit. It's go time.*

Callie turned on her iPhone to the song Dawn wanted as she came into the room. Kevin stood at the bottom of the stairs, waiting for his bride to descend the narrow stairwell. Callie noticed Kevin's face soften and his eyes grow shiny. He grinned like he was the luckiest man on earth. As Dawn reached the final step, he held out his hands to her and drew her in close. Kevin was much taller than Dawn, but since she was on that step, they were the same height. Just inches away from each other, they stood there for a long moment, soaking up the sight of each other. This moment for them, even Callie knew, was the result of a long journey. They'd made it.

And the wedding ceremony was ready to begin.

No sooner had Dawn put her hand in Kevin's to walk toward his father-officiate, proudly waiting for them in front of the fireplace, and POOF! The power in the Creamery went out.

● ● ●

Linc

Back in a minute. Going out to find more candles.

> **Marnie**
>
> Thank you! Don't forget matches. We're running low.

Got it. Text if you need anything else.

> Hurry back! But don't slip on the ice.

Don't worry! This wedding will happen.

Chapter
TWENTY-SIX

Life would be vanilla ice cream without 31 flavors of individuality.

—Heather King, blogger

Marnie could hardly believe how Callie reacted to the power outage in the Creamery. Calm as a cucumber, almost as if she'd been expecting something to go wrong. She'd bought extra candles, and Lincoln brought back more, plus matches, and it wasn't long before the room practically glowed in soft candlelight, helped magnificently by the fire in the fireplace. The gas could run even if the electricity went out, and it kept the room warm. Cozy. When Dawn realized the flames in the fire were real, and Marnie explained that it was Linc's wedding gift to her, she burst into tears. Happy, thankful tears. And soon the wedding ceremony picked back up to carry on.

As soon as Kevin and Dawn finished with their vows, Callie slipped into the kitchen. One moment after Kevin's dad introduced the newly married couple, she reemerged holding a tray of cold champagne and glasses. Maeve took over the pouring of the champagne, and Callie disappeared again. She returned bearing platters of beautifully arranged cheeses, breads, nuts, figs, dried apricots. It was like a choreographed dance. Paul and Linc picked up the chairs and set them at the table settings. Everyone chipped in to help. Leo and his dad, especially. They shadowed Callie to ferry platters from the oven out to the hot grill Callie had prepared by the back door, to keep the entrées warm during the appetizer hour. Somehow, that girl had thought of everything.

But she did it seamlessly. When it was time for the toasts, Callie was there. Just enough time was allowed for appetizers, and then dinner was served. First the salad, lightly dressed, sprinkled with pomegranate seeds. Then the chicken over wild rice, artfully plated with the apricot compote circling the rim.

Absolutely delicious, start to finish. Everything was fine-dining, restaurant quality . . . which shouldn't surprise Marnie. But it did.

Linc used Spotify on his iPhone for music to dance by. After the first dance of Kevin and Dawn, Callie brought out a small wedding cake for them to cut. "I made it," Callie whispered to Marnie, "just in case Dawn had wished she'd had a wedding cake." She went back to the kitchen to cut pieces for the guests.

Marnie followed her in and tried to shoo her out of the kitchen. "Maeve and I can take it from here. You go sit down and enjoy yourself."

Leo was suddenly in between them, peering up at Callie. "Come and dance."

Callie set the knife down. "How can any girl say no to such a handsome cowboy?"

Marnie cut cake and Maeve served the pieces, then they brought mugs of coffee out on a tray. Callie had even pre-thought the coffee. It had been perked and kept hot in carafes. Marnie filled up the last two empty mugs with coffee and went to find Lincoln. She handed him a mug and slipped into her chair. Their eyes met across the table and they smiled, sharing a moment of satisfaction over the entire event. It was hard to talk. The room was surprisingly loud for twenty people. Warm too.

He tipped his head to the dance floor so she would notice Callie, Leo, and Leo's dad, all dancing together. "She seems really happy," Linc shouted over the music.

"She sure does," Marnie shouted back. Boy, she sure did.

Linc came around the table and sat next to Marnie. "He can't keep his eyes off her," he said. "Remember Pong? That old video game? That's what it's been like all night—his head goes this way, that way, as he watches her walk around."

"It's as if they've known each other for a long time," Marnie said. "But they just met."

"Actually, I think they've known each other for a while," Linc said. "That's Bruno Bianco."

Marnie's eyes went wide. "The author? The Saturday class? He's Leo's dad?"

"That's him," Linc said.

"And no one put the two together? Not even Nanette?"

"Nanette knew."

"Why didn't she ever mention it?"

"She said she thought everyone knew."

The music changed to a slow tempo, and Marnie was pleased to see that the trio continued to dance, holding hands together. Hmm, she wondered. An interesting twist to the evening. Cowboy Leo had been besotted with Callie from the start. And so, apparently, was his father.

Seeing Callie so at ease, so cheerful, so alive, so full of a contented glow . . . it made this night all the more perfect. The cherry on top of the sundae. Even the most hopelessly lost people could sometimes get found.

Lincoln set down his mug and put a hand out to Marnie. "May I have this dance?"

She set her coffee mug down and took his hand. "I'd love to."

Linc led her to the dance floor—only four steps away—and put his arm around her waist. He was surprisingly at ease, a good dancer, like he did this kind of thing often. Not so for Marnie. She was acutely aware of his nearness. The contact of his hand on her back sent a warm ripple through her. The way they were leaning into each other felt so comfortable, like they did this all the time, though it was their first dance. She wondered if this was what Maeve meant when she said that things between her and Paul just shifted naturally, from friendship to romance. Something was definitely shifting between her and Linc. She could hardly keep her feet on the ground.

Before the evening came to a close, Callie brought out the last special treat: fancy pops for everyone. Custom made for Dawn and Kevin, with two little chocolate hearts piped on them, intertwined.

Callie, Marnie realized, had some kind of sixth sense for entertaining, and timing, and people . . . because the room had become quite warm, and serving the fancy pops at this point rather than earlier was the perfect answer. Something sweet, something thirst quenching, but not too much.

Marnie had no idea how Callie had managed to cook and bake and churn in that dinky kitchen. It was so limited compared to what she was used to, yet she created a delicious meal, including phenomenal fancy pops.

And no one got sick.

• • •

Upstairs, Callie helped Dawn change out of her wedding dress and into warm clothes and heavy boots. Dawn and Kevin were ready to head over to Linc's pool house. Dawn was determined. She told Kevin that even if they needed to hire a dog and sled, they were going to spend their honeymoon night alone.

Dawn turned her head to the side. "Callie, thank you for everything."

Callie had been unbuttoning tiny little buttons down the back of the wedding dress. "It was my pleasure." These tiny buttons, not so much. So many of them!

"Seriously, this wedding was a dream come true. You made it extraordinary."

Callie smiled. It was a night of dreams coming true for everyone. The entire event had turned out better than she could have imagined.

"So . . . Leo's dad."

Callie's hands stilled.

"Mom said he's the guy who's been teaching the Secret to Happiness class."

"Yes," Callie said.

"I saw the way he looked at you."

She couldn't help it. "How did he look at me?"

Dawn took her time answering, like she was giving that careful thought. "Like the sun came out from behind the clouds."

Did he? The idea of it made her insides feel like quivering jelly. Dancing with Bruno and Leo. The way Bruno smiled at Leo. The three of them together. It felt . . . like they fit. Like they belonged together.

She took a shaky breath. "There. Last button." She helped Dawn step out of the dress. While her cousin threw on warm clothes, she hung the wedding dress carefully on a hanger and placed it in the closet. The dress was a stunner—an off-the-shoulder ivory satin gown with a nipped-in waist, a full skirt poofed out by tulle underneath. Zillions of satin-covered buttons down the back. As Callie zipped up the garment bag, she realized this dress would probably remain in this closet for years and years, never to be worn again. That was okay. It had served its purpose.

When they came downstairs for Kevin and Dawn's departure, Callie was a little disappointed to discover that Bruno and Leo had already left. "Leo couldn't keep his eyes open," Marnie said. "Bruno said to tell you good night."

She felt a tiny bit deflated at that exit. A little stung. But what had she expected? Bruno was a wonderful dad. Leo was tired. It was perfectly reasonable to take him home before it got too late. Perfectly reasonable. Undoing Dawn's minuscule buttons took a ridiculous amount of time.

Still.

An hour later, she collapsed on the air mattress, exhausted. Pleased. She was just starting to nod off when her phone chirped and she leaned over to read it, assuming Jesse was checking in to see how the wedding went. She squinted in the dark. It wasn't Jesse who was texting. It was Bruno.

She sat straight up in bed.

Sunrise tomorrow? Same place, same time?

Sounds good.

That wedding meal. Well done, Chef.

Just another day at the Main Street Creamery . . .

TWENTY-SEVEN

Life is too short not to get the double scoop.

—Unknown

Sunday, March 27

Bruno was waiting for Callie right on the street near the beach. She hurried to meet him, and when she reached him, they looked at each other, and, at the same time, both blurted out, "How did I miss this?" This, as in, how are *you* the person Leo's been talking about all this time? Then they both laughed. Bruno! He laughed. He had a wonderful laugh too. Deep and rumbly. His whole face softened, brightened.

"You never once said a word about having a son."

"You never once mentioned ice cream."

Both were true. Each morning, their sunrise conversations were brief, limited to questions Callie had gathered after reading a chapter or two in his book. Very focused. No time for chitchat. And then he would dash away to his holy moment.

She'd been getting to know Bruno the author through his book. She'd been getting to know Bruno the dad through Leo. She felt as if she were at the optometrist's office, looking through two lenses as the eye doctor clicked the dials and merged the two images into one. One clear image. Two Brunos became one.

They plopped down on the ground in their usual spot. "That son of yours . . . he's quite a boy. He's come to mean a lot to me." More than she could possibly put into words. Leo made her feel so special.

Bruno smiled. A genuine, proud-dad smile. "You've come to mean a lot to him too. He doesn't stop talking about Cowgirl Cal." He coughed a laugh. "I should have started to put the pieces together when he had me looking up odd animal facts. He said you loved them."

"I do!"

"I've noticed. You're a bottomless pit of useless trivia."

"Not entirely useless. I usually win at Trivial Pursuit."

That coaxed another smile out of him. "Callie, you did a fine job yesterday. I don't think your cousin could have asked for anything more."

"And so far, no reports of anyone with food poisoning."

"There's that too." He turned to her. "You're doing well. Very well. I hope you can see that for yourself."

"I can," she said, growing sincere. "I'm in a much better place than when I arrived. You and your book . . . they've been a big help. You've put a lot of things in perspective for me."

His face went a little tender. "Honestly, you've done this all by yourself, Callie. I've just been along for the ride."

Callie had a million questions, but she knew enough about Bruno to not overwhelm him. There were really only two questions she wanted to know the answer to. "Where did you and Leo go for three nights?"

"I had a book event in New York City. Why?"

She pantomimed scissors cutting.

He raked a hand through his now-short hair. "Yeah. My publicist. She's relentless. Constantly trying to make me look more academic and less like a beach bum."

Hardly that. But Callie knew there was a woman behind that haircut! It made her mad. Bruno, of all people, should have the final say on his hair. She had a hunch that woman was the very one who pinched Leo's chubby cheeks. She wanted to ask, but the sun would be up soon and Bruno would dash away and she had a much more important question on her mind. "Would you mind telling me what happened to Leo's mom?"

He hesitated. "What has he told you?"

"That she's in Heaven."

She realized he was holding his breath. He let it out and shoved his hands into his coat pockets, all at once. "Sofia and I met when I was in graduate school. She was a teacher and I was working on my master's degree. I was assigned to provide clinical therapy to a student in her class. We spent some time together, at first just to discuss the student, but it wasn't long before we were spending every spare minute together. We married, and about a year later, got pregnant with Leo. We had a lovely life together."

"So what happened?"

"We were living up in Cambridge while I was finishing my doctorate. It was just an ordinary day. Just an ordinary Tuesday morning. Sofia was about eight months pregnant. I'd kissed her goodbye and went to the car, but forgot my keys. When I went back into the apartment, I found her on the kitchen floor. It turned out she'd had a rupture of an abdominal aortic aneurysm."

"What's that?"

"A ballooning of the aorta—the main artery of the body. It caused massive internal hemorrhaging. They were able to keep her on life support for another week until Leo was ready to be delivered by C-section."

Callie held still and quiet. What could she say? How on earth could she respond? It was beyond anything she had words for. He had said hello to his son and goodbye to his wife on the same day. At last, grasping for something—some acknowledgment of what he was telling her—she whispered, "I am so sorry."

He nodded, staring at the ocean like he was seeing something else. "The best and the worst day of my life." He pulled his hands out of his coat pockets and crossed his arms against his chest.

"So then . . ."

"So then," he continued, "eventually, I finished my dissertation and applied for a teaching position at 4Cs."

"Seems like a guy with a PhD from Harvard could've found a more . . ." How to word that?

"A more prestigious college or university? Possibly. Probably. But it would come with a cost. I didn't want Leo spending his childhood in day care. I needed to find a work situation that worked well for both of us. Someplace safe, someplace neighborly. I wanted Leo to have a normal childhood, full of freedom to roam. Sofia had felt strongly about preserving childhood. She saw it disappearing in American families. Overscheduled children. Distracted parents." He fell quiet again.

After a while, he looked up, seeming to remember she was there. "Chatham was a great choice. Sofia's grandparents had a summer residence in Chatham, and she'd spent a lot of time with them. She'd always loved it here, so I ended up buying the cottage from her grandparents. One day, it'll belong to Leo."

"How in the world did you manage to survive losing your wife?" She couldn't help but think of her own dad.

"The circumstances of Sofia's death were such that there was no one to blame. It just happened. The aneurysm was part of the body she'd been born with."

"Some might say you had a right to be angry with God."

"God gave me Sofia, and he also gave me Leo. Had I not returned for my car keys when I did, I might've lost them both." He lifted one ankle over the other. "Still, it wasn't easy. It took time to find my way to a better place."

"So," she suddenly realized, "that's how you came to study the secret of happiness. Because you wanted to know."

He nodded. "Because I needed to know."

Neither of them spoke, and for the first time ever—maybe in her entire life—that was okay. Callie didn't push against the quiet, or try to fix it, or try to fill it with noise. She just let it surround them, and she stayed right there. They listened to the wind, and the ocean. They watched the sky lighten as the tip of the sun appeared. This time, Bruno didn't rise to his feet and tell Callie he would leave her to her holy moment. Not this morning. He stayed. In a way, *this* was a holy moment.

* * *

Callie
Do you believe in a master plan?

Jesse
A little detail, please?

Like . . . things happen for a reason.

Oh. Yeah, I think I do.

I do too.

And she had to smile, because it was the first time in her life that she actually believed that. What other explanation could there be?

If she hadn't been fired, she wouldn't have let Jesse talk her into temporary work at Penn State's Ice Cream School. And there she found Marnie, who invited her to come to Chatham.

Or maybe Callie invited herself.

Regardless, here she was. And because she was in Chatham, she met Leo. And Bruno.

She was a different person now. A stronger person.

As she was pondering this new way of thinking, she heard the ping of an email. It was from the hotel where she had worked. The subject line read

Update on lawsuit

Her heart started racing. *Please, Lord,* she prayed. *Give me strength. Give me strength to face this.*

Her first true prayer. She took a deep breath and clicked on the email.

Good news. The suit was dropped. Best of luck to you.

Closing her eyes, she released a long, slow breath.

There had to be some kind of master plan.

Chapter

TWENTY-EIGHT

Sweet dreams are made of popsicles.

—Dawn Dixon

Monday, March 28

Two days later, Dawn still had to pinch herself. She and Kevin were married. Married! And their wedding, while not quite what she had originally planned, somehow ended up being even better than she'd imagined. More intimate. Way more. Only twenty people instead of the original seventy-five. But each one was important. Better food, that's for sure. Callie knocked it out of the park.

Kevin had to go to work today, so Dawn decided to head over to the Creamery and properly thank Mom and Callie for all they'd done. She stopped at the grocery store and picked up a bundle of fresh tulips. When she arrived at the Creamery, she couldn't find anyone. She went upstairs and knocked on what was formerly her room and was now officially Callie's room. No answer.

Even after two months, she still worried she'd find Callie dead in the bed. Slowly, she opened the door. The curtains were open, the air mattress was gone, Dawn's bed was made up, the computer was left open. Curious, Dawn went over to see what Callie had been looking at.

The page was open to WebMD on multiple sclerosis. Dawn sat down on the bed. Tab after tab: Multiple Sclerosis. Symptoms. Progression of Disease. Women and Multiple Sclerosis.

"Dawn."

She looked up and shot off the bed at the sight of Callie at the open door. She stared at her, confused. Things started falling into place. Why Callie was depressed. Why she spent so much time on her computer. Why she'd come to live with them in the first place. How had Dawn missed this? How had something this big, right in her own house—her own bedroom, for Pete's sake!—how had it slipped through the cracks? "Are you sick?"

Callie drew her brows down. "Sick?"

"Do you have multiple sclerosis?"

"I don't know. Maybe. But maybe not."

"Oh, Callie," she said, her heart hurting. "Why didn't you tell me?" She sat down and patted the bed next to her.

Callie hesitated. "I didn't want you to feel sorry for me. I still don't."

"Come. Sit." When Callie sat next to her on the bed, Dawn asked, "Why do you think you have MS?"

"I started getting some weird symptoms."

"But you've seen a doctor, right? Please tell me you've seen a doctor."

"I have. But the tests were inconclusive. Very typical of MS. It's diagnosed by ruling everything else out and monitoring symptoms."

"Then . . . it's not definite." So there was hope. Maybe there was a mistake. Dawn's racing heart started slowing down. "Is this why you were fired from your job?"

"Yes and no. I think it's why I made a mistake at the restaurant. I'd been getting these odd symptoms, and one day I got flustered . . . and that's why I made the mistake."

"But what makes you think the odd symptoms mean MS?"

She scrunched up her eyebrows. "Well, because of my mom. She was diagnosed when she was my age. I run a higher chance of getting it."

Aunt Beth. Of course. "I really don't remember much about your mom, other than her electric wheelchair. I thought it was kind of cool."

"It was, in a way. But the reason she needed it wasn't at all cool."

"No, of course it wasn't." What a stupid thing for Dawn to say. "We need to get you to a specialist." She jumped off the bed. "I'm going to go call Lincoln. He has connections everywhere. He'll know who to call for all the latest information. Medical breakthroughs are happening all the time."

Callie seemed amused. "There's not a treatment or a clinical trial that I haven't researched in the last few months. There's no cure for MS."

"What if it *is* something else?"

"Time will tell. If I have what my mom had, then it'll progress pretty fast."

Dawn stared at her. "There's got to be treatments that can help. Slow the disease."

Callie shook her head. "I saw what meds did to my mom. They made her dizzy and nauseous and so tired she couldn't even open her eyes. The worst were the seizures." She shuddered, as if a terrible memory passed through her mind. "I don't want to live like that."

"But you can't live *this* way. Not knowing. It's like waiting for a grenade to go off."

"Actually, I can. I've been learning a lot these last few months. Thanks to you, in fact."

"Me?" Callie gave her too much credit. She always had.

"Yes, you. Dragging me to the Secret to Happiness class. It's taught me all kinds of things. How to live in the present and not worry about what's around the corner. And your mom's been a big help too. With other things. Important things. Like . . . discovering faith. I hadn't given it much thought before I came here."

Still. This enormous burden had been weighing down her cousin, all this time. And Dawn had been oblivious to it. Annoyed by it. "I'm sorry," Dawn said.

"Don't be sorry."

"If I'd known, I would have been nicer to you."

"You were plenty nice! More than nice."

But Dawn wasn't. She resented Callie being here. She'd pushed and prodded her to get out of bed. She'd felt irritated by her presence. She had wanted her room back.

It occurred to her that Mom knew about Callie's symptoms. No wonder Mom had encouraged Dawn to spend time with Callie, to talk to her, to get to know her.

Had Dawn listened? Nope. Instead, she had belittled Callie's depression. That was the worst thing of all. It would be hard to forgive herself for *that*.

● ● ●

Well, how about that? Callie had to smile at the look on Dawn's face when she caught her looking at her computer. She looked like she just stepped on a cat's tail.

This morning, Callie had updated her software on her computer, then it automatically restarted. She hadn't even realized all those old tabs had opened again. She hadn't even looked at those MS pages for days and days. Weeks, maybe.

So ironic. She'd spent the last two months hiding her fear of having MS from Dawn—convinced it would only drive them apart—and it ended up being the very thing that brought them closer. She had underestimated her cousin.

That conversation with Dawn made her think that maybe it was time to let her dad know the truth. Maybe she was finally ready. Ever since Bruno had told her about the death of his wife, she had felt her heart soften toward her dad.

She picked up her phone and pressed on her dad's contact button.

He picked up on the first ring. "Hello, Callie." He sounded curt, like he was still mad at her for hanging up on him that day. He could be petty like that. Hold grudges.

She licked her lips. "Dad, I need you to listen to me. Really listen." Surprisingly, he didn't object.

"First, some good news. The lawsuit was dropped."

Silence, then sputtering, then, "Why . . . that's great news!"

Before he could start in, she took a deep breath and explained more. Why the food poisoning at the restaurant had happened in the first place, why she thought she might have symptoms of MS, though it wasn't at all definite. She carefully detailed out her doctor's response, that she was on a wait-and-see watch. When she finished, she heard only silence on the other end. So silent that she thought the call might have dropped. Finally, she said, "Dad? Are you still there?" She heard him clear his throat.

And then came, in a shaky voice, "We're going to get you to the best doctors."

"I have a great doctor."

With that, her dad exploded. "A great doctor does not let his patient passively wait for the disease to progress. We are not giving up! We'll find the best doctors, the best treatments there are—"

"Dad!" Her abruptness stopped him short. "I have to figure this out," she said, her voice a little softer. "You can't do it for me. You can't fix this. I have to do it myself."

"You're wasting precious time."

Oh no. She wasn't. Time was precious, but she hadn't been wasting it. In fact, the last two months might've been the most purposeful time in her entire life. She couldn't even begin to explain how valuable this time had been for her. "I'll handle things, Dad."

"But are you going to? Are you going to fight this? You don't want to . . ."

When he didn't finish the sentence, she did it for him. "End up just like Mom? Frankly, I'm not sure what's ahead. All I know is that this is my path to figure out. Not yours."

"I can't sit here and watch you die without knowing we did everything we could to prevent it."

As if her dad had ever sat and watched her do anything. She shook her head, and the tears that had been welling in her eyes spilled down her cheeks.

There was a long, quiet pause. "Callie—"

"Dad, I don't want to talk about this anymore," she heard herself say.

"Good idea," her dad said. "We can talk later. I'll do some digging and—"

"No." She shook her head. "I don't want to talk about MS with you at all. Period. Not now. Not ever."

"Wait a minute, Callie. What are you going to do next?"

She nearly smiled. That was her dad. Always making plans. "I'm not sure what I'll be doing in a month or two." Though she was starting to get an inkling about it. "For now, I do have something in mind. You still have Mom's ashes, don't you?"

There was a long, quiet pause, and for a few seconds, Callie thought he was going to say he had no idea what had happened to them. That one of his ex-wives had tossed them out. "Yes. Of course I still have them."

"Good. I want them. I want Mom's ashes." She stared into the long, thin bedroom mirror hanging on the wall as she spoke. She held her own gaze, hardly able to believe that she was the girl in the mirror's reflection. She was the one talking to her dad in such a steady, clear, bold way. "I want to have a ceremony and scatter Mom's ashes. I want to give her a proper goodbye."

She could just imagine the baffled look on her dad's face and nearly smiled. But then she braced for an onslaught of protests.

There was a long, long pause, before he said, "Okay."

"Okay? As in, you'll give them to me?"

"Somehow, I'll get them to you."

"Soon?"

"Soon."

"Thanks, Dad."

"Callie," he said, his voice thick. "I love you."

"What?" she said. "Really?" She put her hand over her mouth. She was pretty sure she'd never heard those words come out of her father's mouth. Not once.

He cleared his throat, then repeated himself. "Yes. I love you."

Wow. She was so unused to hearing this from him that she felt uncomfortable. It couldn't have been easy for him to say that, but she didn't even know how to respond. The silence lengthened, grew more awkward. *Say something, Callie!* "Well, um, I love you too, Dad."

She held on to the phone for a while after he hung up. This was a big moment. Standing up to her dad was surprisingly elating. He could handle it. It didn't drive him away like she'd always been afraid it would. In fact, the opposite had happened. Her dad had actually told her he loved her. Amazing!

Later that day, she realized something else. Something huge. It was the first phone call she'd had with her dad that didn't end with an MS hug squeezing the air out of her lungs.

●　●　●

The next day, Dawn stopped by the Creamery to see if Mom wanted to go see the most recent work done on the old house. She came in the back door and found her mom stuffing towels in the tiny double-stack washing machine under the stairs. "I was just going to drop lunch off to Kevin and come back to make some new batches of ice cream. I won't be long."

"Take Callie," Mom said. "I'll mind the store."

"Is she upstairs?"

"No. She's out front, planting plants in the window boxes."

Dawn had completely forgotten about those window boxes! Last summer, they had been showstoppers. Gorgeous. Full of red geraniums and variegated ivy. She'd had an intention to pack them with daffodils so they'd be blooming in time for Easter . . . but with the wedding and the purchase of the old house . . . she'd completely forgotten.

She pushed open the front door to see Callie on a small step ladder, hands in gloves, stuffing edges of a window box with trailing blue lobelia. "Callie, that looks beautiful!" And it really did. There was a central spike of snapdragons, with ivy bells cascading down, blue lobelia filling in the empty spots.

Callie looked at Dawn with a smile. "I'm hoping there's no more frost." She brushed her hands off. "But if so, I'll just replace the plants."

Interesting. It sounded like Callie wasn't planning to leave. At least, not soon. Dawn felt pleased by that knowledge. Callie made a difference. Her cousin truly was the third leg of a stool. She helped to stabilize the Creamery. She had Mom's finesse and Dawn's attention to detail. Unlike Mom, Callie finished what she started. Unlike Dawn, Callie had a broad set of skills. Dawn was an ice cream maker. A good one. But that's all she really wanted to do in the kitchen.

The Creamery needed aspects of all three women, but unfortunately not full-time. That was the only thing that niggled at Dawn. She wanted Callie to stay in Chatham, but was there enough for her to do? She wasn't sure.

"Want to tag along to the old house? Kevin forgot his lunch and I'm running over to drop it off."

"I thought you'd never ask," Callie said and jumped off the ladder. "I've been dying to see it."

On the drive over, Callie peppered Dawn with all kinds of questions about the house, more than she could answer. Things like, did it have a southern exposure? And was there natural gas in the kitchen? "You'll have to talk with Kevin. He's the house guy. But I don't think we were planning to add a kitchen. Maybe a kitchenette."

"No kitchen?" Callie seemed horrified.

"Well, it's a commercial property. We're hoping someone will come along soon who wants us to customize it for something specific."

"I thought you were restoring an old house."

"We are. We want to retain the architectural integrity of the house. But update it, too, so that it has a new life to live."

Callie tipped her head. "I like that."

"There's a dentist who's shown some interest." Dawn shrugged. "A dentist named Carleton Woods. He's beloved around here. People call him Bud."

As they pulled up to the house, Callie stopped and took in the full house. "It's still a little rough," Dawn said. It did look pretty bleak, especially with the dumpster in the driveway. "Lincoln seems to be just as obsessed with old, broken-down houses as Kevin. Add Mom's design style, and the three of them are just exploding with ideas, like popping corn."

Callie nodded, staring at the house. "I can see its potential."

Inside, enough of the demo had been completed so that you could see through the wall studs. Callie walked around the entire downstairs and back again to where Kevin sat on the floor, bent over some architectural drawings. "So where *was* the kitchen?"

Kevin pointed to the center fireplace. "Other side of that."

Dawn followed Callie to the back of the house. "It overlooks that beautiful field."

Callie turned in a circle. "There is incredible natural lighting in here. Great for cooking." Her voice sounded far away. "You're really thinking of turning this into a dentist's office?"

"Maybe," Dawn said. "Kevin's not keen on that idea. He wants it to be preserved as a home." She walked toward the front windows. "But it is a busy street out there."

Callie joined her at the window to watch the traffic going by. She was quiet for a long time. "So then, it's not too late?"

"For what?"

Callie's gaze swept the room. "Dawn, find Kevin. Let's have a chat."

● ● ●

Daylight savings arrived last Sunday, which meant that the time for the sunrise had to be adjusted. Each evening, Bruno texted Callie about the time to meet up. He brought coffee and a thermos, and they still parted for the holy moment. That was his private time with his Maker. She respected that, and she liked having her own holy moment too.

Plus, she now knew that one of the reasons he kept moving was that he had to get back to the house—which was only a block away—before Leo woke up. There was a neighbor who rose early and kept his eye on the house for Bruno while he went to the beach for the sunrise, but Bruno liked to return to the house before Leo woke.

Callie took a sip of coffee. "I called my dad."

"How'd that go?"

"I told him about the MS symptoms, and that was why I made a mistake at work. And got fired." Funny. She could talk about it now without that tight crunch-feeling in her stomach.

"And?"

"He reacted just like I'd expected him to react. He wanted to send me off to specialists. Start treatments. Blah, blah, blah."

"And you still don't want to take that spinal tap test?"

"I might, but not yet. Not now. I've thought a lot about what you said."

"What's that?"

"You asked me if I would believe the test result . . . or would I always hold on to the fear of MS. I think you're right—that I need to learn to manage the fear. For now, I feel like I'm on the path of healing. Maybe it's just my soul that's healing, but I don't want to interrupt that." She shrugged. "I didn't tell my dad all that. He would send me off to the funny farm." She gazed at the ocean. "I'm pretty sure my mom would understand. I asked Dad for her ashes and he said he'd get them to me. I want to say goodbye to her." She gave him a nudge with her elbow. "You helped me with that too. Thank you. For everything."

"Why do I get the feeling that you're about to say goodbye?"

She laughed. "No. I'm just expressing gratitude. It's from a book I've been reading. A really good book."

Bruno gave her a big smile at that. They were coming more regularly now.

"I do have a plan, though." And she did. She had come to a decision that made her feel, well, joyful. Excited about the future, set free, empowered. She felt strong.

His eyebrows lifted in interest.

"I love to be in the kitchen. But I've also always wanted to teach. I used to think I'd go to college to become a teacher. So I had an epiphany. Mesh the two together. I want to start a cooking school called Intuitive Cooking. Teach people how to trust themselves in the kitchen."

"I like it," he said, nodding. "I could use something like that. I scorched frozen pizza last night. Leo wouldn't touch it."

"Then you can be the first student to sign up for my class."

He snapped his head up. "Here?" His voice cracked, like a fifteen-year-old boy's. "You're going to stay *here*? In Chatham?"

"If everything goes according to my plan."

"What's the plan?"

"That old house that Kevin's working on. I think it might be a perfect place for the cooking school. The location is ideal—commercial zoning, a large enough side area to turn into a parking lot, the interior has been opened up, like a great room."

"A great kitchen, you mean."

"Exactly."

He shifted in the sand to face her. "Are you planning to purchase it?"

"I think I am," she said slowly. Then, more confidently, "Yes, I am." She had plenty of money socked away. Once she'd become an executive chef, her salary had skyrocketed. She'd never known what to do with her fat income, so she just tucked it all in mutual funds. Now, she knew what that money had been waiting for. "At long last, I know what I want. I want that house. I want to start a cooking school in it. I want to stay in Chatham, near Marnie and Dawn and Leo and . . ."

He had turned back to face the ocean, a slight grin on his face. "And Nosy Nanette and Mrs. Nickerson-Eldredge."

She smiled. "Yes. Them, as well." She gave him a nudge with her elbow. "Maybe one or two others." She bent her legs and wrapped her arms around her knees. "I like it here. I like it a lot. I like having a family. I want to help Marnie and Dawn make a success of the Creamery too." She gave him another elbow nudge. "So what do you think?"

He thought about it a minute. Like he wanted to give a careful answer. Like he wanted to say something from the heart. He skooched a little closer to her. "I think," he said, "it sounds like a dream come true." With that, he put his arm around her, and rested his chin on her head. She pressed the side of her face against his chest and they sat there for she didn't know how long. Long enough.

● ● ●

Kevin
Do you really think Callie's serious about buying
the house and turning it into a cooking school?

Dawn
Totally serious.

Good. Because Linc already found another old
house he wants us to buy.

So . . . we're officially in the house flipping
business?

😮😕 House restoration.

Chapter

TWENTY-NINE

Nothing is impopsicle.

—Callie Dixon

Friday, May 27
Memorial Day Weekend

The summer season had officially begun on Cape Cod, and the Main Street Creamery was ready. A lot had happened in the last two months. Callie had expanded the baked goods selection to include a wide variety of muffins and pastries. Dawn handled the ice cream making. Marnie, mostly, handled the customers. She had a way with people.

Callie had something else to add to her good-things list, something she wouldn't have thought possible: She and Dawn began to talk and act like sisters. They shared notes about their lives, comparing memories the way sisters did. Much of their teen years had overlapped at summer camps, but their perspectives had been entirely different. This new, deep relationship with Dawn was an unexpected gift.

And then another gift came in the town of Chatham. It had

undergone a lovely awakening. Its people had returned! Callie enjoyed walking the streets, admiring the gray-shingled houses filling with signs of life. Bright red geraniums in the window boxes, flags snapping in the wind. Stores reopened with the latest gifts and T-shirts and souvenirs to tempt tourists. Painters, standing on ladders, brushed up the crisp white trim of historic buildings. Landscapers mowed lawns and trimmed hedges. Bees flitted above blooming hydrangeas and dipped for pollen. The air blew fresh and breezy, rich with the smell of cut grass and salty sea.

But best of all the gifts of this season came on a gorgeous morning, when her dad arrived at the Creamery. "I'm here," he said, as if she'd been expecting him. In his arms was a bag. "I'm here for the ceremony."

"The ceremony?" Callie stared at him.

He set down the bag he'd been holding and reached in to lift something out of it. An urn.

That ceremony.

Oh. Her stomach tightened.

But she still wanted to do it anyway. Or maybe needed to.

"Get your coat. I rented a boat and skipper at the harbor. I even got an official permit to scatter the ashes from the town of Chatham and that was no easy task. It's all arranged."

So like her dad. No advance warning. No heads up "I'm on my way" call. Arriving at her door full of orders. But he was here. She had to give him that. "I'll get my coat."

An hour later, the skipper led the boat out of the harbor, around the bar, and straight toward the Atlantic Ocean. Three nautical miles from shore, as the law allowed for cremains to be scattered. When the skipper gave them the nod, Callie's dad grabbed the urn and took off the lid. "Okay, here we go."

"Stop!" She reached out to stop him from tipping the contents of the urn right over the boat's edge. "Hold it, Dad. Slow down. Just slow down. We need to say a few words."

"We do?"

"Yes. I'll go first." Callie took the urn from her dad and held it against her chest. "Mom, I know we didn't have the years together that you deserved, and I'm so sorry for that. But you did give me so much. You gave me life, and you gave me faith. And one day we will be together again and I'll fill you in on everything that's happened since you left us." She glanced at her dad.

"Everything?" Dad said, his face tight with guilt.

"Everything," Callie said firmly. "Okay. Your turn. Say something." She handed him the urn. She expected him to say a few brief words and start emptying the urn over the edge of the boat. But he didn't. He seemed at a complete loss.

It was strange to see her dad hesitating, uncertain about what to say. Richard Dixon had always been an unstoppable force—so confident, so determined, so self-possessed. Suddenly, he looked remarkably old to her. Smaller too. For the first time in Callie's life, she felt as if she understood what made her dad the way he was. As long as he kept moving, his feelings couldn't catch up with him.

Today, she wasn't going to rescue him. She was going to make sure he slowed down and felt something.

He looked at the urn. "I'm, uh, Beth, I'm sorry," he started, then stopped. "I'm so sorry. About your illness. About how I handled things. I should've done better." He choked up at that, and looked away, his eyes shiny with tears. "I should've done better with our daughter." He tucked his chin in a sob. Callie put her arms around her dad—who was holding her mom—and they cried together.

Together, they scooped handfuls of Mom's ashes from the urn and scattered them out to sea. Dad even took time for lunch afterward when they returned to the harbor. She told him all about her plans to open up a cooking school and he didn't try to talk her out of it. Well, at first he did, but she held up her hands like a stop sign and he gave up. He even promised to come back to Chatham and take a class. Callie hoped he would. That time together didn't fix everything between Callie and her dad, but it was a start. A very decent start. And she was thankful for it.

Thankful. It was a word that circled in her mind often these days. Especially yesterday. Callie had spent the day in Boston. She sat in a changing room for a long while, waiting for her spinal tap to get underway. A nurse had poked her head in the door and said, "Ready?" And she was. She really was. It was a pretty cool moment to know that whatever it was that had always scared you didn't scare you anymore. It had lost its power. It was as if her soul had risen out of the darkness and into the light. And that was *before* she received the results from the test.

Guess what? No sign of lesions.

This morning, when she told Bruno the news, his smile was enormous. It radiated. It beamed. As bright as the morning sunrise.

Of course, it didn't entirely rule out that she would end up with MS one day, but it did add to her peace of mind. She saw the world through a different lens now. She felt happy. Better than happy. She felt content.

So what was the secret to happiness? First of all, there wasn't just one. Second of all, happiness was an inside job. It was no one else's responsibility. And there were a few more things Callie had learned since she came to Cape Cod:

Pay attention to the good things in each day, because there *are* good things.

What you focus on, you'll find. Good or bad.

Train yourself to stay in the present. To savor it.

Be mindful about who (or what) you let tell your story.

Play every day.

Hunt for awe, for holy moments.

Look for reasons to be grateful. Give thanks. Abundant thanks.

Getting fired from Callie's job in such a public and humiliating way was terrible. The reason for it was even worse. But she wished she had known it wasn't the end of everything. She wished she had known that it was only the beginning.

Because life had become, in a word, awesome.

Discussion Questions

1. When Dawn found out her cousin Callie was coming to stay at the Main Street Creamery for an indeterminate amount of time, it seemed like her worst nightmare had come true. She and Callie, cheered along by their dads, had always been in a lifelong competition with each other. Callie always won. Dawn always lost. Who do you relate to, Callie or Dawn? How so?

2. Be authentic, Bruno Bianco told Callie. She thought she was! Callie thought of herself as a happy person. Everyone did. And then she had some experiences that threatened that self-perception, and she was forced to face the fact that a "happy front" had been her lifelong coping mechanism. Without it, who was she?

3. Callie and Jesse had a text conversation about what it meant to be truly authentic. How would you describe being authentic with your family or friends?

4. Maybe you needed an enforced pause, Bruno told Callie, insinuating that she had *wanted* to be fired from her executive

chef position. Implying that it was easier to let someone else make the decision for her. What is your response to Bruno's remark? Do you think there are times our minds or bodies will find a way for us to take an enforced pause . . . like it or not?

5. Fear is the heart of the matter, Bruno told Callie. She didn't want to get that spinal tap test because she wasn't really sure she'd believe the results. Have you had an experience in your life when you weren't sure you believed something, even when faced with evidence?

6. During the wedding, Dawn came to see how Callie had become the third leg on the Creamery's stool, and she hadn't even known a leg had been missing. To thrive throughout the entire year, the Creamery needed Marnie's design taste, Dawn's attention to detail. And it needed Callie's broad range of skills. She filled in quite nicely. Prior to this, Dawn held a "scarcity view"—there was only so much talent to go around in the family. Callie was a threat to her. Name some ways in which Dawn's scarcity view only hurt herself.

7. Time was precious, Callie noted, but she hadn't been wasting it. Despite spending the majority of the last few months in Dawn's teeny bedroom, how did that time become more valuable to her than all the years she'd been moving at full throttle?

8. Callie's life went from fast paced to . . . slow motion. She realized that it was hard to appreciate things when you were speeding through life, fixing your attention only on what comes next. Slowing down had an advantage. She was starting to notice more. Simple things, like the mournful call of a loon. She'd lived near the Eastern Seaboard all her life yet had never made time for a sunrise on the ocean. Not a

single sunrise! How did slowing down start to change—and improve—her entire outlook? Why did it have that effect?

9. Think of a time you felt overwhelmed by a sense of awe. Looking up at a night sky scattered with stars, standing in front of a vast ocean, hiking a hill and looking behind you at the valley below. Or even something small—the mystery of no two snowflakes being alike. Or no two fingerprints. How would you describe that feeling of awe? Why do you think it fills you with a sense of delight rather than insignificance?

10. Do you think there's a secret to happiness? Or are there many? If so, list one or two that make a difference in your frame of mind.

11. Name three good things from your day today. Make it a habit.

Author Note

Further reading you might enjoy about the secrets to happiness . . .

Carter, Christine, PhD. *The Sweet Spot: How to Find your Groove at Home and Work*. New York: Ballantine Books, 2015.

Gilbert, Daniel. *Stumbling on Happiness*. New York: Knopf, 2006.

Goleman, Daniel. *Emotional Intelligence*. New York: Bantam, 1995.

Haidt, Jonathan. *The Happiness Hypothesis*. New York: Basic Books, 2006.

McBride, Hillary L., PhD. *The Wisdom of Your Body: Finding Healing, Wholeness, and Connection through Embodied Living*. Grand Rapids: Brazos, 2021.

O'Connor, Richard, MSW, PhD. *Happy at Last: The Thinking Person's Guide to Finding Joy*. New York: St. Martin's Press, 2008.

O'Connor, Richard, PhD. *Rewire: Change Your Brain to Break Bad Habits, Overcome Addictions, Conquer Self-Destructive Behavior*. New York: Hudson Street Press, 2014.

Rasmussen, Jamie. *How Joyful People Think: 8 Ways of Thinking that Lead to a Better Life*. Grand Rapids: Baker Books, 2018.

Rubin, Gretchen. *The Happiness Project: Or, Why I Spent a Year Trying to Sing in the Morning, Clean My Closets, Fight Right, Read Aristotle, and Generally Have More Fun*. New York: HarperCollins, 2009.

Sapolsky, Robert M. *Why Zebras Don't Get Ulcers*. New York: W. H. Freeman, 1998.

Seligman, Martin E. P. *Authentic Happiness*. New York: Free Press, 2002.

Satisfy your sweet tooth
with a trip to
Cape Cod Creamery

COMING SOON

Chapter
ONE

Ice cream is duct tape for the heart.
—Anonymous

Fingers hovering over the phone, Brynn Haywood hesitated before texting her best friend. Was Dawn the right person to go to? Brynn had met Dawn as a freshman in college, and she'd never known her to do anything wrong, or stupid, or foolish, or embarrassing. All those adjectives could describe the last twenty-four hours in Brynn's life. Add to the list mortifying, humiliating, impulsive. What happened last night was, by far, the worst thing she'd ever done, so out of character. So shameful.

How would Dawn react? All during college, Brynn and Dawn had been dubbed The Sensible Sisters. They never did anything out of line, nothing crazy. Their majors, and then careers, reflected their rational, logical, left brain-dominant personalities. Dawn was a CPA, Brynn was an engineer.

And then last night happened. Brynn had committed a thoroughly regrettable act. How to untangle it? How to make it all go away? She needed help. Desperately.

Brynn looked up from her phone to see why the long snaking line to get through TSA was barely moving. There was only one TSA agent checking IDs and boarding passes, and he looked as old as Methuselah. Behind him, only one screening machine was open. She blew out an exasperated puff of air and looked down at her phone. She needed Dawn's help.

Brynn
Something terrible has happened.

Dawn
What? Are you OK?

Barely OK.

Can I call you?

No! Don't call!

If she were to hear Dawn's voice, if she had to try to explain herself, she would burst into tears. And once the tears started, they'd never stop.

I just can't talk. I can hardly think straight.

Where are you?

Standing in a TSA line.

Airport? Change your ticket and come to Cape Cod. Stay at the Creamery.

But . . .

Don't overthink. Just come! We'll sort it all out.

Not this time, Brynn thought. This wasn't something that could be easily sorted out. But she did step out of the interminably long TSA line to return to the ticket counter. There, she switched her flight to Boston to a flight that would go straight into Hyannis on Cape Cod.

She knew she was running away from her problem. She knew that what happened last night would require some legal action, but all she could think about was escaping to the beach. From somewhere deep inside of her, she felt a frantic longing to face the ocean, to hear the crash of the waves against the shore. To sense their eternally soothing reminder that everything was going to be okay.

She squeezed her eyes shut, defeated. She had absolutely no idea how to get back to being okay.

• • •

When Dawn picked Brynn up at the Hyannis airport, it was obvious something was truly wrong with her friend. Brynn always looked like she'd stepped right out of *Vogue* magazine, even on a sleepy Sunday morning in a college dorm. She sent her blue jeans to the dry cleaners. She leather-conditioned her purse and shoes. And her personal grooming was impeccable: French manicured nails, long straight hair cut every six weeks, bangs trimmed every three weeks, make-up perfectly applied. Even the wings on her eyeliner looked professional.

But this girl? She was unrecognizable to the girl whom Dawn had roomed with all through college and into their mid-twenties. Brynn had no make-up on, or if she had, it had been washed away with tears. Her hair was pulled into a messy bun, and it wasn't the stylish kind of messy. Her socks were mismatched, her T-shirt had a coffee stain, her beautiful dark doe-eyes were puffy and red.

Dawn couldn't imagine what had happened. Brynn was a civil engineer who worked with tough construction types. Somehow, as small and slender and feminine as she was, she handled them well. But in the back of Dawn's mind was a fear that someone had hurt her, had taken advantage of her, and that worry made her stomach turn over. Then flip back. Brynn was one of Dawn's most beloved persons in the world. She was the sister she'd never had. Brynn's parents had divorced, several times, and were absent more than present. Since the age of eighteen, she'd spent every holiday with the Dixons. If anyone had laid a hand on her, Dawn would hunt him down and . . .

Hold it. She was letting her imagination run wild with dreadful possibilities. Dawn didn't see any bruises, any signs of physical injury. Still . . . *something* had happened to Brynn.

Before Dawn left for the airport, Mom had warned her: Say nothing. Let her talk when she's ready. So as hard as it was to stay silent, Dawn held her tongue. She hugged Brynn, opened the car door to help her in, put her suitcase in the back, and drove away from the small Hyannis airport, all wordlessly.

In Yarmouth, as Dawn flipped on the blinker to turn onto highway 6, Brynn finally spoke up. "Could we go to the beach somewhere, before we go to the Creamery? I don't think I can face anyone right now. Especially your mom."

Dawn flashed her a sympathetic smile. "You bet." She knew of a quiet beach in Chatham that wouldn't be run over with children and dogs. July was the most crowded time on the Cape and today was a picture-perfect day. The population of Chatham swelled fourfold in the summer. Good for an ice cream shop, not so good if you were trying to find a quiet spot on the beach to sob your eyes out.

Dawn knew all about *that.* A few years ago, she'd come to Cape Cod to nurse a broken heart. Her fiancé, Kevin, had broken off their engagement just weeks before the wedding. Dawn had felt the same desperate longing to sit on a beach and watch the waves come in, to absorb the tranquil sounds of the ocean. Time healed her heartbreak, aided by her mother's impetuous purchase of a rundown ice cream shop. And somehow, both time plus the dire needs of the ice cream shop brought Kevin back into her life. Two years later, they had worked through their problems and were happily married. So happily that they'd been trying to start a family.

Trying—without success—for six months. She hadn't found the right moment yet to tell Kevin that she'd made an appointment with a fertility specialist. She knew that her mom had trouble conceiving. Dawn was an only child and there was no way she would be content with raising only one child. Too lonely. Because of that niggling fear, she didn't want to let any more precious time slip away.

Brynn sniffed, wiping her nose with her sleeve (soooo unlike her) and Dawn rummaged one hand through her purse to find a tissue packet to hand to her. When she saw the sign for Harwich, she exited onto Pleasant Lake Avenue, then drove up Queen Anne Road until she came to a narrow lane that led to the beach. Easy to overlook because it seemed like a long driveway with sand along the edges. A perfect hidden spot.

Most people assumed that Cape Cod beaches were one long sandy strip, one wide ribbon. Just the opposite. They were narrow strands of beach, separated from each other by inlets, ponds, bays, jutting sand dunes covered in wild roses. More like a chunky necklace than a wide ribbon.

Dawn parked the car along the side of the lane and the two walked down to the beach. Dawn let Brynn decide where to plop down. There were a few people clustered on the beach but no children, no leashless dogs, and the tide was heading out. Halfway to the water, Brynn dropped to her knees and Dawn followed her lead. She crossed her legs, settled into the warm sand, and patiently waited. She breathed in the salt-scented air, watched the waves as they crashed, admired a bobbing sailboat in the distance, looked at the seagulls circling overhead, noticed the angle of the sun, counted a few puffy clouds floating in the sky. Waiting, waiting, waiting for Brynn to start opening up. Dawn had never been good at waiting. She lasted a full minute before turning to Brynn. "Okay, spill it. What in the world happened to make you so upset?"

Eyes squeezed shut, Brynn tensed up and, suddenly, the dam broke. Big, choking sobs. Shoulder-shaking gasps. Struggling breaths. Dawn rubbed her back in gentle circles and let her cry it out. As Brynn started to recover, she mumbled something.

"You did *what*?" Too harsh. Dawn had triggered another crying jag.

When that jag ebbed, Brynn repeated herself, more clearly.

Dawn's mind could hardly grasp what Brynn was trying to tell her. She leaned back, elbows digging into the sand, gobsmacked. "You got married . . . to a stranger?"

Acknowledgments

It takes a village to get a book out. My readers are my village, and I am so appreciative of each one who reads my book and especially so for those who recommend it to others. I'm grateful! Like Callie, gratefulness is on my mind a lot lately.

When we quit cultivating gratitude, we begin to forget how dependent we are on the grace of God, and when we forget how much we need grace, we quit seeking what only grace can give. Gratitude is huge. Foundational. Transformative.

I'm deeply grateful to my daughter, Lindsey, for sharing a couple of pivotal stories with me that helped bring this story together. She has her master's degree in food safety, and knew of an actual food poisoning that had occurred at the Food Safety Summit. Such irony! It was just begging to be Callie's backstory.

And then there were Lindsey's neighbors while living in Washington. She observed, firsthand, a young mom's rapid decline from multiple sclerosis. Through the living room window, she saw the paramedics' arrivals in the night to whisk the mom off to the hospital. She saw the effect of the mom's illness on her daughter (about Callie's same age). She felt sorrow for the little girl when there came a time when the mom didn't return from the hospital and went, instead, to a nursing facility.

Another friend, Kim Ray, shared the experience of her mom's journey with MS. Kim's mom was older when diagnosed, in her fifties, but the impact on the family was still profound. I remember when Kim once said that nearly every family vacation had to be cut short because of an unexpected health crisis for her mom.

And can I just take a moment to thank all the Bookstagrammers, and bloggers, and online reviewers and readers out there who took a chance on my books, and then loved them, and then helped spread the word in one way or another? Books live or die on word of mouth. If you have ever done anything to encourage anyone to read something I've written, thank you. It mattered. I'm still here because of you.

I am grateful beyond words to my beloved publisher, Revell, for all the ways they've believed in me and supported me and become the most wonderful home. I'm so thankful to be there, and so lucky to get to work with such talented, hardworking people: Andrea Doering, Barb Barnes, Karen Steele, Michele Misiak . . . and so many more. I also—always—want to thank my agent, Joyce Hart, for her unwavering support over so many years. She took me on and changed everything.

Suzanne Woods Fisher is an award-winning, bestselling author of more than forty books, including *The Sweet Life*, *The Moonlight School*, and *Anything but Plain*, as well as the Three Sisters Island, Nantucket Legacy, Amish Beginnings, The Bishop's Family, The Deacon's Family, and The Inn at Eagle Hill series. She is also the author of several nonfiction books about the Amish, including *Amish Peace* and *Amish Proverbs*. She lives in California. Learn more at www.suzannewoodsfisher.com and follow Suzanne on Facebook @SuzanneWoodsFisherAuthor and Twitter @suzannewfisher.

"*The Sweet Life* is a wonderful beach read, set at the Cape, with lots of ice cream sprinkled throughout. Nothing could be better on a hot summer day!"

—*ROMANCE JUNKIES*

Jilted by her fiancé, Dawn Dixon escapes to beautiful Cape Cod on a groomless honeymoon, with her mother. But she didn't expect to end up risking everything for a rundown ice cream shop—in need of her ex's help.

Revell
a division of Baker Publishing Group
www.RevellBooks.com

Available wherever books and ebooks are sold.

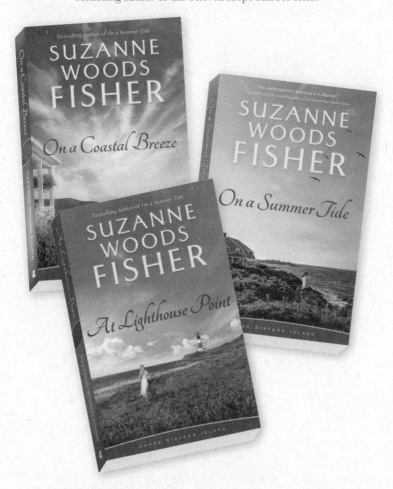

"An unforgettable story about love and the transforming power of words and community. Deeply moving and uplifting!"

—LAURA FRANTZ,
Christy Award–winning author of *Tidewater Bride*

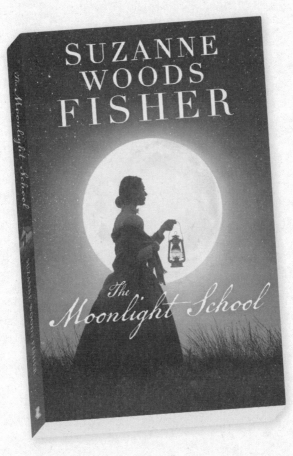

Based on true events, a young woman used to the finer things in life arrives in a small Appalachian town in 1911 to help her formidable cousin combat adult illiteracy by opening moonlight schools.

Revell
a division of Baker Publishing Group
www.RevellBooks.com

Connect with SUZANNE

www.SuzanneWoodsFisher.com